BLOOD NECKLACE

Thomas S. Mulvaugh

ISBN 978-0-9794767-9-2

First Edition

© 2015 Paul Herd

Golden Roads Publishing, a division of PAH Publishing

Acknowledgements/Dedication

To my darling wife Karla, without her help this book could have not been written; for being there when I would want to just give up but she would not let me, she always encouraged me, and also for reading this story over and over through its changes and offering suggestions; you are the love of my life.

This book is dedicated in the memory of my big brother George, who I can always remember for that beaming smile and hearty laugh, who like any older brother would pester and tease, but when I needed him he was always there to give me the greatest big brother advice, and since I still use that every day, he is always there with me.

BLOOD NECKLACE

"It is said that God forgives all sins, but some sins are so secret that some people are willing to die for them, others willing to kill for them. What are secrets and what would you do so no one would ever know?"

Chapter 1

Annalisa was the love of Rick Ryder's life, childhood friend, high school sweetheart, and now she was dead, murdered. Found crumpled behind the wheel of his 458 Italia Spider, a three-foot long yellow Ethernet cable tied around her neck; the other end wrapped around the leather steering wheel of the sports car. The bright red Ferrari was as much a victim as its driver. A rock placed on the accelerator, the powerful engine screaming as it raced in between the picnic tables, and leaping headfirst into the cold waters of Roaring River, the motor gurgling, and finally dying as it drowned beneath the waters and the spirit of the car rose up as a cloud of steam. It was three minutes after midnight when a park ranger found her. The beautiful blonde's neck was broken, her head at an odd angle, dangling just inches above the water that filled the car's interior.

Early Tuesday morning, it felt a little a bit strange to be turning left on Locust Street once again and be comforted by the security blanket of the shade of the Kansas City, Missouri Police Headquarters.

It had been almost been three years since he had walked out those double glass doors. He had spent ten years of his life here, as a homicide detective including the biggest case of his career: the serial killer known as the Kansas City Butcher-who brutally massacred 13 people. It was a different time back then, the citizens of the city locked away behind their doors, afraid to venture outside, as he worked with an F.B.I. agent trying to track down the killer. He was never comfortable about that arrest, but the killing did stop, so maybe it was the right guy. However it was the eyes of the last victim, looking up at him in that ghostly stare, that changed him forever. They were no longer a piece of the puzzle; they each had a name. He tossed the badge down and walked out, and his life changed forever.

After walking out, he bought a Mega Powerball ticket and won the biggest lottery jackpot of all time: One billion dollars. At that moment he went from serving Kansas City to being served by Kansas City, being the guest of all the powerbrokers of the city, including last night as a special guest of the Chiefs at Arrowhead Stadium to toss out a football to the kicker.

1

His build was like a professional quarterback, tall and fit, with broad shoulders, because at one time that was what he was. In high school he was all American leading the Cassville Wildcats to three years in a row state championship, and the Mizzou Tigers to a National Championship before being drafted by the Chiefs; he played a half a season before being injured in a play that went wrong. He now walked with a slight limp, he could chase criminals but he couldn't out run 350 pound linebackers anymore.

After winning the lottery work shoe leather was replaced with Italian loafers. Hand stitched suits and custom-made shirts covered his broad shoulders. His saddle brown hair was now personally styled; costing what would be a day's wages when he was a detective. Designer glasses replaced the discount tree sunglasses.

 Now he was back 'in the box': the interrogation room. A small room with no windows, plain gray walls, with sound absorbing panels and only a simple table and three fold away chairs in the center of the room; two on one side and one on the other that faced a two way mirror. How many times had he been here making them wait, and now, ironically, it was he who sat waiting for an officer to question him about Annalisa's murder. He sat in the hardback chair, his elbows resting on the table, staring at the two chairs on the other side of the table. He slowly twisted the gold ring with its round dark blue sapphire center stone, which matched his eyes, on the ring finger of his right hand; he glared up at the two way mirror and stared directly into it. He motioned with his hand for them to come on in as he said. "Let's just get this over with." Ryder said his voice low and calm.

The door opened and in walked Captain Craig Grosstree, a heavy set career man who had spent his entire life as a law enforcement officer in Kansas City, and sitting in a chair most of the day was beginning make his back spread to match his belly. His once dark hair was beginning to show streaks of silver, which would have been wiry like his mustache, if he let it grow out instead of being buzz cut. He was also the first commander to choose and build his own team of detectives; one of his proudest choices was Ryder, and he wasn't going to let some rural deputy railroad him.

Directly behind him was a round faced deputy from Barry County, dressed in khaki pants and chocolate brown short sleeve shirt. As the deputy walked over to the table, Ryder's eyebrows drew down in bewilderment. The man looked familiar, but he just couldn't come up with the name.

"Ryder, this is Brian Thompson." Captain Grosstree said, introducing the deputy. "He wants to ask you a few questions about Annalisa." He sat down in one of the chairs and continued. "I am here to make sure that everything goes well. " He looked over at Ryder. "He may not wear a shield anymore, but he is still one of my guys."

Ryder grew up in the small Ozark town of Cassville, Missouri, a town of a little over three thousand and just under 200 miles south of Kansas City, it was the county seat of Barry County. "Thompson? Are you any kin to Teeny Tiny Thompson?" Ryder asked remembering his old classmate and fellow football teammate.

"He is my big brother."

"Too Thin?" Ryder asked finally recognizing and shocked by his now hefty appearance.

Deputy Thompson sat down in the other chair. Ryder could see the same round face, broad smile, and sandy crimson hair brushed straight back and parted on the side that was like his older brother, of course being that he was the center of the football team that was not the end of his brother the Ryder saw the most.

 "Once a Wildcat." The deputy raised his hand up and acting as if it were claws he swatted toward Ryder and mocked a growl. A salute that was made up by Ryder's class the year they were ranked the number one high school football team in the United States.

"Always a Wildcat." Ryder said mimicking the same actions; it was a sign of respect, which was shown to former members of the Cassville R-4 school district. Ryder twisted his head slightly, looking the man over. "You are no longer too thin, what happened to you?"

"I have put on a few pounds since then." Deputy Thompson laughed patting his belly as he added. "Too many Texan burgers at the Family Room; best in the county. You know, Thom is the county coroner now."

"Heard you got a new sheriff."

"You believe it?" Deputy Thompson said with disbelief. "An outsider from San Diego! Worked with US Customs before coming here. Not a bit of law enforcement experience."

"What happen to Sheriff Matthews?"

"Died behind his desk two days before the election. Heart attack, so they say. The word is your pal the congressman bought the election."

"He is no friend of mine." Ryder said as he pushed himself up in the chair and faced the deputy eye to eye. He knew how this game worked; he had played it so many times before he knew every move. First you do chit-chat, maybe even make a joke, all to make the person feel at ease. Then you start with a simple but direct question. Ryder prepared himself for it.

"But his wife, Annalisa was. Wasn't she?"

Now he was going to watch Ryder's body language, to see if he was tense, stubborn, frightened, it would decide how the next question would be asked. Tense, the tone would be comforting, stubborn, harsher, frightened, the tone would be friendly. The most difficult suspect was the one that showed no emotion, there, only the skill of the investigator would count. Ryder drew his hand up to his chin and looked across the table at him. Ryder's face was blank, his eyes fixed directly onto the deputy as he calmly said. "Yes."

"And much more."

"A long time ago."

Deputy Thompson laid the case folder down on the table in front of him. Ryder offered an impish grin and twisted the ring on his finger. "Deputy Thompson?" Ryder asked, dropping his gaze down to the file, then back up to him. "Do you have much experience in interrogation?"

"Some."

Ryder leaned forward, crossing his hands on the table. "My dear mother told me 'you don't go into a bear's cave and poke him with a stick unless you have a big gun behind your back.' "

"What does that mean?"

"This is my cave."

It was clear from the confused look on the deputy's face he didn't understand so Ryder explained further. "You know how many times I have sat in that chair? Looked across at the evil that crawled out of the oozing underworld of humankind? I see exactly what you are doing. You are doing it step by step, just like out of the book." Ryder leaned in closer to the deputy and noticed a bead of sweat dripping down from the man's forehead. Ryder leaned back and twisted the gold ring on the finger of his right hand. He stared down into the bright blue sapphire stone, before looking back up to the deputy and asking. "What about the most sinful of all crimes…" He paused briefly before adding. "…murder?"

"I have had some robbery cases."

"Oh my gosh!" Ryder said, shocked. "You are a virgin! This is your first homicide case." Ryder couldn't believe it; they sent a ham-fisted deputy to investigate Annalisa's murder. Ryder looked down at the file again. "You know the only reason I am here. I want to look at that file."

"I can't do that." Deputy Thompson said, placing his hand on top of the file.

"Then I guess we are done here." Ryder said standing up. "Arrest me, or…" He glared at the deputy before continuing. "Or we can make a deal. I answer your questions, than I get to look at the file." Ryder placed his hands on the back of the chair and prepared to shove it under the table. "What is it going to be? Or do you want to go back and tell your sheriff that you couldn't do it?" Ryder knew, it didn't matter if it was a small county sheriff, Kansas City, or the hard streets of Manhattan itself, the one thing a cop didn't want to do was tell their superior 'I couldn't get it.'

"I don't know…" Deputy Thompson said hesitantly as he opened the file. Ryder glanced down at the file, it was a police report done by Barry County. Over the years he had gotten very good at reading upside down. *'Apparent cause of death- asphyxiation- due to strangulation, corner inquiry still open and under investigation.'*

"Deputy, look at it this way, it is not like you are letting the general public see this." Captain Grosstree said and pointed at Ryder. "I trained this man. He was the best detective I ever had. Ninety-eight percent closure rate. That is because he is one stubborn bull-headed…" The captain's voice was rising in tone, and then he calmed back down. "Look at it this way. You might need help with this." The captain's lips twisted around to the side. "Besides, you know this man. Do you really think he could have killed Annalisa?"

"No." He said with a shake of his head. "No, I know what she meant to him. But the prosecutor… he is demanding answers, and since it was your car…"

"What does that matter?" Ryder asked and Deputy Thompson dropped his gaze away from Ryder and to the table. Ryder knew there was something that he wasn't telling him. "Who is the D.A. there?"

"Jonathan Price." The deputy answered as he looked back up. It was a name from Ryder's past, the quarterback from a rival school, the Monett Cubs. It was his senior year and the Wildcats met the Monett Cubs for the district championship and whoever won that game would go to the state championship. Monett was ahead but Ryder brought the Cats back to win the game, something Price always held over him, for ruining his life.

"Oh, him." Ryder said spitefully. "All right, get on with it."

"Where were you between the hours of six p.m. and midnight yesterday?"

"You are kidding, right?" Ryder asked, amazed that he had not seen him throw out a ceremonial pass to the kicker at Arrowhead. That was not a usual thing, but when you give two million to the team's charity, they make exceptions. "You weren't watching the game?"

"I am more of a Rams fan."

"Oh! You are the one." Ryder joked. "You do realize you are behind enemy lines here?"

"How long were you there?"

"Till around eleven thirty."

"And after that?" The deputy pushed for more answers. Ryder was only willing to give only so much.

6

"I went home and found that my Ferrari was missing." Ryder leaned back in his chair.

"Is this your car?" Deputy Thompson asked picking up a photo from the file and sliding it across the table to him. It was the wrecked Ferrari, the front twisted to the passenger side, the interior soaked and stained with water.

"Yes."

"Is there some reason she could have been found dead in it?"

"She took it."

"What didn't you report it stolen?"

"This wasn't the first time she took my car. She took my car in high school and disappeared for two days. I didn't want to get her in trouble. Besides, if she wanted it, she could have it." Ryder looked over at the file; he could see a photo of Annalisa's body in the car. A yellow cable tied around her neck, her head tilted over strangely, clearly her neck was broken. A red high-heeled shoe placed on her left foot, with the other shoe missing. Her golden hair was soaking wet, plastered to her beauty queen sculptured face that was stained with blood, baby blue eyes frozen in death, covered in a haze, staring up at him. He closed his eyes and swallowed his breath. The human in him didn't want to see any more, but the detective in him demanded more.

"Did you see Annalisa yesterday?"

Ryder stood up and walked around to the other side of the table and sat down on the edge, crossing him arms over his chest. "Yes, around ten in the morning."

"What did she want?"

"I don't know…" Ryder paused and rubbed his hand over his rough day's growth of whiskers. "She didn't say." He stood and walked over towards the door with his back to them. He brought his clutched hands up to his lips. "You have to understand who Annalisa is—"he quickly corrected himself. "—who she was." He turned back to them and dropped his hands down to his sides. "It could have been that she found out she was dying, or that they no longer sell your favorite color of nail polish." He was doing his best to show no emotion, and he turned away from them again and gathered his composure. "She kept saying that she wanted to give me something 'that would change our lives forever.' "Ryder went around to the other side of the table and glanced down at the file. "I need to see that."

"Just a few more questions."

"No more!" Ryder barked firmly there was only one reason he was here. "I want to see that file now."

"Just a couple more questions."

"No more questions!"

Captain Grosstree, placing his hand down on the file said. "I am going to ask the questions now. What motive would my man have to murder this woman?"

"Price is saying it is jealousy, because she turned you down when you asked her to marry you."

"When was this?" The captain asked, turning and looking at Ryder.

"When we were eighteen."

"Eighteen!" Captain Grosstree said, amazed as he turned back to the deputy. "Really? That is your motive?" That was twenty-two years ago. Wasn't she married to the Speaker of the House Congressman Warner? Why would he be doing this now?"

"Do you know why she turned me down?" Ryder asked, grabbing the chair, twisting it around and straddling it. He looked over at the deputy who shook his head. "It was religion. You do know she was Jewish. I am not." Ryder's tone was soft and he paused for a moment, his mind racing back to that night when she told him she could not marry him but she wanted to keep his ring so that she would never forget him. He twisted the ring on his finger again and remembered that she gave it to him, he wore it for the same reason: that he would never forget her. "If she married me she could no longer be Jewish. That was more important to her." His tone once again became forceful. "I want that file."

8

Deputy Thompson closed the file, placed his hand down on it then leaned back and said. "I can't do that. If I were to let you see this they would fire me."

"You know deputy, when Ryder won the lottery he bought us a fancy coffee maker, and a whole kitchen. If you would like we can go and try it. And since you wouldn't want to get anything spilled on it you could just leave that file lying right here." Captain Grosstree smiled as he got up from his chair and placed his hand on the deputy's back. The deputy stood up and the captain continued. "Come on. You can get anything from a plain cup of Joe to a latte to an espresso. He turned to Ryder and smiled. "You won't read that file, will you Ryder?"

"I can promise you I will not read that file in this room. Ryder said, holding his hand up.

They walked out and closed the door behind them. Ryder reached over and pulled the file over to him, then reached in his jacket pocket for his cell phone, and clicked on the phone. He opened up the file and began to photographing the pages. He heard the sounds of footsteps on the tile floor approaching the door, it was not the gate of a man, it was a woman, and she was quickly approaching the interrogation room. He quickly photographed the last page and closed the folder, then slid it back over to the other side of the table. He shoved the phone back into the inside pocket of his dark navy jacket, and leaned back in the chair just as the door opened. He dropped his gaze down to the table.

It hit him like a slap across the face, the strong aroma of Red Door perfume, not put on in a small dab, but at least three solid sprays, one behind each ear and then another on one of her wrists rubbed together, first counterclockwise, then clockwise. The door closed with a soft click of its latch and the smell of the perfume grew stronger.

Ryder let his gaze drift over across the gray floor tile floor and on to a pair of doeskin loafers with a small one inch heel, for just a moment he imagined Annalisa as it was the type of shoe she would wear. His gaze drifted upward to pair of shapely legs protruding out from under a business gray wrap around skirt that ended just above the knees and a matching gray jacket and white silk blouse that had the top two buttons unbuttoned, revealing a long well tanned neck. Her milk chocolate hair was streaked with golden highlights, framing a beautiful face, which seemed to have belonged on the catwalks of Paris instead of holding a badge. It was Special Agent Isabelle Alexander, but she went by Alex. He watched her as she walked around the table and sat down across from him.

His mind flashed back to when they were together, working on the Kansas City Butcher case, all those long nights huddled together in an unmarked cruiser. Maybe it was the cold wind blowing off the river, or it was the heat that was between them, but things changed that night, and there was no way either of them could put in the report why they didn't see the killing that happened only a hundred feet away from them.

"Well! Hello there, detective." She said, turning sideways in the chair and crossing her legs; her voice was smooth and he remembered her skin being that way too. He also remembered that she would say or do anything to get what she wanted.

"Good Morning, Alex." Ryder said as he let his gaze drop back down to her feet, and one of her shoes was dangling from her foot. "Never seen you in anything but high heels."

"This is all I had." She said, looking down at her shoes and wiggling her foot, barely keeping the shoe on and revealing her bare heel. "Had a beautiful pair but, they got ruined last night." She looked back up at him and added with a crooked smile. "You know the awful stuff that the F.B.I. runs into."

"Yeah, getting blood out is really hard." Ryder smirked and brought his hand up and rested his chin on his hand. "What are you doing here?"

Alex uncrossed her legs and turned and faced him as she placed her hand on the file and her tone became harsher, that same tone he had heard from her when she was questioning a suspect. "The wife of the Speaker of the House was murdered; what do you think I am doing here?" She slid the file off the table as she stood up. "You really think Attorney General Baker is going to allow the good ole boys of Barry County to try to solve this? He has given this to professionals." She stepped away from the table and towards the door.

"Yeah." Ryder quipped as he turned to her. "We wouldn't want anyone asking Speaker Warner. *Why did you kill you wife?*" Ryder's tone increased. She grabbed the door handle, but stopped and turned back around as she clutched the file to her chest. He could see the command that she had already been given- 'blame it on somebody, but make sure it is not the speaker.' Ryder rubbed his hand over his whiskers in frustration. "Come on, Alex! You know when a wife is murdered the first suspect is always the husband. Or have you gotten so 'D.C'. that you don't care about the truth anymore?"

"And what would his motive be? That she was *still in love with you*?" She said softly as she turned back to him, as a strand of hair fell down in front of her eyes that were a mix of gray and green. She pushed her hair back and knocked on the door for someone to let her out. Just as she stepped out of the room she added. "Just stay out of it, Ricky. Please! Just stay out of it."

The door was left open and Ryder stood up from the table. He tugged at the tail of his jacket, pulling it back down into place, walking out of the room. He looked around the squad room, at the desks all line up in neat little rows, each with a busy detective behind it. He looked over where his desk had been, a young man sat behind it now. The phone rang and he answered it, jotting down the information, grabbing his jacket off the back of the chair and dashing for the elevators. It was at that moment there was a little of him that missed all of this.

"You going to stay out of this like she said?" He heard Captain Grosstree say as he walked up beside him, holding a mug of coffee in his hands.

"What do you think, Captain?" Ryder asked, turning to him and looking slightly down because the Captain was four inches shorter than Ryder's six foot four frame. "

Captain Grosstree raised the mug to his lips and took a sip of the hot black liquid and stared out across the squad room. "I think that you will piss somebody off and even though I am not your boss I will hear about it."

Chapter 2

Ryder pushed the glass doors of police headquarters open, standing on the top step outside of police headquarters he looked down at the gold ring on his hand and stroked it with his thumb. He didn't hear a sound, so unusual for downtown KC, no screaming sirens that smothered the songs of robins that were hopping about in the criss-cross manicured pattern of the city hall lawn. Even the air didn't breathe, not a leaf on the trees moved.

A bright flash of light filled his eyes and the silence was shattered as a pack of reporters descended upon him. "Mr. Ryder, what were you questioned for?"

"Does it have something to do with the murder of Speaker of the House Scott Warner's wife?"

"What was your relationship with her? Were you two having an affair?"

"Are you considered a suspect?"

"Mr. Ryder! Mr. Ryder!"

Ryder didn't say a word as he walked down the steps, past the reporters, refusing to answer their questions. How they had changed from timid little purring kittens running up to the saucer of warm milk he would put out for them when he gave money away, to the rabid dogs now snapping and biting each other just to get closer so they could ask a question that would deliver the fatal bite.

"Did you kill her Mr. Ryder?" A blonde haired reporter from FOX NEWS said as she pushed her way through the crowd and shoved a microphone at him. He turned to her. He slipped on his Ray-Ban sunglasses. His lips curled into a snarl as he said. "No, but I am going to find out who did." He opened the door to a sleek dark green Jaguar sedan.

"And what will you do when you find them?" The reporter asked again.

Ryder lowered his sunglasses and turned and looked at the reporter and said. "Bring them to justice."

"Is that criminal justice, or your justice?"

"I guess." Ryder said sitting down in the seat of the Jaguar and closing the door. He rolled down the window and added. "You will have to wait and find out." He quickly drove off.

If there is anything that is close to the heat of the fires of hell it has to be August in Missouri, unless of course it comes in September, the sun viciously beating down, the pavement bubbling up like a witch's cauldron weaving a spell of sticking tires leaving behind a trail for others to follow. Only a few small fluffy clouds drifting across the bright blue sky would occasionally hide the sun, giving only a moment when a relieving breath could be exhaled, and eyes could open wider, only to squint back down as the sun ended its game of peek-a-boo, and once again appeared.

The tires on the Jaguar squealed as Ryder turned into the underground parking garage of his apartment building. The thermometer on the wall read 101 as he stopped in front of the gate. A thin framed teenager with a large amount of curly dark hair was the attendant in a small room. It was Charlie Spears; he had just graduated from high school earlier this year, and he was headed to Missouri University in Columbia this fall, thanks to Ryder's influence.

"Good afternoon Mr. Ryder, good to see you." Charlie said with his always pleasant tone. He leaned over the counter and handed Ryder a ticket that was given to everyone when they arrived or left the garage. Ryder looked at it. The time stamped on it. *1:00 p.m. Tuesday September 14.*

"Charlie." Ryder said, looking up at the attendant. "Were you on duty yesterday?"

"Of course."

"Did you check my Spyder?"

"Yes." He said sounding ashamed that an expensive car was stolen and he had let it happened. "I didn't mean—if I knew—I thought since she had the keys it was..."

"It is okay Charlie, it was just a car. Do you remember seeing her?"

"The blonde? Oh yes, I remember her, reminded me of Blair from the 'Facts of Life'. She told me..."

13

"Do you know what time that was?"

"Sure; it was eleven o/clock the morning. A 'Facts of Life' marathon had just begun."

"Mad crush on Blair?" Ryder asked because of his reference to the character before, and that he had noticed the resemblance too.

"No, more of on Jo." Charlie's face twisted up. "You know, it was so strange. She was laughing and giggling, telling me a story of how you two tied a fire extinguisher to a skate board and sent it rocketing down the hallway during finals week. And how you and the football team put the vice principal's car into the gym as a senior prank. Ryder laughed, remembering a line of students walking by, to get a look at that bright yellow Beetle right under the basket ball hoop. "How did you get it there?"

"You can unbolt the center post in the double door."

"She told me then you all tried to get in inside of it, and then have your photo taken. Then it happened."

"What?"

"She saw a strange van drive by."

"What van?" Ryder asked, puzzled.

"A white Dodge. One of those new Rams. It had blacked out windows. It was really strange."

"What was so strange about it?"

"It slowed down, and then parked right on the side of the road just a few feet away. Then she took out of here like a bat out of hell. The van turned around and chased after her."

"Charlie, did you happen to get a license number?"

He shook his head. "Oh! I remember!" Charlie said with excitement. "Just before she left." He leaned back into the cubical and grabbed a piece of paper off the wall and handed it to Ryder. "She told me to give this to you." Ryder took it: it was a register sales slip for a Wal-Mart store in Cassville where she had bought a 14 GB USB flash drive. Written on the back was

'Meet me at Mother Ross's Bar-B-Que. Annalisa.'

Kansas City offers a vast array of choices for every discerning palate, from the five-star restaurant where a reservation was a must to the little hole in the wall places, that required you to only come in and sit down, then you ordered by the aroma that was drifting out of the kitchen. Ryder had tried them all. However, his favorite was a little place downtown that served the 'best darn ribs there is.' It was a little hard to find, and tourists were truly lucky if they stumbled onto it, as you had to drive down an alley and at the end of the alley, go into in the first floor of a red brick building. The only sign was three by four feet and read: Mother Ross's Bar-B-Que.

The restaurant was only accessible by a single green metal door. As soon as he pulled the door open, the sense of smell was met with ecstasy. The sweet aroma of apple wood smoke drifted out like the slender fingers of a comely prostitute waving the next victim into her lair. It was not that well lit, but sight was not required to find your way, you just followed the moans of delight, of customers eating pork that fell from the bones, and melted in your mouth nearly before you could even swallow, as a sauce that was tangy, yet sweet as honey dripped down their chins, that they did not dare wipe away, but instead licked away, not wanting to miss one drop.

Owned and operated by the Hall of Famer former Chief's running back Michael Ross, who got the nickname of Mother as the defensive player would curse as he would break through the line for first down, just when the Chiefs needed it. He had developed his own special Bar-B-Que sauce, and would slow cook the ribs and beef brisket over a low wood fed heat. The sweet iced tea served in quart size mason jars, and there were always fresh homemade rolls that were as large as a man's fist served with honey butter. Even in busy times it never took long before a waitress was coming over and ready to take your order. If you dared to ask for a menu they knew you were a visitor, as most regulars knew exactly what to order and had the usual, and there were in some cases, their usual spots. For Ryder it was the third booth back.

"So what will it be, honey?" The waitress asked as she walked up to his table. Ryder had his head down at first, staring at the table. His mind was racing with memories of Annalisa. Of playing house and eating her famous sandwiches; American cheese and a slice of tomato with mustard on a hamburger bun, it was all that the seven-year old could make. Of hot summers just like today, when they would ride their bikes and go swimming in Snake Creek. Sitting in the back seat of the bus bouncing up and down when it went over a bump, for that was where the biggest bump would be. Of lying out on a blanket staring up at the starry night sky, telling tales of the dreams they wanted to share.

"My usual, Denise." Ryder said, without lifting his head. He looked up at her and slowly added. "And and answer."

"Ryder!" The woman exclaimed out loud. "Long time no see!" She turned her head and shouted towards the kitchen. "Mother! Get out here. Ryder is here." There was a clang of pots from the kitchen, and the double doors from the kitchen swung open and a tall stout-built man with very dark skin appeared. He was dress in white pants and a t-shirt with a white apron over that. He pulled the cap from his head as he walked towards Ryder's table. He grinned and his white teeth shown up through his tightly curled beard.

"Ryder, you old son-of-a biscuit eater you!" Mother said with a cheerful tone, holding out his hand as walked up to the table. Ryder stood up and took the man's hand, and he pulled Ryder towards him and embraced Ryder and patted him on the back. "Haven't seen you since you won the big bucks, thought you had forgotten all us working slobs." He released him and Ryder sat down on the bench.

"Half slab of ribs with Moms special sauce. Onion rings, coleslaw, and sweet ice tea with a half twist of lemon." The waitress wrote down his order and left, while Mother sat down on the bench across from Ryder. "Saw you last night on the TV. You gotta get a little more arch on that ball."

"Next time I'll let you do it, Mother."

"Nah." He said with a shake of his head. "Running was my game." Ryder glanced down at the man's huge hands and at the large diamond encrusted Super Bowl ring. He paused for a brief moment before adding. "And I know what your game is." Ryder lifted his gazed back to the man's face. "It is about the girl that was murdered isn't it?"

"Mother, was she in here yesterday?"

"There were a lot of people here, including blonde women. But I remembered her." He leaned his elbows on the table and turned to his wife Denise. "Go get it." He looked back over the table at Ryder. "Those piercing blue eyes? How could I forget 'em? Besides, we don't get too many Jewish people in here. You know the pork thing. "

"How did you know she was Jewish?" Ryder asked as he cupped the Mason jar in his between his hands.

"She was wearing a medallion around her wrist. I had a friend on the team, he was Jewish and so was his wife, she wore the same thing. I believe it is the hand of Moses' sister. Suppose to be some sort of good luck charm or something."

Ryder lifted up the Mason jar and took a sip of the sweet lemony tea, and set the jar back down on the table. He slowly twisted the glass in his hands. "She is the one, ain't she?" Mother asked making Ryder look up. "The one you told me about. The one that you can't get over? The one that every other woman is compared to but…. " She was that one girl that he could never get out of his mind. The one when he would see a fluff of blonde hair and he would think it might be her. When he walked by a perfume counter and you catch a whiff of what she wore, and instantly she is there in his thoughts. She was what he measured every other woman up to."

"Doesn't measure up?" Ryder said, interrupting, as Mother nodded.

Denise returned with a white business sized envelope and handed it to her husband, before sitting down beside him. "She left this here for you." Mother said, sliding the envelope across the table. Written on the front was her handwriting that read '*My Dearest Ricky*.' He picked up the envelope and sniffed it for the delicate floral scent that she wore. He flipped it over. On the flap were symbols, it was Hebrew, many times Annalisa had tried teach him, but he could never read it. He started to open it, but changed his mind, thinking that this might be the last thing she had written to him, he couldn't face it, at least not with anyone watching. He folded the envelope in half and stuffed it into the breast pocket of his jacket.

Back behind the counter where customers would pay the bill a TV was on, turned to a cable news channel. A male news reporter was talking:

"Israeli Ambassador Hiram Weinstein was demanding answers about the fact that IDF had found a group of Hamas terrorists armed with US made military weapons. Senate Majority Leader Wallace Goodwin assures the Ambassador that Israel is America's ally, and has vowed to 'get to the bottom of this'. And assures him America is not arming terrorists. We have learned that this may be in connection with a militant group known as Black Midnight. The biggest news of the day is still the suspected murder of the wife of long time Speaker of the House Scott Warner. Just awhile ago authorities questioned former Kansas City detective Richard Ryder about the Speaker's wife."

Ryder looked up at the TV and saw the tape of him coming out of police headquarters. He lifted the Mason jar and took a drink, as the reporter continued. *"Mr. Ryder was a long time friend of Ms. Warner however, Captain Craig Grosstree from the Kansas City police department and the Barry county sheriff's department assure us that Mr. Ryder is not a suspect in the Congressman's wife's murder."*

"Her name is Annalisa, you moron." Ryder grumbled, setting the jar back down on the table.

"Breaking news we have just learned that the F.B.I. has formed a special team that has taken over the case of the murder of Speaker of the House Scott Warner's wife. And earlier today the Speaker had this to say:

"I am deeply saddened by the loss of my wife. But I put my faith and trust in the Department of Justice, that they will solve her murder. And bring all those responsible to justice. I also want to thank all of my constituents and all those around America who have offered comforting thoughts and prayers, and ask that the press will give us our privacy through this difficult time."

"Can't you even say her name?" Ryder said under his breath, before standing. "Suddenly I think I have lost my appetite." Ryder pulled out his wallet and began to pay.

"No." Mother said grabbing his hand. "You are family here. You don't charge family." He grabbed Ryder in an embrace again and added. "You just keep them in your prayers." He released Ryder and said, pointing his finger at him. "And if you need anything even if it is two o'clock in the morning, you just let your old Mother know."

After walking back to the Jaguar Ryder sat down in the driver's seat of his car and laid his head back on the headrest. Again his mind filled with images of Annalisa, from the time she was a little girl pretending to be a bride, carrying her doll around, to leading her out at half time on the football field as the Wildcat's new homecoming queen, to seeing her rip her dress in grief at her grandfather's funeral. He let out a ragged breath, holding back the tears; he reached into his jacket pocket and pulled out the envelope, and tore it open.

Inside was a folded up piece of paper. His face screwed up in puzzlement as he unfolded it, there was nothing on it, and he turned the paper over- nothing. *Why did you do this?"* He thought to himself as he lowered his head on the steering wheel. *Why didn't you leave me something? Why a blank piece of paper?* He rose up and looked into the rear view mirror, as he carefully folded the paper into thirds before tossing it to the floor on the passenger's side. "What are you trying to tell me?" He said out loud. "What does a blank piece of paper mean?" A flash of lightning filled the sky. A storm was coming.

Chapter 3

He wasn't sure how many streets he had been on or even if he knew where he was going. It just seemed all he knew was to drive into the night and keep on going. He found himself driving through Hyde Park, the warm colors of the street lights painting over him, the sound of the city still beating its drum loudly in his ears. The giant towering skyscrapers were closing in on him, the headlights of the other cars trying to peer through the windshield, trying to get a peek at his life, those on the sidewalks seeming to stop and listen to his heartbeat, which was pounding like the thunder rumbling in the sky. His fingers tightened on the leather steering wheel, while it seemed the seat belt was a boa constrictor squeezing the life out of him. Turning onto a street and the traffic thinned. The tightness was leaving. He let out a relieved breath, as only the cool blue lights of the instrument panel of the Jaguar bathed him now, and the headlights of the Jaguar were all alone reaching out to the pavement, only being interrupted with a fork of lightning streaking down from the sky, followed by the roaring applause of thunder. It was through the flash of lightning that he saw the street sign. *Blue River Road.*

If Interstate 70 was the aorta that brought life blood to the city and I 670 was the main vein, Blue River Road was a capillary, seeming not necessary but vital if you need to get to where you wanted to go. It was nothing more than a narrow twisting ribbon of pavement that was mostly striped with a double yellow streak down the middle of its spine, not that it was the coward, but more that timid drivers should not attempt to pass on this road. Trees guarded it on both sides and made a tunnel in the middle, keeping the sky from looking down on the road.

Ryder pushed down on the throttle and the Jaguar responded, digging its rubber claws into the pavement. The motor was purring as he forced it down a straight stretch, then growling as he shifted the car down a gear and twisted the steering wheel on the car, its claws digging deeper into the pavement, hanging on as the wind whipped the leaves off the trees as if they were confetti in a celebration of his misery. He shifted the gear back up and the car shot under I-435 overpass and for just a moment he was drawn back into the city. With a flash of lightning he left the noise behind, and rain began to fall. At first it was gentle, just a drop here and there, soon it was a free fall, the wipers swatting at full speed, and he could only see a few feet in front of him.

More curves, and the headlights caught sight of a sign, something about *Inspiration Point*. He turned hard to the right and the car slid around in the road. The rain was rolling down the hill of Chestnut Avenue; at the top of the hill to the left was a church. He had never been here, nor did he even know it was here, but it was just somewhere and that was all he wanted, to be somewhere.

He guided the car up into the parking lot, drove around the church, and stopped, putting it in park. He sat there for a moment staring out into the valley as lightning flashed and streamed across the sky. He sat there listening to the rain as if it were hundreds of fingernails tapping on the roof, each drop asking him "what is wrong? Why can't you mourn for her?" The drops swirled down and spattered up on the glass roof, pouring as if it were tears from the sky. Heaven was mourning for her; why couldn't he?

He took the cell phone from his jacket pocket, and pulled up the photos of the file he taken. Again he looked at the photo of Annalisa dead in the car. The seat pushed all the way up, her body jammed in between the seat and the steering wheel, the red high heel shoe on one foot, the other bare. *Where is the other shoe?* He thought. He moved to another page. There was no mention of the shoe being found in the list of evidence. Tire tracks show the car was speeding straight from F-highway into the river; there were no other tracks or foot prints located. He flipped to another photo; it reported there were no fingerprints found on the steering wheel or dash; *this was strange*. He drove that car just the day before; his prints should have been there, and where were Annalisa's? Someone had to wipe the car clean, but why?

He moved to another page, it was Annalisa's body lying on the coroner's table. She was pale looking, her eyes closed. It suddenly hit him, she was gone. He leaned his head back and looked up through the roof again. The rain poured even harder. He could feel his chest ache, it was so empty inside, each memory of her just brought more pain. He wanted to just forget, so there would be no more pain, but he couldn't stop. The dam of emotions burst and for the first time since hearing she had been murdered, he wept.

Chapter 4

Ryder was awakened the next morning by a phone call from Yakira, Annalisa's younger sister; she told him that Annalisa's body was released by the authorities and being prepared for burial at ten o'clock tomorrow morning. At first Ryder told her he didn't want to come, he preferred to just grieve by himself, but she begged him saying she *'needed him there.'* He assured her; he would be leaving later today, and would arrive that evening.

It was the time of *avel*, the time of mourning. In Jewish culture it was the pulling away from life toward death, when the person was mourned and remembered. Ryder had gone through this all before when Annalisa's grandfather passed away. According to Jewish culture her body was not to be embalmed, instead the *Chervah Kadisha*,- the Holy Society- would clean her body, wash her by pouring three buckets of water over her, they would then wrap her in a *tachrichin*,-a simple burial shroud- without pockets, 'for you came into the world with nothing and you take nothing with you'. Then they would place the body in a simple wooden casket, where all the lining would be stripped from it, a fringe on her prayer shawl cut off, so that it may no longer be used and it would be buried with her. Dirt from Israel would be sprinkled over her, and the casket would be sealed shut, as the guardian- the *shomer*-would stay with her till the burial.

Ryder went back up to his condo-the penthouse. It was perfectly decorated in the latest style, of what was "in", modern and stylish with a hint of an industrial look. Chrome and glass-topped tables, and an aquarium, filled with exotic colorful fish that doubled as a coffee table that sat in front of a dark blue ostrich skin love seat. It was good enough to be in the latest design magazine, the problem was, it wasn't him, he just put down the money and told the designer 'do what she does best.'

He missed his old two bedroom bungalow that was next to the river. The only thing he had brought from the place was his old walnut desk, with its scratched up drawers, and chipped off corner; it looked out-of-place here, but it was the only thing that was him. It was his mother's old desk; it was where each month she got the check book out and paid the bills. He stroked his finger over the chipped off corner and remembered when it happened. He had just gotten a bicycle for Christmas. A beautiful green metallic stingray with a white banana seat and extra high sissy bar, but it was a white Christmas: ten inches of snow and he couldn't ride outside. Annalisa, who lived just down the road with her grandmother, had come up. She wanted to go for a bike ride. She climbed on the bike with him and they took a spin through the house. They turned the corner and BAM, right into the desk, knocking the tip of the corner off. His father was furious and jerked his belt off, but his mother told his father to cool it, that 'what he did, he did for love.'

He opened the bottom drawer on the right hand side and pulled out his old service weapon, a Glock 30SS flat black with matching checked plastic handles. It was short, less than seven inches in length and with the stopping power of a 45 caliber and with a ten round clip it was the perfect conceal and carry weapon; it was his choice as a side arm when he was a detective. He put it into a leather holster and tossed it in the bag of clothes he had packed, along with a couple of 45 caliber clips. He reached back into the drawer and produced a small cedar wood box, with a red velvet lining; he lifted up the brightly plated Smith and Wesson 500 magnum revolver that was inside. Laying the revolver down beside the box on top of the desk, he picked up the small card wedged inside of the lid. It read:

"Merry Christmas and Happy Chanukah! Love, your little sister Yakira.

She had always been like his little sister, even when she was following him and Annalisa around town as if she were a puppy; trying to do everything they did, including having to have her picture made with them the night of the prom. Ryder picked up the one of the photos on the desk and looked at it, of him Annalisa and an eight year old Yakira. Next to it was a photo of Annalisa, in a round silver frame. He set the first photo down and picked up the other photo and held it in his hands, as he lovingly let his finger trace over the photo of Annalisa's face. He turned the frame over and removed the photo and shoved it into the inside breast pocket of his jacket.

He reached back into the drawer and pulled out a leather shoulder strap holster, and shoved the SW 500 in it then tossed it into his bag also. Reaching into the drawer again he pulled out a box of bullets for the SW 500 and tossed them in the bag. He pushed the drawer back in place, and sat there for a moment, staring out over the apartment. At the leather-bound books of titles he never wanted to read when assigned to him the first time in school. At antique vases that cost more than he made in one year as a detective. Paintings hung on the walls that were done by the latest great artist, but really looked like something a kindergartener would paint. He walked to the door, holding it open, giving his apartment one last look before he walked out, and closing the door behind him. Inside there was a small little voice telling him he wasn't coming back here.

Once again he found the towering giants of concrete and steel looking down upon him, judging him harshly with the gleam of sunlight off the windows. Were they disapproving of him leaving, or was it their way of saying goodbye? Soon the towering giants stood behind him, getting smaller and smaller in the rear view mirror. The locomotives were all lined up proudly facing into the wind, CSX car carriers, with the newest models tucked away behind their protective doors, with only a hint to the treasure hiding within them, grain cars waiting with hungry open mouths to gorge themselves on the grain in the bins.

With the winding and twisting of the road, the city just didn't want to let go, holding on to him, surrounding him with multiple lanes of traffic, crossing over the Missouri River, blending in with the semis, cargo vans, and mothers tooling along in minivans and SUVs. The city finally giving a gentle wave of farewell as the wide string of insanity gave way to four lanes of uninspiring pavement heading into the beauty of the Ozarks.

Straight south, then to I-44 and headed for the highway 37 off ramp, winding through the notorious speed traps and then through Monett, passing by the large old brick house full of history in the town. All Ryder knew was it large, old, and likely was haunted, after all that was what his Uncle Tony told him when he was a kid.

The highway took a hard turn to the right and to the left was Broadway that ran right through the middle of town. However, it was the building over to the left before this intersection that was getting his attention-the Family Room Steak House, the place that Deputy Thompson was talking about and how good their burgers were. Having not eaten anything since yesterday, his stomach was demanding he stop.

It had gone through different names, from the Black Kettle to some other place that Ryder couldn't remember when he was last here. It was fresh and inviting, painted white with black and red stripes. He parked the car, and walked around to the side where the entrance was. Stepping inside he reached up and removed his sunglasses and glanced down at the daily specials written on a stand up blackboard. 12 ounce rib steak, it was beef, but that wasn't what he was wanting. He continued up a sloping walk and through another door.

Inside it was bright and cheerful, with good lighting and the white theme continued with arched shaped openings that allowed one to see clear through to the other side of the restaurant. The other wall to his right was bright red, he didn't know why it was but the color red always made him think of blood, and blood always brought his thoughts to murder. All around the restaurant were messages of encouragement that family was greater than anything else, yet the only family, by blood, he had left was a uncle. He had a father, but where he was Ryder didn't know nor care. Ryder glared at the sign behind the checkout counter where you paid, it read.

"The more you complain the longer God makes you live."

"Wouldn't you just hate if that is true." He heard a woman say. It was the hostess. She was an attractive young woman, in her early twenties, with auburn hair that would normally flow down her back but was held back in a loose ponytail. She smiled and revealed the sprinkling of freckles around her emerald colored eyes.

"If it is, politicians will never die." She began to lead him into the next room, with tables and chairs, where a middle-aged couple sat enjoying their meal. "Can I have a booth instead?" Ryder asked, glancing across the room into another room with a row of high back booths up next to the windows. She led him into the other room that was divided by the arch shaped openings. Ryder picked the third booth from his left and sat down facing another bright red wall.

"What do you want to drink?"

"Iced tea. Sweet, with a half-twist of lemon." He said, placing the menu down on the table. "A friend of mine recommended a burger here. But I don't see it listed here."

"Who's your friend?"

"Deputy Thompson."

Kathy grinned showing her crooked smile and said. "Oh yes, that is a specialty burger. She took the menu from him and added. "It is not on the menu, we only make for our special customers. It is a Texan Burger. Two beef patties on thick cut Texas toast, with grilled onions, America cheese, lettuce and tomato, and our special homemade Barbecue sauce."

"Spicy?"

"No, more sweet and mild."

"Good, because I hate spicy." Ryder grinning slightly before adding. "Except of course, women."Kathy returned the grin as she slightly blushed. "I like them sweet with a little bit of the *right spice.*" His tone made her cheeks glow even more. "Am I special enough for that?"

"Since you're a friend of Brian's, okay."

"And can I get dill pickles with that too?"

"Sure thing." Kathy said writing the order down on a pad, as the color came back to her face. "How about fries?"

"Naw. You don't eat fries alone."

"That is what I think. They are meant to be shared." Kathy turned and left, walking towards the kitchen. She returned and placed the glass of iced tea in front of him and said "That is an excellent choice. I made the sweet tea today. It is really sweet. If you need anything, just let me know."

Ryder nodded and she turned and started to walk away. "Anything?" Ryder asked.

"Well, within reason." She said, turning back to him again a pinkish glow coming over her cheeks. She walked back to the booth. "Oh heck, you are a cutie." She added with a large smile. "Anything!"

"How about answering a question?"

"No, I am not married." She laughed.

"Well, that is good to know." He said as he reached into his jacket pocket and pulled out the photo of Annalisa. He held it up. "Have you seen this woman?"

"Oh my God!" She said, taking the picture and steadying herself with her other hand she sat down in the in the booth across from him. "This is the woman that was murdered at Roaring River." She looked up from the photo and added. "The congressman's wife." She handed the photo back to him and he slipped it back into his jacket pocket. "I saw her earlier that day. She drove into the parking lot, and wanted something to drink." Ryder could see it was difficult for her to talk and slid the glass of tea over to her. "Thank you." She said and took a sip before continuing. "We had a water line break that day. It was a mess so we were closed that day; as we were cleaning up, she drove up."

"What time was that?"

"It was a little before four in the afternoon."

"Are you sure?"

"Positive! Brunettes in Mercedes, BMW's, blondes in Mustang convertibles, we get. Pretty blondes in red Ferrari's we don't get. Not that kind of car and not in this area. Anyway Jamie saw her and got her a drink and even made her a sandwich."

"Jamie? Who is that?"

"The owner, she is a good person with a big heart, didn't even charge her for it, because she was acting so strange."

"How so?"

Kathy began to choke up as she spoke. "She was so sweet and kind. How could anyone kill her?"

"That is what I am trying to find out."

"Are you a cop?"

"No, just someone who is trying to find out the truth, you said she was acting strange, why was that?"

Kathy took a larger drink of the iced tea and said. "We were out in the parking lot talking about all kinds of things. Men, women, and the stupid things we all do for love. Then it happened."

"What?"

"She saw this white van slow down, and she tore out of here like a bat out of Hades. She had to be doing seventy when she hit the curve, I didn't know you could take it that fast!" Kathy stood up and added. "I better get back to work." She picked up the glass and added. "I will get you a new glass of tea."

She quickly returned with the glass of tea, it was so sweet, that it almost seemed addictive, as one sip called for another and another, he was quickly becoming a 'teahead'; he had gone through two glasses before Kathy returned once again and set the plate down in front of him.

He picked up the salt shaker and salted his dill pickles before placing them on the burger. He picked up the burger; it was a handful, even for his large hands. He bit into it and a sweet savory flavor of the homemade barbecue sauce filled his mouth. It wasn't overwhelming with spice, and the sweetness with the saltiness of the burger just demanded another bite. Kathy returned with a pitcher and picked up the glass and poured him another glass of tea.

"I just remembered something else that she said." Kathy set his glass back down on the table. "It was something really strange."

"What was it?" Ryder asked as he put the burger down on the plate.

"She asked me- do you think that God can forgive all sins? Even those that you can't even confess to him?"

28

"What did she mean by that?"

"I don't know. But I told her all are forgivable if you ask. She told me this one she couldn't ask forgiveness for. I told her He knows already."

Kathy had left when Ryder heard a distinctive voice that made his skin draw up like a bullfrog in the Arizona sun; he just wanted to hide under the table.

"Oh my goodness..." He glanced up and there was a tall curvy blonde woman who was twenty years older than he was, it was Maureen Ryder, his step mother, along with another woman. "Richard!" Suddenly Ryder's appetite faded like sunshine behind storm clouds. "We will just take this seat right here with my son." She said. "It is so nice to see you, Richard." She continued as they sat down across from him. "I have my son back here now." She reached over and patted his hand. "So what are you doing back in town?"

"You are not my mother!" Ryder said, pulling his hand back away from hers. He looked at the other woman; she was about the same age as Maureen, shorter, thin with long dreary looking hair. He recognized her as Maureen's good friend Pamela Williams, her neighbor from across the street. "You are the woman who married the man who my mother was married to." Ryder in no way hid his distaste for his step mother and wanted no connection to her. His mother had died when he was twelve. He was there holding her hand, when she took her last breath, his so-called father was with this woman, and married her hardly before the flowers wilted on his mother's grave. He had never forgiven his father for this and as for Maureen, "I have told you before; I have no need of you."

"So what are you doing here, Richard?"

"I am here for Annalisa's funeral." He said, taking another sip of the tea, even as sweet as it was it seemed bitter as he swallowed it and he looked right at Maureen as she dotted the tears from her piercing blue eyes. "Oh no you don't!" He shouted wiping his mouth and tossing his napkin down on the plate, making the customers in the restaurant look. "You don't have a right to shed any tears over her."

"But she was such a sweet child. I—" She sobbed. He could not believe what he was hearing. How could this woman say this? She hated Annalisa. It was her that had such a problem with them being together.

"No! Not after what you did!" "Ryder stood up, interrupting her.

"I just did what I thought was best, if…"

"No! " He shouted again, drawing Kathy's attention and she approached the table.

"Is there a problem here?" She asked.

"No, no problem." Ryder said. "The food is good." He turned and looked at Maureen. "It is just the company that is lousy." He turned back to Kathy and said. "I need a to-go box and cup" Kathy turned and went back to the kitchen. Ryder gritted his teeth together as he said. "I am going to find out who killed her, and when I do…"

"Haven't you heard? They made an arrest."

"Who? Warner?"

"No, her little sister." The woman replied back. Ryder's eyes drew down her as if he was aiming through anger through the sights of gun.

"Yakira?" Ryder demanded. "Why?"

"I don't know I just heard that the prosecutor was going to file charges on her."

"Price!" Ryder said angrily, as he took the box from Kathy and tossed the burger into box and poured his drink into a foam cup. "He is going to be sorry he did that." He closed the box and handed the server a fifty, telling her what was left was to be for a tip. He pulled out his phone and began scanning under the contact list. He pressed the send button. As he walked out of the restaurant he said into the phone: "Remember that favor I did for you? Well, I need one now."

Chapter 5

For Yakira Rosen Cassville had always been home, she knew no other , and she barely ventured out of the area, maybe occasionally go to Springfield or Joplin, but little Rock was as far away from home as she ever got.

Cassville's greatest claim to fame was that it was home to some of the best trout fishing in the state, but it was the city's nickname- the City of Seven Valleys- that drew her grandfather here. Seven Valleys, it just 'sounded so right'. Seven, God's perfect number, it just 'sounded as if it was where a proud Jew should live.' Her father would always say that when he told the story of their travels from New York to here.

For the most part the Rosen family may not have found a 'Promised Land' here, but they did find a home. Her father, an expert tailor, even found a place for his shop- Pascal's Fine Suits- right there on the town square, between the drug store and a furniture store. His skills were so fine, that customers came from as far away as Little Rock, Arkansas just to have one of his suits, plus the farmers around the area had to have a Sunday going to church, getting married, getting buried suit.

Even Yakira herself enjoyed business success with her gun shop out on highway 112. *Rosen's Outdoor Sports* was a favorite with all the local hunters and fishermen. If there was big fish tale, or a yarn about a twenty-point buck that just couldn't be taken down, she had heard it, and most likely more than once. Now the biggest tale in town was her sister's murder and that she had been arrested for it.

Ten years younger than her older sister, Yakira was the complete opposite of Annalisa. Thin, with feminine curves that only showed when she turned to her side, hair straight and dark as the night itself, except for the ends which were dyed red; it flowed down her back just below her shoulder blades. Her face shown no age, even though she was on her way to 30, she still looked like a teenager. Her dark eyes were like that of a fawn, with such gentleness to them. Her skin was flawless, with a slight exotic completion, which gleamed against pink clothing, which was what she always wore. Her nose was large, clearly showing her Jewish background. While Annalisa was well more than half way over the five foot mark, Yakira just barely topped that mark, by only two inches.

As Ryder pushed the pedal down on the Jaguar, memories flowed of that cute little girl, wanting to go everywhere he went, always wanting to eat what they were eating. Oh how she would worm her way into them taking her to the movies, having to have a burger at the local drive inn, even staying up all night to wait for he and Annalisa to return on prom night and dance with him. Ryder had never had any siblings of his own so it was just natural to see her as a little sister. He jerked the steering wheel and the Jaguar zoomed off the main highway and onto the business route that headed into town.

He zoomed by the small little white churches and tall evergreen trees dotted along the ribbon of pavement that suddenly became main street. Twisting the steering wheel the Jaguar sped around the square, heading straight down West Street till he came to the Barry County Judicial Center. He parked the car in the front of the red and white brick building and stormed inside.

"Can I help you?" The guard asked as he leaned on the counter.

"Prosecutors office: where is it?"

"What is your concern?"

"Legal matters! Where is it?" Ryder said, removing his sunglasses.

He couldn't be sure if it was Ryder's size; the look on his face, the tone of his voice or something else but the guard straightened up and kindly offered. "Down the hall to the right, sir."

Ryder passed through the metal detector and he turned back to guard. A phone call is coming in about five minutes. You make sure you put it right through."

"Yes sir."

Ryder walked down the hall and pushed open the door, walking past the secretary and into the inner office. A tall skinny man with thinning gray hair stood up from behind his desk as he looked at Ryder and a quirky grin spread across his lips. Ryder asked in an irritated tone, "Price, where the hell do you get off pressing charges on Yakira?" His secretary had followed Ryder in and asked if she should call for the guard.

"No, it is quite all right." Price said with a smirk. "Don't you know who we have here? This is the great' Pale Ryder', that led the Wildcats to three state championships in a row including placing the Cassville Wildcats as the number one team in the United States his senior year. With the number one draft from the Missouri Tigers to the Kansas City Chiefs?" Price smiled a cocky smile trying his best to upset Ryder, bringing him back to that night. "Then there was the blind side hit, right Ryder?" His secretary left and closed the door behind her.

Ryder was taken back to that night, Monday Night Football. Millions were watching. He was driving the Chiefs downfield, against the Broncos for the fifth time in a row, scoring every time, bringing that famous air attack that had given the Missouri Tiger's two Championships in a row, to Arrowhead. He drew back and threw, touchdown. It was a late hit, and it drew the flag, next thing Ryder remember was staring up into, the stadium light beaming down on him, closing his eyes from the pain, surrounded by the other players, some kneeling down to pray, including those on the other team. He remembered the stillness of the crowd, the cheering had stopped. It was that eerie silence that was the last thing he heard before disappearing into the tunnel on the cart. He shook the memory from his mind and went back on attack.

"Answer me, Price!"

The man stood up behind his desk, shuffling through the papers on his desk. "Oh, now what case was it you were interested in?" He picked up a paper and held it out. "Oh yes, poor Annalisa's murder, it seems to me that I have this case all wrapped up. I have witnesses that show her and her sister got into a fight. They heard them arguing."

"Really, Price? That is all you got? Siblings fighting!" Ryder said as he moved closer to the desk. "You have her prints on the cable? Prints on the car? What is the motive?" Ryder asked and suddenly the phone rang. Ryder grinned. *Right on time.* It rang again. "You might want to get that. It is not good for your career to make Superior Court Judge Walker wait."

Puzzled, Price picked up the receiver and said "Price here." The expression of smugness washed away on his face as he heard the voice on the other end. His lips tightened as he glared at Ryder and said. "Yes, your honor I understand. I will your honor. Yes, your honor. I will." He slammed the receiver down. "I've just been ordered to drop all charges on Yakira. How did you manage that?"

It was simple. The good judge had had one too many and Ryder, instead of arresting him, took him home. "Let's just say it was favor paid. Ryder slipped his sunglasses back on to his face and continued. "Now you call over to the S.D. and they better have her ready to go when I get there or I am going to call in another favor."

"You know, something really stinks here Ryder."

"You noticed that too?" Ryder grinned. "You really should get this place cleaned up." Ryder walked over to the door and looked back at him. "Make that call, Price."

Chapter 6

It was typical county jail, made of concrete blocks with no thought to style, it was made to be a jail, built to keep and hold prisoners and not to attract attention, even the block lettering over the opening seem so cold. "I am here for Yakira Rosen." Ryder said as he walked up to the counter in the lobby. A woman, in her late twenties named Clarice, with her platinum hair piled up on top of her head was hurriedly flipping through papers, looking through her cat eye glasses that made her green eyes look slightly crossed. "Is she ready?"

"No, Mr. Ryder. But she will be." Clarice apologized. She turned and yelled at the woman deputy. "For gosh sakes Lucie get her out here!" She turned back to Ryder. "It will be just a couple of minutes."

Ryder pulled his sunglasses off and laid them down on the counter, He picked up a brochure about a cruise ship from San Diego called the Virgin Princess.

"The sheriff's brother is the captain of that ship." Clarice said. Ryder laid the brochure down and looked at the woman.

"One hundred seventeen seconds and counting." He said calmly.

"I will see if I can hurry her up." Clarice said and walked back through the door that separated the outer office and the jail.

"Well, if you had this much power when you were a cop, you must have been one heck of a detective. " Ryder heard someone say from behind him. He turned around; a man was standing there. Stocky built, in his late forties, brown hair that was slicked back over on the side and parted on the right, with a well trimmed full goatee and mustache that was showing hints of gray. Clutched in his hand was a brightly plated revolver; a 32 caliber Saturday night special in his right hand and polishing it with a cloth in the other hand. "I have never seen my people move that fast in my life." He added with a smile as he placed the gun down on the counter and held his hand out. "Jeff Hart, I am the sheriff here." Ryder shook the man's hand.

"Rick Ryder. Nice revolver there."

"Yes it is." Sheriff Hart replied holding it up. One of a kind, I am sort of a collector. "

"Where did you get it?"

"A little pawn shop here in town."

"Where do you get off arresting Yakira?" Ryder demanded. "You should be questioning the congressman, after all, just last week wasn't a charge was made on Congressman Scott Warner's credit card for one Ethernet cable?"

"Now how would you know that?" Sheriff Hart asked surprised.

"I still have connections in the department."

"Is that how you broke the Kansas City Butcher case?" Ryder was relieved by his comment, as most people recognized him as the big lottery winner, which resulted in a plea for money. He had given away some and invested in others, such as three million to the guy who wanted to start a store that would have all the good things people remembered from childhood, like pop in a cooler, Banquet cream pies, and candy bars whose names had been long forgotten. It was nice being remembered for his work.

"Not exactly." Ryder drew out his words that could have made Dirty Harry proud

Sheriff Hart walked behind the counter and pulled open a drawer and slipped the revolver into it, then pushed it closed. Unlike the other deputies he was not in a uniform, instead he was dressed in a light blue western inspired suit, gray cowboy hat and black cowboy boots. "I asked the Speaker about it." Sheriff Hart said as he stepped back out from behind the counter. "He told me it was his son L.J. who bought it."

"L.J.?" Ryder hadn't heard this name before.

"London James." Deputy Thompson said as he walked into the room. "You know he was married before Annalisa?" Ryder shook his head; he did not know that tidbit of information. "His former wife's dad owned the sorghum mill and the ranch that he now lives at." The deputy poured himself a cup of coffee from the pot that was sitting on a table behind the counter. He lifted the pot as an offering to Ryder. Ryder again shook his head and Deputy Thompson continued. "London." He mocked. "Silly name for a man, don't you think? He sortta runs the mill now, when it is open. Other times he spends a lot of time in here."

"We questioned Speaker Warner on where he was." Sheriff Hart said as he walked back and picked up the trash bag, there were several foam cups and paper bags foam the local McDonalds and Sonic plus an empty package from a Tracfone, the phone removed. "It is unbreakable; he was doing a remote broadcast from Springfield." He said as he twisted the bag of trash around and tied it in a knot.

"You have a witness to this?"

"Yes, it is his assistant Susan Glenn and a reporter in Arizona for the ten o'clock news report there."

"And what about you?" Ryder asked still with that low tone to his voice

"You are accusing me?!" Sheriff Hart asked, shocked that he would even be considered a suspect. "I barely knew the woman. Why would I want to kill her?"

"Where were you?"

"I was here working except for around seven to eight I went on a call for an alarm at the Sorghum Mill."

"Ricky." He heard a soft voice say from behind him. He turned around and saw Yakira standing there, dressed in blue jeans and a pink blouse with a white collar. He moved in front of her, her head barely reached his shoulder. Standing there she still looked like the little sister he envisioned her being, but as she looked up at him with those big eyes there was something different about her, there was a hint of womanhood there. "*Shalom*." She said barely parting her lips, revealing her slightly larger front teeth.

"*Shalom*." He replied back. "You ready to go?"

"More than ever." She said, raising her head and making her hair fall back over her shoulders. She grabbed him, buried her face in his chest and said "I knew you would rescue me." He lifted his hand, up towards the back of her head, holding it there, but not touching her. His fingers closed together in a fist, shaking, confused as to what to do. If it had been Annalisa he would have just held her and assured her that everything was going to be okay. This was different; his fingers unclenched as he patted her on the back and pushed her away a little.

"Let's get going." He said as he picked up his sunglasses and slipped them on his face. He held the glass front door open for her. He turned back to the sheriff. "Just to let you know sheriff, I am going to be staying in town for a while."

"Doing little fishing or hunting?"

"Yeah, a little hunting, for a killer. I am going find who murdered Annalisa." He stepped out the door and added. "I owe that to her." Then he let the door shut behind him.

Ryder and Yakira got in the Jaguar and again headed north on main street. They had just passed by the courthouse in the middle of town when Yakira spoke up. "Can we go somewhere before you take me home?" She asked, looking over at him. "There is something I have to do."

"Where?"

"Bubbie's old house." She said, and he nodded. "But first there is something I need to get at Wal-Mart." She looked down on the floor at the foam box; she picked it up and opened it. "Is this a Texan burger? From Family Room Steakhouse?"

"Yeah. I would give you the other half. But it is not kosher. It has cheese." Growing up with his best friend being Jewish, he knew a few things about the culture and meat and dairy at the same time was not allowed.

"Oh, honey." She said patting his arm, smiling and raising up one eyebrow. Her tone was that of a 90-year-old Jewish woman and a twenty something, with just a hint of a hillbilly accent thrown in. "I kind of bounce off the kosher wagon every now and then." As she said that she took a bite of the uneaten half of the sandwich. "Just don't tell anyone. Our secret, okay?" She turned her head sideways and looked at him and grinned. She handed him the other half that he had taken a few bites from. It was cold and greasy, but the sweetness of the sauce, or maybe it was just being hungry made him want another bite. "Sweet?" She asked, picking up the cup of tea that was in the cup holder.

"Of course!" Ryder could stand tea without sugar it made him gag.

Yakira leaned her head back on the seat, and turned her head, watching the scenes go by, till they got close to an old abandoned house at the crossroads. Ryder turned left onto a small county road; it was now paved, but he remembered when it was nothing but a single lane dirt road, it was when he lived here.

It was home for the first twelve years of his life. In a two story flagstone home, that as he remembered was huge, and could be anything he wanted it to be from a hotel to a hospital or a police station, only limited by his imagination. It was down the road about a mile then take a left and follow another narrow dirt road, under 'pucker your butt' bridge-so named because of how narrow it was- that reduced travel to a crawl, to keep from knocking the mirrors off your car, then straight across to another set of crossroads and down another half mile. Ryder hadn't been back here since Mr. Roberts had bought the farm for his horses. That was shortly after his mother died. There wasn't much left of his old home, the flagstone stolen, the aging decaying wood slats were showing through, and the floorboards ached from the bales of hay stacked in it. It seemed so small now, how could he have thought it was huge? His bedroom was barely wide enough for his bed; you had to kneel on the foot of the bed just to open the windows. The once soft green yard, that was his duty since seven years old to mow, was now grown up, over taken with weeds, the big old walnut tree in the front yard had fallen in a wind storm. Still tied to the limb was the old rope that was used with an old tire as the swing. It was so much fun back then, he and Annalisa swinging as high as they could, on the upswing he could see the roof of the barn, and the back swing gave him such a wondrous feeling, just before it would stop and swing forward again.

Just down the road a couple of hundred feet, and across from the old barn, was Bubbie's old house. A three-wire barbed-wire fence surrounded the house. Ryder pulled the car off the road in the drive. He held up a wire and Yakira crawled through, and he followed her. It was so still that the beat of a meadowlark's wing could be heard as it took flight from a field next to the house. The fence that once surround the yard was broken down, the wood picket slabs half-rotten, others broken in half, their sharpen points bent down as if they were the spears of guards daring anyone to enter. A wooden gate at the front next to the old well house was ajar, tilted over to the side, and hanging on only with the bottom hinge, that moaned as he pushed it open.

A swarm of grasshoppers took flight as they flew towards the old mobile home, painted putrid green, with porches built on the front and back, with the front facing the south. The weathering lumber creaked as they walked up to the front door, once bright white, faded and stained with rust. He gripped the knob and twisted and pulled back, the bottom digging in the wood planks of the porch, but it opened just wide enough so that they could squeeze through.

Empty beer and soda cans littered the floor, and he kicked them out of the way. The trailer was fourteen feet across, and 60 feet long, with a bedroom at each end, and the living room dominating the biggest part was in the center of trailer, the only bathroom being next to the master bedroom at the eastern end. Most of the walls of the bedroom had been pulled off and lay in a heap on the floor, and the copper wiring stolen and sold years ago. There was only one wall that was left intact, that was the northern wall in the living room, and Yakira stood holding a plastic sack in her hand as she stood staring at the wall.

"They have no idea what this means to us." She said as he walked up behind her and looked at the swastika spray painted in black paint. "I just got through scrubbing this off my gun shop yesterday. And Dad's place the week before."

"Who is doing it?"

"Some putz name Watterson that moved here from `Frisco." She said, turning to him as she reached down into the sack and pulled out a can of pink spray paint she had bought. "We used to not have problems here but lately—." She turned back to the graffiti and popped the lid off the spray can and began to shake it up. She began to paint over the mark, connecting the lines together, till it was four separate squares. In the squares she painted the letters L-O-V-E. "Through the window of love even the ugliest thing can become beautiful." She said turning to him with a grin. "You know who taught me that? He shook his head. Her voice broke, trying to hold the tears back. "My sister."

"You okay?" He asked but she quickly turned and dashed outside and he followed her. She stood at the edge of the front porch starting out across the front yard to a small storage building. It was 10 foot square, the sides covered with ruby colored roofing shingles. Yakira's grandfather had built it, and Annalisa used it as a playhouse, and her bedroom. In the winter you huddled together, buried under ten heavy quilts. If you had to pee, you just held it.

40

Summers, it was too hot to sleep inside; instead you took one of the quilts and spread it out on the grass. That sense of loss was coming back to him. He couldn't let her see; he lifted his head and stared up at the orange red sky that was gleaming from the setting sun.

"I just miss her so much." Yakira said. She wiped the tears from her eyes using the back of her hand and turned back and shivered with rage as she cursed in Yiddish and said. "I can't believe he is going to get away with it!"

"Who?" Ryder wondered if she had she had anyone else in mind, after all no one knew Annalisa better than her little sister.

"That damn Scott." Her word just confirmed Ryder's suspicions as she walked back down into the yard, making the grasshoppers jump and the large brown ones call out as they took to flight and landed on the remains of an old wood pile next to the fence line. She turned back to him as he followed behind her. "I know he killed her! And they are not going to do anything about it. He is the stinking Speaker of the House and my sister was…"

"The greatest person I ever knew." Ryder said, interrupting her as he walked past her and held the wire up for her once again. She crawled through and she turned to look back at him, as he added. "Don't let anything ever change that." He crawled through and held the door of the Jaguar open for her.

"Those stupid cops." She said as he climbed in behind the steering wheel. "They arrested me before I could ask him who she was."

"Who, who was?" He asked as he backed the Jaguar onto the road.

"He was having affair, Ricky." Her words made him turn and look at her and he brought the car to a stop in the middle of the road. The sun was illuminating Clifford woods behind them, casting long finger-like shadows over them. "Annalisa told me so. She just didn't know who it was. Isn't that a motive for murder?" She turned to him. "We can't let him get away with this. And I am going to stop him before he hurts anybody else."

Chapter 7

Pascal opened his shop the day Annalisa was born, three days after Ryder was born. It took five and half years to get his store to make a profit and another six and half years before he could afford to move out of his mother's trailer and to a house on Tenth Street in town. Up to that day, there was not a day that went by that Ryder and Annalisa would not see each other. Lost in a world that that only they could see, they built cities in their minds, the cats and dogs all part of their make-believe world, they were never bored; there was always something they could do. Then their world shattered when Ryder's mother passed away, they sat under the trio of pine trees, and she comforted him, even giving him his first kiss, but the land of make-believe was no more.

The Rosen's home set on a large corner lot at 10th and Oak Hill. The white house was one of the largest homes on the street, two stories high with large pillars on the full width front porch, predominated by a bay windows on each side of the front door. Three steps led up to the large inset red door, attached to the inside of the door frame was the *mezuzah*; a small wooden box attached about two-thirds of the way up, slanting inward at the top towards the top of the door. On the front at the top of the box was a small window in the shape of a square, revealing the parchment, with the word '*shaddai*' written on it. Written on the scrolled up parchment were the words:

'Love the Lord your God with all your heart, and with all your soul, and with all your strength.' - Deuteronomy 6:5.

"I don't know about this." Ryder said as Yakira reached for the front door handle. He placed his hand in front of her. "I really don't belong here."

"You were part of her life." She replied, looking up at him. "Besides..." She looked down and slipped her fingers in between his. "...I need you here." She glanced up at him. "I need a friend." She opened the door and they walked into the entry way. Every mirror in the house, including the large one that hung on the wall just above the hall tree where the coats were hung was covered with black cloth, 'so that others may not see themselves and instead remember the one who has died.' It was all part of the Jewish culture. Strange to someone who grew up in the Catholic faith, but hadn't darkened the doorstep of any church since he left this town, and that was twenty two years ago.

At the end of the entryway was the main staircase that led up to the second floor. Two rooms were on each side of entryway; the dining room to the right and the living room to the left. The family had gathered in the living room. Pascal; a squatty set man with graying hair along the sides of his head, the bald spot covered with a red and yellow colored *kipah*-skullcap. Ryder made this mistake, of calling it a beanie when he was a kid and got a lesson on what it meant. *'To honor God. You are to cover your head in order that the fear of heaven may be upon you.'* That was somewhere out of the bible, but exactly where he didn't know, or really care.

As always, Pascal was wearing a suit, one of his own that he had made, draped around his shoulders was a bright white prayer shawl with dark blue stripes and fringe on the ends; he was reading from the book of Psalms. He glanced up and stopped reading as he saw them standing there. He got up and walked over to them. According to Jewish customs Ryder was not to greet him, but to wait for Pascal to greet him.

"Yakira!" He said with great joy as he embraced her. "We have been praying for your release. They would not set bail. How did you get out?"

"Ricky got me out." She replied as she gazed up at Ryder. "You should have seen them Abba, they were *plotzing* all over the place to get me out of there."

Pascal turned to Ryder and offered his hand to him. "*Shalom Aleichem sheli ben.*"

"Peace unto you, Pascal." Ryder replied back, shaking the man's hand.

"I will be forever in your debt for saving my only daughter. How can this be repaid?"

"Allow me to mourn with you." Ryder said as he looked down at Yakira. "I have no one else." Ryder knew this was time that only the family was allowed to be here, it would be later those others would be allowed to give their respects.

"Rick you have always been family to us." Pascal said reaching into his jacket pocket and producing a white skullcap and handing it to Ryder. "And you always will be." Ryder unfolded it, and put it on top of his head and then entered the living room. Ryder stood next to Yakira, waiting for someone to say something before he spoke. "I was out in the garage the other day and saw that old bicycle you fixed up for her. You and your mother must have worked for a month on that. So she could have it for her birthday .I couldn't even afford a bike for my kid back then. I may have been poor but I was blessed with good friends and neighbors."

"Well I just got tired of having her on the back of my bike and having to take her everywhere." Ryder grinned.

"You remember that day, Rebekah, how happy Annalisa was?"

Rebekah, the mother, favored her youngest daughter in her face, and yet she lacked the sparkle that Yakira had. She was heavier-set with raven hair that was tightly premed and dyed. She looked at Ryder and nodded but didn't say a word. Try as he might he couldn't get rid of that memory of twenty-two years ago, right here in the living room, that Annalisa proudly showed her the engagement ring as she had her arm wrapped around his waist. Pascal gave his blessing, but it was Rebekah and Maureen that stood there clothed in their robes, their hair put up in curlers. Saying 'this cannot be allowed."

To her right seated on the sofa was Anna, Rebekah's older sister, who sat with her arms crossed in front of her as she stared at him, and their younger sister Leesabeth, who was thin as a rail, and she grinned like a Cheshire cat at him. Seated in another chair that faced Pascal was the matriarch of the family, his mother-Seraphina-Bubbie- the grandmother. Dressed in a red and white robe, she looked every bit like a queen. He remembered her that night also, standing at the bottom of the stairs as he left, not saying a word.

"How you doing, *Motek*?" Bubbie said, offering a term of affection to him. She held her hand up to him. He took her hand and he felt her elderly fingers grip around his as she guided him around in front of her. He had known this woman all his life, when he got sick she always brought him a bowl of matzo ball soup, that always seem to work miracles. His mother wanted her to hold him when he was christened, 'Richard Thomas Allen Ryder' but the church, the Catholic Church, would not have it. So instead, there on the farm they had their own private christening, with his uncle Anthony performing the service, going against his own church.

Ryder kneeled down in front her and dropped his head down, trying not to let her see the tears that were forming in his eyes as he spoke. "You know what she meant to me, Bubbie." He raised his head and looked into her big soulful eyes. "I promise you I am going to find out who killed her. And when I do, I am going to make them pay."

"Don't do that!" He heard Rebekah say, as he stood up and turned to her.

"You don't want to know who killed Annalisa?" Yakira snapped at her mother.

"There is no need to be angry, Yakira. We should be honoring your sister. 'Whatever the Merciful One does, He does for the best.' This is so even when those we love die. "

Yakira swung her head around, closing her eyes and gritting her teeth in frustration. "Annalisa did not just die! She was murdered! This isn't due to Yahweh's will. He strangled the life out of her. "

"Who are talking about, dear?" Pascal asked.

"Look around." Yakira said. "Do you see your wonderful son-in-law here?"

"He had business in D.C. He will be here for the funeral."

"Oh geeze, Mother! How stupid can you be?"

"Do not call your mother names." Pascal said. "Show her respect."

"I am trying, but she won't…." Yakira again shook her head in frustration. "Don't you get it; Scott was cheating on her. He is a stupid pile of…" She turned to Ryder and looked up at him then back to her mother. "There is only one man who ever really loved her and it wasn't that one who… Forget it!" Yakira turned and walked out of the room then sat down on the bottom step of the stairs.

Ryder, feeling uncomfortable, pulled the skullcap from his head and handed it back to Pascal. "I think it would be best if I leave."

"Yes, I agree." Rebekah said pushing herself out of her chair. "It would be best if you left. We don't need to be bringing up that marriage thing again."

Yakira glared intensively at her mother and twisted her head once again as she took in a deep breath.

"Pascal, you need anything. I mean anything, you just ask." Ryder said and walking out of the room, he had just reached the entryway when Yakira yelled out.

"Wait! I will I go with you."

"Yakira." Her mother spoke up as Yakira glared at her, standing at the entryway to the living room. "We must honor your sister's memory. It is our faith."

Yakira stopped and twisted back to face her mother and said. "Right now I don't care about faith! I just want to know who killed my sister." She turned around, standing for a moment, before she turned back to face her mother again. "And when I do…" She tuned and headed towards the door and followed Ryder outside.

They walked back to the car and she didn't say a word as he held the door open for her, until he was seated behind the steering wheel. Staring straight ahead, she said. "Let's go to the lake house."

"Okay, but first we'll need to stop for some food and other supplies."

They stopped at the local super market for groceries and other supplies, which Yakira made a list of on the piece of paper she found lying on the floor of the car. It had been dark more than a couple of hours when they turned off the small county road that was somewhere between Golden and Shell Knob. The headlights of the car picked their way through the dotting of black walnut, pine and oak trees that were on each side of the narrow road that twisted its way through the woods. The tall grass swiped at the sides of the car as playfully as a kitten would with a bright sparkly ball. The road bent hard to the right and slightly up hill, the car bucked as the tires rolled over the remains of a stump at the top of the hill. At the bottom of the hill was Table Rock Lake and Ryder's lake home.

The headlights caught sight of the double pane glass of the A framed Lake House and winked at them just before he shut them off. They stepped out of the car, and only the dim glow of the interior light spilled through the darkness that was growing. Ryder scooped up the four paper bags of groceries from the back seat and shut the door, and the glow was gone, and they took a couple of steps towards the front porch, then just like being stars on center stage, the motion lights tucked under the peak of the roof came on and covered them in light. It was these lights and the fact that the place was owned by a cop that kept teenagers from trashing it. It took a few seconds before his eyes adjusted to the bright light; by that time Yakira had carried Ryder's suitcase to the porch and used her keys to open the front door and switch on the light inside.

The front door led into the kitchen, it was a straightforward design with gray slate flooring and a single cabinet along the side of the wall. With a refrigerator, range, dishwasher and sink, the only storage space was that in the upper cabinets. To one side of the house were the bedrooms and the bathrooms; to the other side was the great room, with an oak dining table at the far end and a fireplace at the other end. The wall that overlooked the lake, in the great room, was mostly windows with sliding glass doors next to the fireplace and the dining table.

Ryder put the sacks down on top of the counter. He noticed the trash can was full of sacks from fast food places. The freezer had several frozen TV dinners that he had to move around to fit in the packages of meat they had bought. When is the last time you've been down here?"

He continued to empty the sacks, with cans of vegetables, a carton of eggs, bread, chocolate candy bars, cream, packets of sun dried tomatoes, sack of potatoes and a six pack of Coke among all the other necessities that one needs to stay comfortable and clean. He placed a couple of rib eye steaks on the counter. He pulled one of the frozen dinners out of the freezer. It was the cheap type that was occasionally put on sale. They were nothing he would buy; it meant someone was staying here.   "When is the last time you've been down here?" He repeated.

"I have been staying here." She mumbled as she stepped into the great room and turned on another light, revealing its modest furnishings that consisted of a couple of chairs that faced each other, and a sofa that faced a large flat screen TV that was on the only part of the wall that was not windows. In front of the sofa was a coffee table littered with fishing and car magazines. ""I lost the lease on my apartment about a month ago. Hope you don't mind. I have been staying in the back bedroom."

He closed the freezer door on the refrigerator and stepped into the living room just in time to see her walk over to the glass door and gape out into the night, her reflection in the glass stared back at her, and Ryder could see the sadness in her eyes. "You can stay here as long as you want. You are my little sister." She looked over her shoulder and offered a small smile.

"Go on out to the deck and relax while I fix the steaks." He told her as he went back into the kitchen and placed the package of rib-eyes out on the counter and tore them open. "I know how you like yours." She slid the glass door open and walked out onto the deck. Meanwhile Ryder washed a couple of potatoes, rolled them in salt and wrapped them in paper towels and cooked them in the microwave. While the potatoes were cooking, he took kosher salt and poured it on one of the steaks and then wrapped it in a paper towel, and placed it on a plate. The other steak he poured about a quarter cup of salt into a glass bowl and mixed it with water, then submerged the steak to soak out the blood, for Yakira, so it would be according to Jewish customs, this was the closest he could get as there were no kosher stores within a hundred miles. The microwave went off and he took out the potatoes, they were still firm, and he wrapped them in tin foil and placed them on the plates.

He turned and went out on the deck and saw Yakira standing, her hands resting on the rail as she stood seemingly in her own world, just glaring at the lake. She didn't say a word, nor did he. On the deck was a pair of lounge chairs and a small glass-topped table with chairs around it, and over next to the house was a propane gas grill, that he fired up. With the grill hot he returned to the kitchen and pulled the steak out of the bloody water. He patted the steak dry and removed the paper towel from the other steak which had soaked up some of the juice and dry aged it slightly. He took another paper towel and patted the other steak dry and placed them on a pan where he brushed both sides of the meat with vegetable oil. He picked up the pan with the steaks and the plates with the potatoes and returned to the grill. He placed the steaks down on the grill; with a sizzling hiss smoke rose up and tickled his nose.

He heard her sigh heavily and then speak. "Can you love someone and at the same time hate them?"

"Of course you can." He said walking over to her "You are talking about Annalisa, aren't you?" She nodded, but didn't say anything. "I know how you feel."

"Don't get me wrong." She said as she turned and looked up at him. "I loved her dearly. And anyone who would say anything bad about her, I will put them in the ground, but…" She turned back as if she couldn't face him and tell him this; then she stared back out across the lake. "…you know what a pain in the butt it was having her as a sister? Following in her footsteps all the way through school, she was the smart one, the popular one, in all the clubs, cheerleader, homecoming queen …" She leaned down, resting her elbows on the rail. Then she continued in a mocking tone "….All I would hear was Annalisa would never do that, Annalisa would never say that. Annalisa is the good little Jewish girl. Annalisa this, Annalisa that!" She paused and took a deep breath before saying in a normal tone. "I could never measure up to her."

He leaned down on the rail next to her as he looked out across the lake, the waves smacked against the bank, as if a drum keeping time with the buzzing song of the jar flies high up in the limbs of the sycamores, with that of katydids joining in on the rousing chorus, and a pair of bullfrogs bringing in the bass, with an off-key solo by a night heron topping off the night opera.

"This is also the same girl that got suspended for starting a food fight. And tossed Doug Harkin into a window down by the gym because he called her…well, a name I don't repeat. The sweet mellow sound of the steaks sizzling on the grill caught his attention making him walk back to the grill. He flipped over the steaks, revealing the heavy charred sides. He went back, leaned on the rail.

"I am having one of the worst days of my life." She said, still staring out across the lake. She turned to him and added. "And the one person I always called…" She lowered her gaze and shook her head as she sobbed "…I can't call any more." She turned back and gazed out over the lake once again. She reached over to place her hand upon his, but he was gone. He was over next to the grill, removing one of the steaks and placing it on one of the plates next to the potato as he let the other steak cook.

"You never asked me." Yakira said as she walked over to him.

49

"Asked you what?" He said with a tranquil tone as he removed the other steak and placed it on the other plate. He took the plates and went back inside and set them down on the table.

"About why Annalisa and I were fighting?" Yakira asked calmly as she went to the kitchen and grabbed flatware, steak knives, and a tub of margarine from the refrigerator and placed them on the table.

He pulled her chair out for her and she sat down and he seated himself at the head of table. He cut into his steak and the warm red juices flowed out, soaking into the potato skin. He turned to her and said. "I thought you would tell me when you were ready." He removed the tinfoil from his potato and slit it open and added a heaping amount of margarine.

"Well, I am ready." She said somberly staring down at her well done steak.

"Check your steak."

She cut into her steak and as she mumbled out "It is kind of hard to say."

"It is not done enough?"

"No, the steak is fine." She said laying her fork and knife down beside her plate. She cupped her fist inside her other hand and rested her chin on her fingers. "It is what the fight was about."

"So what was it about?" He asked, chewing on a piece of steak.

"It wasn't a what." She said lifting her head up. "It was a who, it was you."

Ryder swallowed hard, and grabbed a napkin and wiped his mouth as he said, thunderstruck. "Me?"

"I met her up at the football field." Yakira said putting margarine on her potato.

"What time was that?"

"Around five, maybe."

"What did she want?" It vital he knew, the last moments of a victims life some of the most important to determine why they were murdered, it was a text book he learned that from it was Captain Grosstree.

"She wanted me to bring her something."

"What was that?"

"A gun." She said plainly and waited for his reaction. He knew that Annalisa was not a fan of guns; she didn't own one and as far as he knew had never fired one. He sat there staring at her. His eyes not blinking in the dim glow of the lamp that hung over the table.

"What did she want a gun for?"

"That is what I asked her. She told me I didn't need to know. That it was best. She didn't say it but I could see she was scared."

"So where do I come into this?"

"Right now." She said as she took a bite of steak. "I told her if she was in trouble she needed to call you. She said…" She paused long enough to swallow the bite of meat. "She tried but you didn't want anything to do with us anymore. I told her that was a lie. You wouldn't do that. She said I was a silly little girl who didn't know what I was talking about and if I thought you were so great. I could have you."

"What did she mean, you could have me?"

Yakira gasped back embarrassment, not wanting to face him; she stared straight ahead and looked at her reflection in the windows. "Oh she got it in her silly head that…" She turned quickly and looked at him. "…there was something between us." She forced a mock laugh and asked. "That is silly, isn't it?"

"Of course. You are like a little sister to me." He said as he went into the kitchen, got a couple of glasses, filled them with ice and split a can of Coke He brought the glasses back and stood next to the table. He set a glass down in front of her. "You don't think there is anything between us, do you?"

"No, of course not. It was just…" she stumbled over her words before finally spitting out, "…of course not."

"So where is the fight? Is this the fight that they are talking about?"

"I guess, but I did yell at her when she called me silly little girl. I am not a little girl." Yakira picked up the glass of soda and took a drink and set it back down before continuing. "I gave her the gun and showed her how to use it. Then just before she left she hugged me and told me 'if anything happened to her I was to hang on to you and let my dreams come true.' "

"What does that mean?"

"I don't know!" Yakira answered excitedly as she stood up and took the plate into the kitchen. "You know how she was, crazy as a loon sometimes." She rinsed the plate under the faucet and then placed it in the drainer on the counter. "Ricky, I am really tired of talking about this, I am going to bed. You can have the front bedroom. *Layla tovey!*" She said in Hebrew, meaning Goodnight.

"Good night." Ryder said.

Yakira sat down on the edge of the bed and pulled her boots off and let them fall to the floor. Pulling her blouse up and over her head she unhooked her bra and tossed it and her blouse over the cedar chest that was at the foot of the bed. She stood, and unfastened the button on her jeans, and twisted out of them, and tossed them also on the chest. Opening the closet door she took out an old Wildcat football jersey, black with a gold number 7 on it. Slipping it over her head, she tossed her hair down over her shoulders and crawled under the sheet and the tan woven blanket, before turning off the lamp on the night stand next to the bed.

She lay there waiting for sleep to come to her, staring up at the darkness, closing her eyes she did what she had always done when she was sad, she imagined in her mind how life could be, it always filled her mind with light. She would be the perfect one; the one that always got mom's praise, the one that graduated with honors, and the one that all the boys wanted, the one that Ryder wanted. She heard a board creak from outside the window on the deck. Her eyes flew open; again she was enclosed in darkness. It could have been any number of things, from boards just settling, to an animal hunting for something to eat; raccoons were common visitors at the lake. She slowly turned over and faced the window, she gasped as she saw a shadow pass by the window- a human shadow.

Yakira lifted the covers up and crept out of bed; even through her black cotton socks, she could feel the coolness of the hardwood floor. She heard the creak on the deck again and she pushed the bedroom door open and looked out; the only light was the greenish glow from a nightlight in the kitchen hallway. The water heater heaved in and out, like a beast huffing behind the slatted bi-fold doors. She quickly stepped past the laundry closet, and through the kitchen, turned to the right.

Suddenly she was looking down the barrel of a Glock. "What are you doing up?" Ryder asked as he lowered the pistol to his side. She let out a relieving breath.

"I heard something." She whispered back. "There is somebody out there." He moved and looked out the window, letting the moonlight bathe over him, revealing he was dressed in nothing but a pair of dark blue silk sleep pants. His hairy chest was well toned and his shoulders were broad and his biceps bulged, as he gripped the butt of the Glock and moved towards the front door. Holding the pistol in his right hand, his back up against the wall, he used his left hand to open the door. He turned back to her. "Lock the door behind me and don't open it unless it is me."

Gripping the gun with both hands he disappeared out onto the deck. She shut the door and tried to lock it behind him, but the dead bolt wouldn't turn. She saw Ryder pass by the windows, with his back as close to the house as possible, to avoid making the security lights coming on. Twisting her head, she pressed her forehead up against the glass, watching as he leaped over the deck railing and crept around the other side of the house out of her sight.

There was dead stillness as she lowered herself to the floor and could feel the coldness of the tile floor through her lace panties. The only sound she could hear her was own heart beating. She hugged herself, remembering the gun that she had in the kitchen drawer, a snub nose Bulldog 357 magnum. She pulled the drawer open and picked up the revolver. Beside it was a box of shells. She flipped open the chamber and begin putting in the shells.

Blood Necklace

The sound of two gunshots rang out, breaking the tranquility. She could tell by the sound that they were from a 45 caliber, *he might need help.* She thought and she began shoving the bullets in quicker, loaded, she flipped the chamber back into place and pulled the hammer back. The door knob twisted and the door creaked open. She clutched the Bulldog in both hands and aimed, ready for a kill shot, her finger gripped around the trigger.

Chapter 8

"It's me!" Ryder said. He breathed a sigh of relief as she lowered the weapon to her side, slowly lowered the hammer.

"Who was it?"

"Don't know." He said as walked over to the kitchen counter and laid the Glock down on the counter, then reached down and took the revolver from her and placed it up on the counter next to the Glock. "Looked like an old Chevrolet pickup, I hit the passenger's side tail light, before they got away. Most likely kids looking for a place to party; don't think they will be back." He looked over at her. "I forgot how good you are with a gun." He added as she looked up at him. "I am lucky to be alive, huh kid sister?" He joked as he reached over and rubbed her hair. "Let's get some sleep; we have a big day tomorrow."

****

Ryder awoke the next morning coughing, and the smoke alarm was buzzing. He opened the door and the house was covered in smoke; he heard the words "Oh shoot" from the kitchen, followed by a loud hiss. He looked around the corner; there standing in front of the sink, was Yakira. Still dressed in his jersey, her hair tied back in a loose ponytail, her bangs dropping down over her grease- smudged forehead. Steam was rising up from the frying pan that she had just poured water on. She looked at him and blew her hair out of her eye and said. "I was just trying to fix breakfast for a surprise for you." He walked up to a pan on the stove filled with black lumpy stuff that was seared to the skillet; it was supposed to be scrambled eggs.

"Well, it certainly is a surprise." Ryder said taking a fork and trying to scoop up the charcoaled remains. "Did you use butter?"

"Butter?" She asked confused. "You might want to be careful. There might be shells in there."

He looked in another pot, there was a spoon sticking out of it and he picked it up, raising the pot. "Oatmeal." She said looking into the pot.

"Did you follow the directions?"

"Directions?" She asked, puzzled. "I just got some water and poured in a box of oats and boiled it till it was thick. That is how you do it, isn't it?"

"And that in the sink?"

"Bacon." She replied, coughing from the smoke that was hanging in the air. "I kept it on high to get it crisp. Because that is the way you like it." She reached up on her tippy-toes and got a cup and poured him a cup of coffee. She fixed it just the way he liked it, one cream and two sugars. She stirred it and handed it to him. It smelled like coffee. It looked like coffee. He took a sip. He gagged and then spit it into the sink.

"Did you use a filter?" He said spitting out the coffee grounds that were in his teeth. He reached up into the cabinet and got a small juice glass and filled it with water that he used to further rinse the grounds from his mouth.

"Filter? I just thought you put the coffee in the water." She said as he opened the back of the coffee maker and looked down inside and saw the coffee grounds floating on top of the dark colored water. Ryder coughed as he walked over and opened the front door to let the smoke out. "Guess I am not a good cook." Frustrated she pushed herself up on one of the stools at the breakfast bar and buried her face in her hands as she said. "Oh, great! Another thing my sister was better at than me. If I was to die right now, I couldn't do it as good as she did."

"Well you did get something right." He said as he placed a small juice glass down on the bar using the paper that Yakira had used to make the shopping list on as a coaster. "You do make a mean glass of O.J." He laughed softly.

"Oh, great! I am capable of pouring a glass of juice." She sighed. "And I spilled that when I poured it. I am such a *shmuck*." She pushed the glass away. "Tell me one thing I can do better than she ever could."

He sat down on the stool next to her. "When you got out of jail you said 'I rescued you.' "She swiveled around on the stool and faced him. "Annalisa always needed rescuing. I saw how you handled yourself last night." He reached over and pushed the strands of hair back out of her face. "You don't need me to rescue you. You rescue yourself. " He looked over at the dishes then back to her. "I will make you a deal. I will do the cooking. You do the cleaning."

"Cleaning?" She asked timidly, looking at the mess she had just made. "This?"

He patted her leg as he stood up. "We will start with new stuff. Go get dressed and I'll take you out for breakfast.

Chapter 9

Death is life's mistress. She is cold, calculating, with eyes of hot blazing coal, a fine wine that is elegant, yet bitter to taste in the mouths of mourners. Ryder couldn't taste the flavor of death anymore. As a detective he made it a point to attend every funeral of every victim, not where anyone could see him, he would just stand and watch them. Today wasn't any different, that was what he kept telling himself, but even he knew that was lie. This wasn't some piece of a puzzle that he had to put back together, or even a name, it was memories, everywhere he looked, everyone he saw, there was some memory attached to this woman.

He stood under the cool whispering shade of three pine trees remembering his first kiss and gazing out over the headstones all facing the sun that was still rising in the sky and graves lined up like soldiers waiting for their command to 'raise up.' His stared at the dark gray stone that held his mother's name and at the open grave on the next row that would soon hold Annalisa, the dark glasses over his eyes shielded the tears of what he was feeling.

The sound of gravel crunching under tires made him turn and watch as a bright white hearse rolled up with an SUV behind it, containing the pallbearers. They were all men of Jewish faith, as they opened up the rear door of the hearse the white family limo pulled in, followed by a string of other vehicles all paraded with the headlights on. He watched as Yakira stepped out of the limo; she was wearing a light weight gray dress with a pink sash around her waist and bright red high heeled shoes. He watched as she walked through the gate following behind the casket that was being carried by the Jewish men. They stopped and quoted in Hebrew the first word of Psalm 91:11. *"Kiy"*

"Shouldn't you be up there?" He heard a voice say from beside him. He turned and saw a heavy set man with a round face, hiding behind a pair of heavy black framed glasses. His once sandy crimson hair had heavy hints of silver and on top of his head was a large bald spot. It was the funeral director: Thom Thompson.

"Double T! Why aren't you up there offering up boxed condolences? Isn't that your job?"

"I resent that! She was my friend too."

"I am sorry, Double T."He knew than to say that, they had all attended the same school from kindergarten to graduation, and cruised Main Street as teenagers, she was his friend.

"Talk around town is that you're here to find out who murdered her." He said as they both watched the men carrying the casket stop and they spoke the first two words of the Psalms. *"Kiy mal'äkhäyw"*

Ryder glared at Speaker Warner, dressed all in black, while the rest of the family dressed in all shades. One didn't wear black for a Jewish funeral. He knew better, but it made better photos for the press. At each stop the pallbearers would make he would drop his gaze slightly down, but still trying to look as if he was still in control of his emotions. The men stopped for the third time and spoke. *"Kiy mal'äkhäyw y'tzaûeh'"*

"Then there is something you need to know. Annalisa didn't die exactly the way the report said she did."

"What do you mean?" Ryder demanded as he turned back to him.

"Somebody is trying to cover up something." Thom said staring at Speaker Warner, as Ryder pulled his sunglasses down on his nose. "Say a congressman who has his sights on a higher office next year." Ryder pushed the sunglasses back up on his nose and watched as the men carrying the casket stopped again and quoted four words of the verse in Hebrew. *Kiy mal'äkhäyw y'tzaûeh-Läkh'*

"Was she murdered?"

"Without a doubt!" He exclaimed and Ryder turned back to him; his face twisted in puzzlement at Thom's words. "It is too complicated to explain here. Stop by the funeral home after the services. I will explain it all. " Thom walked away, as Ryder continued to watch the men carrying the casket, they would stop and recite the verse in Hebrew.

"Kiy mal'äkhäyw y'tzaûeh-Läkh' lish'mär'khä"

Ryder's mind was now racing faster than his Ferrari could have ever gone, he felt that excitement pumping through him once again, a feeling he hadn't since he had quit the force, the feeling that he might be on the edge of breaking the case wide open and that soon he would have it solved. He watched as the men carrying the casket stopped once again and spoke.

"Kiy mal'äkhäyw y'tzaûeh-Läkh' lish'mär'khä B'khäl"

Then it hit him once again. This wasn't just some Vic; this was Annalisa in that casket. The excitement, like a tide rolling in on the beach rolled back and left emptiness instead just as the men reached the grave and all there repeated the entire verse of Psalms 91:11 both in Hebrew and in English as Ryder repeated *"For he shall give his angels charge over thee, to keep thee in all thy ways."* Yakira join him in Hebrew.

He looked down at the red shoes she was wearing. They were the same ones that Annalisa was wearing when she was murdered. "Those are some shoes; where did you get them?"

"Daddy special ordered them."

"Shouldn't you be up there with your family?"

"You should know by now I don't always do what I am supposed to." She smiled, parting her lips enough so that the bottom of her front teeth showed. "Besides, you're *mishpucha*. Family." She said as she draped a white scarf with pink stripes over her head and her shoulders as the services began. She grabbed his hand, letting her fingers entwine with his. Jewish funerals were always something to behold, there were no flowers, not one bouquet, not even one long stemmed rose. No one wore black, the colors were dull.

All the mourners, including Yakira and Ryder said "Blessed are you, Lord our God, King of the Universe, the true Judge." Before tearing their garments, Yakira reach up with her left hand, grabbed her dress and ripped the right sleeve down, exposing her bare shoulder. She reached up, grabbing the right breast pocket of his jacket, and ripped it down.

He tried to catch the envelope that was in his pocket before it hit the ground. She quickly scooped up the envelope and saw the writing on it. "My Dearest Ricky?" With a tone mixed with disillusion as it was curiosity. She looked from the envelope to him and asked. "This is Annalisa's writing, she gave you a note?"

"I thought so." He said, still disappointed as he took the envelope back and shoved it into a side pocket of the jacket. "But the paper inside was blank."

"Can I see that envelope again?"

He handed it to her. She turned it over and saw the word on the back of the envelope. "You see this! This is the word for secret. Don't you remember how you and Annalisa passed notes in school?" His mind raced back to grade school when she would write on a piece of white typing paper with a white crayon, to read the message they used water colors to paint over it, revealing the message. "Where is the note?"

"You made a shopping list out of it last night."

"*Oy Vey!*" She slapped her forehead. "It is down at the lake house." The casket was being lowered by the lowering device operated by Pascal and he said:

'May she come to her place in peace.' It was last words of the services. The straps from the lowering device were removed and a shovel was brought out as a line of ten Jewish men lined up around the grave. 'From dust she came; to dust she returns'. It was *Stamata HaGolel*- the sealing of the grave. A Jewish man would pick up the shovel, scoop a shovel full of dirt and throw it down on the casket, which landed with a thud. Each man would do three shovelfuls, and then lay the shovel down, and the next man would pick up the shovel and throw in another three shovelfuls, this continued on till the casket was completely covered, then everyone there, including Ryder and Yakira, recited three times.

"Yet he was merciful; he forgave their iniquities and did not destroy them. Time after time he restrained his anger and did not stir up his full wrath." Psalms 78:38.

The visitors formed two lines as the mourners passed between them. Ryder stood in the line, next to him was Yakira. As the family passed by those in the lines said:

"May the Omnipresent One comfort you among all these who mourn for Zion and Jerusalem." Ryder stared and watched as Speaker Warner passed in between the lines. Ryder held out his hand to the Speaker's, who was flanked by two federal agents; they looked like as if they had been made in a factory, the same suit, same expression, and same smell- bargain store after shave- Agent Peter Chris and Agent Herbert Simms.

"Well, Mr. Ryder." Speaker Warner said. "I hear that we have you to thank for our little Yakira getting out of jail." Ryder shook the man's hand but didn't say a word. "With the F.B.I now in charge, I am sure they will catch the real killer soon."

"If they know where to look." Yakira muttered, cocking her head sideways, looking at the speaker.

"It is no longer detective, is that *right?*" Speaker Warner added with a pretentious tone.

"Actually, it is detective." Ryder said, watching as the congressman's arrogant smile quickly vanished. "I have been hired by the family to investigate Annalisa's murder." He looked over at Yakira and said. "A dollar a day? I will pay the expenses. "

"I am sure it would be best if the…."

"To have the feds investigate, Mr. Speaker." Ryder interrupted, and gave a sideways smile. He lowered his voice and whispered in the speaker's ear. "So they won't find out what really killed Annalisa?" Ryder leaned back away from the speaker and the speaker's face became a reddish pallor, before he became angry.

"Are you accusing me?" He shouted at Ryder; his eyes glancing over at the sea of TV cameras, microphones, and phones that were recording everything that they were saying; the reporters were moving in closer. He flashed a phony smile that could only be found on a politician. "I assure you I did not kill my beloved wife. I loved her dearly and no one will ever be able to take her place." The same smug smile he had before reappeared as he continued. "Besides, Mr. Ryder, I have a strong alibi. I was doing a remote broadcast." He stiffened up and jutted out his jaw and proudly claimed. "For my *Full Grace Foundation.*" He turned directly to a camera and added. "So that we may 'feed the world with one spoonful at a time', using Ozark Golden Sorghum. As my dear wife wanted we are sending our shipments to Palestine and Israel with hope that it may bring peace." He turned back to Ryder." He spoke slowly and powerfully, enunciating his words. "I guess we have a lot in common, Mr. Ryder." Ryder's insides twitched as if he might throw up right there, being compared to a politician, they were no way alike. He flashed a faux grin as he added. "We both loved the same woman."

Chapter 10

It was only a short drive back to town and to the Thompson Funeral Parlor. It looked like a large old house, and at one time it was the funeral parlor on the bottom and home on the top, but over the years and as the owners changed, it was all business now. He parked in the back.

As he turned off the ignition he turned to Yakira. "I really think you should stay in the car."

"Why?" She asked, starting to open the door.

"This is about your sister." He leaned over in the seat and placed his hand on hers. "You really don't need to see this. You need to remember her as she was." He pulled his hand back.

"It is too late. I was the one who identified her." Yakira said as she opened the passenger door and looked across the glass roof of the car. "You can't save me from that." She shut the door. "I have already seen it."

They walked up to the back door into the business, and he removed his sunglasses as he held the door open for Yakira, and then followed her in. Ryder looked around, he had seen Thom's car in the parking lot and knew he was here. Ryder called out. "Double T!"

"Back here."

He followed the voice back into the funeral parlor. Thom was in the small room off to the side used for the family during funerals. He was bending over, his wide bottom pushing at the seams of his khaki trousers. "Now that is a sight I won't forget!" Ryder said standing behind him. Thom had just picked up a colorful vase when Ryder stood behind him and shouted "Twenty-one gold! Hike! " Just as he had in the state championship game. With the precision of a machine, Thom heaved the vase between his legs. Ryder quickly caught the vase.

"Still have those magical hands, huh Ryder?" Thom said standing up and turning around. "Good to see you again, my friend."

Thom turned to Ryder and grinned, a smile that seem to sweep all over his face from his droopy hound dog-like cheeks to the gleam in his eyes. He placed his hand on Ryder's shoulder and added "So what are you here for? Oh! I know! You want to plan your funeral. With all your money I could retire after that." He laughed heartily.

"No, I'm here for your other expertise."

"Women?" He joked. "I have been married three times, now on the fourth, I am the kiss of death to marriage. "He laughed again, slapping at Ryder's ribs. "Besides…" He looked over at Yakira. "Looks like you are in pretty good shape."

"We are just friends." Ryder said pulling out a note pad from his jacket. "I am here because of what you said in the cemetery."

"Just like you, all business." Thom said walking around him and he motioned for them to follow him back down the hall. "It is in the basement." Thom stopped in front the elevator doors, he pressed the button on the wall and the doors opened. He pressed the button for the basement. The doors opened into a room with smooth, slick white walls. With the cold air blowing down from the ceiling vents, it felt like they were inside a refrigerator. The steel racks were empty, there were no dead bodies. They followed Thom to the back of the room where a row of gray four drawer file cabinets were. He pulled open the drawer marked O-R. He went through the files till he came to a file that read Rosen, Warner Annalisa, Elise.

"Shouldn't she be in the W-Z drawer?"

"I figured she would be more at home in this drawer. Warner never suited her." He said, pulling out the file and shutting the drawer. It was a large manila envelope. He opened it and dumped the contents out on a table. Ryder felt sort of strange looking down at the photos of Annalisa's body as Thom laid the pictures in a row across the table. Of her dressed, then nude. "You see something missing here? " Thom asked, waving his hand over the photos as if he were a spokes model describing the grand prize showcase. "She doesn't have a blood necklace." He said as he picked up a close up photo of Annalisa's neck.

"A what?" Yakira asked, puzzled.

"A reddish bruise that is made from strangulation." Ryder said as he picked up the photo and looked carefully at it. He had seen this kind of death before, and heard the phrase.

"But the official death report states asphyxiation due to strangulation. Are you saying she didn't die from that?" Ryder laid the photo down and Yakira picked it up.

"No, the official cause of death is asphyxiation. She shows all the signs." Thom picked up a close up photo of her face. "She has petechial hemorrhaging." Small red spots of blood had pooled in the whites of her eyes. "Very dark red blood. Edema of the lungs and dilation to the side of the heart. All signs of asphyxiation." He put the photo back down and said. "

"So did he strangle my sister?"

"He?" Thom asked letting his gaze drifting quickly to her.

"Speaker Warner." Ryder said as he picked up another photo, noticing Annalisa's bruised and battered face.

"Oh, him." Thom said with distain. "Strangulation is only one way. There was smothering and acute poisoning."

"Poisoning?" Yakira said shaken. "He poisoned my sister?"

"Well, I see great minds think alike. We all think Warner did it. I just can't prove it."

"Back to the poisoning." Ryder said. "What do you mean? What kind of poison?"

Thom picked up a toxicology report. "Look at the levels of sodium pentothal."

"Truth serum?" Yakira asked, unbelieving. "That is what they use in the movies." She paused and then asked. "But that doesn't work, does it?"

Ryder began writing in the notebook he was holding in his hand. 'In some cases, yes it can, if it is done right. The F.B.I has used it, unofficially, of course. " Thom said as he picked up another photo, a close up of Annalisa's arm.

66

"There were two injection sites; the first one was for the Pentothal. Who ever gave it to her knew what they were doing."

Ryder looked at the report. "According to this report the levels of Pentothal were not lethal."

Thom turned the page and said. "Look at the levels of Amtyal." Thom grabbed up another photo of a close up of Annalisa's elbow. "You see this large bruise. This is where the injection of Amtyal was given, it was sloppy; it was even in her tissues. Whoever did this didn't have a clue at what they were doing. It was done with a large bore needle. Guess you could say she was bored to death."

Ryder didn't know why it was that all M.E.'s or coroners seem to have the same weird sense of humor. He didn't know if it was the job, and it was just the way to keep them from going crazy, or they were already crazy, and they didn't know better. He knew only one way to react, cock his head slightly and raise his eyebrows. It always made them explain more. "As you can see the dose of Amtyal was at least 1000mg."

"One thousand" Ryder said with shock. "That would be enough to put a grizzly bear down."

"Papa Bear, Mama Bear, and Baby Bear too, along with Goldilocks herself." Thom joked as he gathered up the photos and put them back into the envelope.

Ryder picked up a photo of Annalisa's face. Swollen and battered with heavy dark bruises around her eyes, her lower lip cut and swollen twice its size. "She was worked over pretty good. "

"Severe bruising and minor abrasions around the eyes, laceration to the lower labium plus there a section of skin torn away from the third digit of her right hand. However, the avulsion to the area around the nostril area caused severe bleeding. The septum was shattered and the ethmoid was broken, shattered, and sinus cavities filled with blood. There was a lot of blood; anyone around her was covered in it." Thom explained

Ryder looked at the photo; he laid it back down. "Sure these didn't happen in the accident?"

"Positive." Thom said as Yakira picked up the photo.

"The report said her hyoid bone was broken. The photos clearly show that her neck was broken."

"Yes, my friend, but there was no sign of pooling of blood, her neck was broken after she was dead." Thom picked up an autopsy photo of Annalisa's neck-cut open and the hypoid bone removed. How many times had it been Ryder had seen photos like these, or to be right there and watch it all happen. It wasn't that he was feeling sick, like the first one he saw, but it was an uneasy feeling. "You okay?" Ryder nodded and Thom continued. "My guess is it happened when the car went into the river. The cord was tied around her neck. Sheer impact snapped her neck. I can't say for sure. But I do know she was dead when it happened. Once you die the heart no longer pumps blood. The blood starts to pool in the lowest areas."

He picked up another photo, a close up of her bare feet. "You see this dark coloring and swelling in her feet. Heard about dying with your boots on? Well she died with no shoes on."

"How do you know that?"

"Yakira, can I see one of your shoes?"

Yakira placed her hand on Ryder's shoulder so that she could lift her leg up and pull off her one of her shoes and handed it to Thom. He took it and pulled the top of the shoe back. "You see this elastic under the stitching? If she had these shoes on that mark would be on top of her foot." He pointed down at Yakira's bare foot, and the red mark across her foot. And that is being alive."

"What was the time of death?"

"She was found at midnight, but she was dead at least two hours before that; could be as much as six hours." He picked up a small yellow envelope, opened it, and poured out a small bracelet into his palm. Ryder picked it up. It had a red braid for the chain and the one small pendant, a silver hand with an eye in the middle. "She had a death grip on this. I had to pry it out of her hand."

"Here, "he said, handing him another envelope. "This is all her personal effects. I tried to tell all this to that pretty F.B.I. agent, but she didn't want to hear it. Told me the official cause of death on the report would be by asphyxiation due to strangulation and if I knew what was good for me I would keep my mouth shut, but I never knew what was good for me."

Yakira picked up the pendant attached to a red braided ribbon for the chain, the pendant looked like a palm of a hand. "She had this in her hand?" She asked, looking over at Thom. "She must have been scared to death." She held the charm up and looked at it. Ryder noticed how intensely she was looking at it.

"What is that?"

"This is a *Kabbalah Hamsa* bracelet. It is the hand of Miriam-the sister of Moses." She looked up from the charm and to him. "Bubbie gave this to her. It is used to ward off the evil eye." Yakira's attention turned back to the charm and then back to Ryder. "It is what a four-leaf clover is to you. It is to bring good luck. But it also…" She paused and clutched it in her own hand. "Gives comfort in time of—." Yakira opened her hand and picked the bracelet up and wrapped it around her wrist. She sniffed sadly. "If she was hanging on to this, she knew what was happening to her. She knew she was going to die." She fastened the lobster clasp.

"You believe how I said she died?" Thom asked, turning to Ryder.

"Of course." Ryder shot back, he had been one his best friends in school, and his center. A quarterback has to know his center they have to have an unspoken bond, and Ryder and Double T had that.

"Then you might believe me about the casket."

"What?" Ryder asked wondering where this was going to go now, as it was getting stranger every minute.

"The night before her funeral, I found the person that was supposed to be staying with her out cold, the lid of the coffin had been opened, and somebody was searching for something."

"The *shomer*?" Yakira asked suddenly, drawing her attention away from the bracelet. "Was the dirt on her disturbed? The dirt from Israel!"

"Yes, but I made sure it was back on her before sealing the casket closed."
It was important that the dirt of the homeland be placed on her body; it was
the way of guiding her home.

"What happened?" Ryder wrote down everything that Thom was telling
him on his notepad. "What time was it?"

"It was around ten. Someone brought in a sandwich. It was half eaten, lying
beside her. Before you even ask, I don't know who brought it. But I do know
what was in the sandwich. Gamma Hydroxybutyric Acid. I would say
Rohypnol, as it wouldn't have any taste."

"What is that?" Yakira asked.

"It is a date rape drug, knocks the person out cold."

Chapter 11

It was the middle of September and the summer just wouldn't let go of the Ozarks. Be it the insects that were buzzing around that should have been dying off or the smothering heat. Rain had not been lacking this year, and the humidity just made it hotter, seeming to hang in the air, slapping you across the face like a jealous lover every time you went out.

They were heading back to her parents house and Yakira fidgeted in her seat, she just couldn't get comfortable. Then again, maybe it wasn't the heat of the afternoon sun, but the heat of hearing her mother's words going over and over in her head. *'When are you going to find a nice man and get married? I am not getting any younger; I would like to have grandchildren.'*

"Well I guess that is something I could do that Annalisa never did." She said in a low tone.

"What?" Ryder asked as he pulled the Jaguar off the street on the side of the front yard, parking on the edge of the dark green grass, of the Rosen's home.

"Nothing, just…" Yakira said as she rolled her eyes up. "Guilt. Something that mothers do."

"All mothers." Ryder agreed remembering how his mother could just look at him when he did something wrong and he would admit it.

Yeah but *Elohim* gives Jewish mothers a triple dose of it."She looked over at him. "Believe me; they are very good at it."

"Are you going to be that way when you are a mother?" Ryder asked as he got out of the car. He walked around and opened the car door for her.

"I hope not." Yakira said as she got out of the car and turned and looked at the house. "So what about you? What kind of father would you be?"

"Me?" Ryder asked, puzzled with almost a bitter tone, as he shut the car door. "A father?" He had never seen himself as this.

"Surely you and Annalisa you talked about having kids?"

"I don't think I would be a good one." He said as they walked towards the front of the house. "I didn't have the greatest role model for that." Ryder's lips twisted in anger, his eyebrows drawing down in a frown as memories of his father flashed through his mind. Not one good memory, he was never there for Ryder, and not there for his mom when she needed him the most.

"You are not like him." She said as she placed her hand on his arm. The memories made Ryder uncomfortable and he quickly switched the conversation back to the investigation.

"Who was the *shomer*?"

"Aunt Leesabeth. They are probably all around in the back yard." They headed across the yard and around beside the garage. "Mom wants me to get married and have kids. How can I do that when I haven't had a date in two years?"

"Two years!" He said in disbelief.

"Okay, it has been three years." They went around the back of the house. The yard was typical middle class suburban. With freshly mowed green grass and evergreen bushes lining along the border between the property lines and a fish pond. Sliding glass doors from the kitchen led out onto a red brick patio, complete with a large stainless steel propane grill, and white iron patio furniture, at the edge of the yard under the shade of a pine tree. When they moved here there were two trees, now only one remained, the one planted in honor of Yakira, the one that had been planted in honor of Annalisa, had been cut down and a chest was made and given to her on her wedding day. "Oh all right, four years." Yakira admitted.

"How is that possible? You are an attractive girl."

"You think I am pretty?" She asked hopefully, stopping and grabbing his sleeve again to make him face her. "Really? You think I am pretty? Maybe if I did something with my hair?" She fluffed her hair between her fingers and continued, with the excitement of middle school girl noticing boys for the first time. "Wear a little bit more makeup, maybe wore something else, a dress. I would be considered sexy?"

"Yeah, I guess." He answered uncomfortably. "You know, for a little sister."

"Little sister again." She mumbled under her breath. Not hearing her he pulled away from her grip and walked toward Leesabeth who was sitting in a lawn chair between Pascal and Maureen, under the shade of the remaining pine tree.

What is she doing here? He thought as he walked up to them with Yakira beside him.

"Get yourselves a plate and join us." Pascal said.

"I am here to talk to Leesabeth, Pascal."

"Well I don't have to have anything to say to you." She replied, lifting up a spoonful of lentils from her plate.

He kneeled down beside her and whispered. "About *last night.*" As soon as he mentioned those words, the corners of her mouth dropped down and she let her spoon fall back to the plate. She stood up; placing the plate on the seat of her chair, without saying a word she walked over next to the border of evergreens. Ryder and Yakira followed her.

"What do you know?" She asked turning and facing him, making sure they were far enough away that no one else could hear.

"Yakira." Ryder said with a nonchalant tone. "Correct me if I wrong as I am not that knowledgeable in Jewish culture. But the main duty of the guardian is to make sure…" He turned and faced Leesabeth and his tone become more solemn as he continued. "…the casket isn't opened!"

"It was your fault that the dirt of the Holy Land was disturbed." Yakira said grabbing her aunt's arm. "Because of you she may not be able to find her way to peace."

"Okay. Okay! You can't tell anyone." Leesabeth whispered. She leaned in towards him. "Please!"

"If you answer our questions, so what happened?"

"I didn't mean to fall asleep." She explained. "I just got tired. Right after I ate. I shouldn't have eaten that sandwich."

73

"You are right, you shouldn't have. It was drugged."

"Drugged!" She said, loudly, her face filled with fear and shock. She looked around to see Pascal getting up from his chair, because he had heard her shout.

"Do you remember anything? Who brought you the sandwich?" Ryder pulled out his note pad, and began writing.

"I can't believe she would do that!"

"Who, Aunt Leesabeth?"

"Susan Glenn. Scott's assistant." She sighed heavily and added. "I should have known when I saw it was ham."

Susan Glenn was the assistant to Speaker Warner for the past three terms. It was usually easy to find her, if you looked for him you would find her by his side. However, today that didn't seem to be the case. Neither one of them could be found; the office in town was closed. It wasn't until later that evening that Deputy Thompson told them he had seen Susan at the Emery Melton Inn at Roaring River.

One of the shining jewels of the Ozarks was Roaring River State Park; it is located seven miles southeast of Cassville, on highway 112, which snakes its way through the rolling hills of Barry County before dropping off into a canyon-like valley that is nearly hidden by the deep growth of forests on the Ozark Mountains on all sides.

The river was fed by a natural underground spring that poured out over twenty million gallons of water each day, in a fern lined grotto at the base of a dolomite bluff. The water of the spring ended in a crystal clear lake, that made all prospective anglers a little anxious when they see the large rainbow trout swimming about, tantalizing them, for there is 'no fishing' here in the pool.

Campers, RVs and tents dotted all along the campgrounds, and fishermen lined up along the banks of the cold water stream, flipping out the line and pulling it back, hoping to get the rainbow trout to bite, some pulling in a winning catch, others, measured but thrown back when they don't meet the mark. Darkness was beginning to cover the park and most anglers now were back at the campsite frying up today's catch or sitting telling tales of the one that got away and assuring everyone they would reel it in tomorrow.

It was eight thirty p.m. by the clock in the car when Ryder down shifted the Jaguar, and it stalked its way down into the park. Ryder open his mouth wide and swallowed to keep his ears from popping, for they were descending fast; as they reached the bottom of the hill, he up-shifted the Jaguar and drove across Dry Hollow Bridge.

Catching first sight of the hotel with the golden light peering out from the solid top pane of glass on the top floor, it appeared as if there were mighty eyes glaring down at them, watching as the Jaguar drove past. He turned to the right, up a winding drive into the parking lot and parked the car in the first empty spot they came to.

He held the car door open for her. As they walked across the parking lot, the high-pitched constant buzz of jar flies clinging to leaves high up in the sycamore trees, their song never seeming to end, when it got to the point where, the song would wind down, it was replaced with the chatter of crickets, hiding along the brick path that led up to the rustic looking inn.

Located between Dry Hollow and Piber Hollow, just off highway 112, the Inn was one of the newest structures in the park, and was a perfect blend of modern architecture, yet remained true to the character of the park, with its geometrical stone façade, and aged looking wooden beams that gave it a rustic hunting lodge feel. It reminded him of a lodge up in the mountains of Colorado where he went to hunt in the winter. All that was missing was the snow and the roaring fire in the fireplace that was flanked by overstuffed leather sofas and chairs, painted with the warm glow of the table lights that just invited one to stop and relax, but he had no time for that, as the clang of dishware and the aroma of food guided him back further towards the restaurant.

"We are about ready to close, but just the two of you?" The teenage hostess said as she met them at the door.

"Yeah."

"Booth or table?"

"Doesn't matter." Ryder didn't care, he knew the food was good, but he wasn't here to eat.

The hostess grabbed two menus and led them into the restaurant. The style of the dining room could have been considered dated with the lower half of the wall having stained bead board paneling and the upper half painted creamy white, but it just seemed to fit the place with the faux grapevines entwined around the beams on the ceiling and the fishing décor on the walls it was clear to see what the specialty of the house was before even looking at a menu.

The young hostess lead Ryder and Yakira past the rows of country-style oak tables and towards the end booth next to the windows, when Ryder saw who he was here to see, Susan Glenn, sitting in a booth, having a late supper, across from her was Agent Chris, they both were enjoying the specialty-rainbow trout.

"Can we have the table here instead?" Ryder asked pointing to a small rectangular table that was catty cornered to the booth where Susan was sitting. He sat down in one of the Windsor chairs, turning slightly so that he could look right at her. Yakira sat down in the chair next to him.

"I am Missy; I will be your server for the evening." He heard another woman say, but he didn't look up, he just sat watching the woman at the table. Susan was in her early forties, painfully thin with long skinny legs, a long neck and short-cropped raven black hair, and with her long hook shaped nose; surely she had a cackle for a laugh too. "What can I get you to drink?"

"Just two waters, please." He said as he looked up the server. "And do you have *ham sandwiches.*" He added loudly, watching Susan drop her fork onto the plate. "I thought it might help me sleep."

"We have a club sandwich that I would recommend."

"We'll take a look at the menu." Ryder stood up and walked over to the booth. "What about it Susan, do you eat ham sandwiches, or just deliver them?" Agent Chris stood up and Ryder looked over at him. "Agent, take a walk."

"You don't tell me what to do. I am a federal agent. I tell you what to do."

"Calm down, Spot, nobody pulled your chain." Ryder said to the agent, and then looked down at Susan as he said with a low tone to his voice. "Unless you don't mind him being here."

The agent looked over at Susan. "Go on." She said softly. "Yakira is the sister of the speaker's late wife, and Ryder is a dear friend of the family; I am sure that they just want to offer their blessings." The agent left.

"Who ordered it, Susan?" Ryder asked as Yakira moved into the booth across from her, then he sat down beside Yakira.

"I don't know what you are talking about." She said nervously, picking up her glass and taking a sip, nearly spilling it when she set the glass back down.

"She remembers you bringing the sandwich to her. Last night."

"I don't know what you are talking about. I was home all night last night." Susan picked up the glass again.

"Give it up, Susan. I have the sack you brought it in. It has your prints on it." Yes, that was a lie, but she didn't know it.

She set the glass down on the table and it turned over; she quickly grabbed a napkin and started sopping it up. The server grabbed a rag and quickly wiped up the spilled liquid, and then she took the empty glass. "I'll get you another one." The server said. "It was a Root Suicide. Half root beer then a shot of everything else? "

"Can you forget it and just bring me a glass of wine?"

"What would you like?"

"It doesn't matter!" Susan replied annoyed. "Just bring me whatever is open."

Susan said softly as she leaned over the table. "I was only told to deliver it." The server returned with a glass of red wine and Susan became silent till she left.

"Who told you to deliver it?" Ryder asked as he wrote in his notebook.

"I don't know."

"So some stranger walking down the street came up to you and told you to deliver a ham sandwich to a Jewish woman. Do you not find that odd?"

"Okay. Okay." She said reaching across the table and placing her hand on top of it. "I will tell you. But you have to believe me; I didn't know it was drugged." She lifted her hand up and took a sip of the wine before she continued. "Shawn O'Malley gave it to me."

"Who is Shawn O'Malley?"

"He is the foreman of Warner's Ranch." She lowered her voice even more, leaning over the table again. "I really thought I was doing something good, okay? I didn't know it was drugged till she passed out and I got scared and I left." She drank the rest of the wine in her glass and wiped her mouth with her napkin. She ordered more wine and then said. "And before you ask I saw Annalisa the day she was murdered. It was right before the Speaker and I left for Springfield, She was in that car of yours."

"What time was that?"

"I don't know. Okay, it would have to be before five thirty. That is when we left."

"What did she say? What did she do?"

The server brought her another glass of wine and she took a big swig before saying. "She must have lost her mind." She took another big swig of the wine before continuing. . "She held up a flash drive. She said she wanted a divorce and "two hundred and fifty thousand dollars. She said 'she knew what he is doing' if he didn't do exactly as she said, she would release the information. And he would be hanging at the end of a rope."

"How did Warner react to that?"

"I can't tell you that."

"Then I am calling in the F.B.I. and not your pal, but his boss Special Agent Alexander, I am sure she can get it out of you."

Susan downed the rest of the glass of wine and ordered yet another one. "Okay, he freaked out. He tried to grab the flash drive and she…" She paused just as the server brought up the glass of wine and set it down in front of her.

She took another drink. "…she pulled a gun on him and told him that he had till tomorrow morning or he would…" she took another drink of the wine. "…be seeing a report that would end his career, if not his life." She swigged the rest of the glass of wine down and ordered another one. "But you have to believe me. I didn't strangle Annalisa."

Chapter 12

The full moon was dressed as a bride with a thin veil of haze covering her face; it was going to be another warm night, be thankful for air conditioning. "Remember our deal. " Ryder said as he stopped the Jaguar in front of the lake house. She turned to him, confused. What deal could he be talking about? As she dropped her gaze away from him, he knew that she knew what he was talking about. "I cook." He said, opening the car door and getting out. "You…"

"I clean." She said, finishing the sentence reluctantly, as he opened the car door for her. "I would." She smirked. "But we don't have any pans." She got out of the car. "Remember, you had me throw them away."

"I bought some more along with a new coffee maker." He said opening the trunk and revealing several large boxes.

"Okay, I clean."

The house looked so good, the soft bed waiting for him, it had only been a day, but it seemed that they had been gone for a week. "It all makes sense." Yakira said as she used her key to open the front door.

"What are you talking about?" He said, lifting up one of the boxes.

"The note she left you. She was trying to tell you something." She continued to talk as he stepped up on the deck. "What she had on Warner." She turned around and looked up at him as he entered the house. "I looked over the evidence in that file on your phone. They found no flash drive. That means that Warner found it or…." She paused if she were actor on the stage doing it for dramatic effect "… she hid it for you to find."

"That is good detective work. But they don't have it." He said as she turned around and disappeared out the room. He heard the banging of cabinet doors.

"Just keep talking, I can hear you." She shouted.

"I was saying that he couldn't have found it." Ryder said, raising his voice so she could hear. She reappeared with something in her hand. It was a plastic box of old watercolors.

"I remembered seeing these down here. " She said laying the paint set out on the cabinet. "You were saying?" She reached up for a glass in the cabinet and filled it with water, then dipped the brush in the water.

"I was saying that because they searched her coffin, means they didn't take it from her." Ryder said handing her the paper that was lying on the bar. "You may be right about the note. She might have hidden the drive somewhere."

She took the paper and tried to smooth it out as best she could. She opened the box and turned her head, then looked at him and smiled as she picked up the paint brush "What color should we use?"

"My favorite, red." He replied, leaning a bit closer and looking down over her shoulder as she took the cheap nylon bristle brush and mixed up a small amount of paint and water, till it was just right. "You know how many notes we passed in school like this?" Yakira began to paint across the paper; he moved his hand from her shoulder and wrapped his arm around the back of her neck. His fingers caressed her upper arm. "It was the greatest way to share…" She turned and tilted her head back, looking up into his eyes. They were nose to nose, and the brush nearly slipped from her grasp.

"…secrets." She said softly, before she swallowed hard and quickly pulled back and he lifted his hand from her shoulder. "Yeah, she showed me." Yakira drew back and begin to quickly brush the paint over the paper; nothing was showing up, except the wrinkles in the paper. She dipped the brush back into the paint and went across the paper again. Something was beginning to appear. It wasn't letters, it was symbols and lines. She kept painting, going back, and putting more paint on the brush and painting across the entire paper till the message showed up.

אוצמל תא בלה יבג לע הזה

מש ולכות אוצמל ותוא רתסומ ךותב Heart

"Heart?" Ryder asked seeing the one word he recognized.

"It is Hebrew!" She said as she continued to paint.

"Why would she send me a message in Hebrew knowing I can't read it?"

"But I can read it." She around and face him. "She wanted us to do it together. That is what she meant by she would let me have you. She wanted me to help you.

"So what does it say?

Hebrew had been taught to her starting at an early age, ideally it would have been done at a Hebrew school, but instead it was Bubbie who taught both her and Annalisa. She turned back around. The first thing that is taught is that Hebrew is read not from left to right but from right to left.

"Find the heart on top the chest. There you shall find it hidden within heart." She said, sounding unsure of her translation.

"Are you sure?"

"Yes, well it could be Chest on my heart to find hidden within it find you there heart. " She said, picking up the piece of paper and looking at it again. "Annalisa had the habit of translating single words instead of the entire phrase. " Yakira shook her head. She turned back to him and said confidently. Yes, I am sure. 'Find the heart on top the chest. There you shall find it hidden within heart.' "

"Why all the Hebrew, then the word Heart in English?"

"I haven't got a clue there."

"I can't think on an empty stomach. Don't know about you, but I am hungry." He said getting up and pulling the refrigerator door open and looking inside. "How about some scrambled eggs?" He pulled out a carton of eggs. "Maybe with a little fresh chives and sun-dried tomatoes?"

"Yeah, okay." Her tone seemed distant, as if she was lost in thought. She turned around, placing her hands on the counter as she looked down at the message on the paper. Meanwhile Ryder broke four eggs into a clear glass bowl, and using a French whip, whipped them together. He returned the egg carton to the refrigerator, and pulled out a package of fresh chives. Using a chef's knife he finely chopped up the chives on a cutting board.

"Wash up one of those new skillets." He asked, but she didn't respond. He looked over at her, she had a pen and she was transcribing the note, writing the words under the Hebrew words. "Yakira!" She turned to him. "Remember? I cook, you wash."

"Oh, yes." She said, opening the box and pulling out a skillet and washing it in the sink. She dried it, and then handed it to him. He put a pat of butter into the skillet and placed it on the stove, allowing it to melt and bubble slightly around the edges, and then poured in the eggs and chives, while he chopped up the sun-dried tomatoes and placed them on top of the eggs then mixed it all together. While she went outside, he heard the car door slam and she returned with the copy of the file that Thom has given Ryder. She walked into the great room, and opened the envelope and dumped the contents out onto the table. She started sorting the photos of Annalisa's body out in front of her. Ryder carried in two plates of fluffy eggs, and set them down on the table. She sat there staring at the photos "Yakira, it is ready. Yakira!" He looked down at the photos. "And no more looking at these." He added forcefully quickly picking them up and shoving them back into the envelope. "You need to eat."

She gave the *SheHakol* blessing "Blessed are you Lord, our God King of the Universe, through whose Word came into being." She picked up the fork and looked over at Ryder who was already eating. "You don't say a blessing? " She said, disappointed.

"Don't believe in that faith stuff so much anymore. Praying is just a waste of time."

"I don't believe that."

"You haven't had the life I have had. Now eat before your eggs get cold."

Yakira scooped up some eggs and took a bite, then dropped the fork down on the plate. Thinking there was something wrong with the eggs he turned and faced her. "What could she have been involved in?" Ryder put his fork down. "You said it; she wasn't the innocent girl I thought she was. What if she was involved in something illegal?"

"She may have been the one who would tell you a joke to make you laugh hard enough to pee your pants, but she would have never been in anything illegal."

They went back to eating their eggs and had almost finished when she turned and asked "How do you know? How do you know she wouldn't have done anything illegal? You haven't seen her since you were eighteen. People change."

"I have seen her many times since then." Ryder laid his fork down again and leaned back in the chair. "Even before she married Warner, I begged her not to do it. But she said she couldn't."

"Why? Because of faith? Scott is not Jewish. And she is still accepted by the family."

"I know." Ryder said humbly dropping his gaze down to the last bite of eggs on his plate. He picked his fork back up and scooped up the last bite and ate it. "I just assumed that being the wife of a congressman was better than that of a cop's. Then when I won the lottery I called her and told her we could just run away that we didn't have to get married. But she said no way." He pushed the plate out of the way. "It was always about faith with her. I mean, what other couples were getting in the back seat…well, we never did."

'It is just like Bubbie said…" Yakira said as she stood "'…sometimes the more educated someone is the dumber they are." She picked up the plates and walked into the kitchen and placed them in the sink. . "She graduated at the top of her class, and got her degree in education. And was a teacher at school. Yet she was still dumb."

"Why was she dumb?" He asked, walking up beside her.

"She chose faith over love." She turned to him. "I would never do that. If I am in love with a man, Bubbie, mom, dad, not the angels in heaven itself will stop me from marrying him."

"Well, the guy who gets you will be a lucky man" He gave her a brotherly kiss on the cheek as he added. . "But he better not hurt my little sister." He turned around and walked back into the great room and began to look at the autopsy photos again.

"Yeah, little sister." She mumbled as she washed all the dishes then placed them in the drainer next to the sink. "That is all I am to you. That is all I will ever be."

84

"Did you say something?"

"No," she replied picking up a towel and drying her hands as she walked back into the great room and sat down at the table next to him. "I was saying I wonder what Annalisa wanted us to see." He looked over at her. "You know the secret note she left us?"

"Oh yeah." Ryder said as his gaze fell on the small envelope lying on the table that held Annalisa's personal effects. He scooted it over to her. "You should be the one to open it". She tore it open and dumped the contents out before her. Annalisa's wallet, her wrists watch that her mom and dad got her when she graduated from high school, her wedding ring, the Star of David necklace. "It is not here." She went through the items again looking to see if it could be stuck in the envelope "It is not here!"

"What?"

"The ring you gave her. The one that matches that one you wear." She said as he looked over at her again. "The heart-shaped blue sapphire. She never took it off. Even taking a shower, she never took it off. It was something that was a part of her." He looked down at the ring on his finger.

"Can I see that ring?" She asked. He pulled the ring from his finger and handed it to her. There was only one thing engraved on the inside of the ring shank-a heart. "She put a heart on everything she loved. It was proof it was hers. Her toys, her clothes, and you." She handed the ring back to him. "As long as you wear that ring, you belong to her." She stood up. "I am tired; I am going to go to bed." She walked out of the room.

Ryder sat there studying the photos of the autopsy and the crime scene. There was something that was wrong here, but he just couldn't figure out what it was. It was getting late, three a.m., as he stood and rubbed his sore neck. He walked over and pushed the sliding glass doors open and stepped out on to the deck. He walked over to the rail and stared out into the darkness, hearing the water slap up against the bank. He walked over to the chaise on the deck and lay down. He stared up into the starry sky. He closed his eyes and soon sleep overtook him.

****

BOOM! Ryder awakened to the sound of a fiery blast the next morning. BOOM! It sounded again. He quickly rose up from the chaise lounge. He shielded his eyes from the morning sun, trying to figure out where the sounds were coming from. He stood up and BOOM, it sounded again. It was gunfire and it was coming from around the back of the house. He walked down the wooden steps from the deck that led to the yard.

The yard was huge, almost a whole acre and a ten-acre field was directly behind the yard, separated by a barbed wire fence, and accessed by a tall wooden plank gate. Right along the edge of the fence row was a wide row of evergreen trees, cedars and pine trees that could be used as a wind break in the winter and offered a cooling shade in the summer. Twenty feet away was a wrecked 1972 Dodge Charger Special Edition model, its nose crumpled, after hitting a tree, it had been his car in high school.

He walked through the gate and felt the cool breath of the pine trees on him as he stood under them, watching Yakira. She was dressed in a pink and white striped tank top with white shorts that hugged around whatever little bit of hips she had, standing there in bright pink tennis shoes with bright green laces. She picked up a news magazine and walked out into the tall weeds to the group of trees that formed a semi-circle that consisted of oak, hickory, walnut and a tall old sycamore that had been stuck by lightning a couple of years ago and was beginning to die. Using a nail that was in the trunk of the old tree, she hung up the magazine with the cover facing outward. On the cover was a photo of Speaker Warner.

She walked back to the car and picked up the Smith and Wesson 500, the nickel plating gleaming. She held it up and pulled back the hammer with a click. Her head twisted slightly and she glared down the sight, and squeezed the trigger. "BOOM!" The revolver went off. Yakira's body jerked with the recoil, as blue smoke bellowed out of the barrel. The slug ripped into the magazine, and into the trunk of the tree, as a shower of bits of colored paper and dead bark rained down on the ground. She raised the weapon again, preparing to fire it, and the smell of gun powder drifted over to him, filling his nostrils. The gun shook in her grip and the barrel dipped down as she lowered the hammer, and placed the gun on the hood of the car. He heard her voice quiver and her hand trembled as she brought it up to her face. "Die, you…"

He walked up beside her and she turned to him. He didn't speak, just glanced over to the magazine hanging on the tree and saw that the slug had hit the picture of the congressman in the left eye. He turned and looked at other magazine covers lying on the hood of the car. They were all photos of the congressman, all shot between the eyes. She turned to her side, resting her hands on the fender of the car. She began to cry.

"I hate that man." He reached down and laid his hand down on top of hers. She turned her hand over, wrapping her fingers around his as she turned to him, but didn't look at him as she spoke. "I wish he was dead. And I could be the one who killed him!" She shook with anger; letting go of his hand she grabbed the revolver up off the hood of the car with both hands. Turned and fired: BOOM! The slug plowed into the magazine, turning it into confetti. He reached up and took the huge weapon from her hands, and placed it on the roof of the car.

"I know he murdered my sister." She said, leaning down on the car again. "And I think I know why." She turned back to him. "You know how Warner's family made their money? They made moonshine. I think she found out and he had her killed."

"You think Warner was running shine?" Ryder asked with disbelief.

"The modern version of it, drugs. What if he is running drugs in the cans of sorghum? And Annalisa found out. Would that not be motive to kill her?"

Chapter 13

Warner Ranch was a sprawling 1500 acres of rolling pasture with a rippling creek, streaming with perch and goggle eyes that tucked away safely under the shade of a large wooded area. There were two houses, the first was a huge two-story five bedroom and five and a half bath monstrosity made of limestone with a three car garage, complete with a gated garden area lined with rose bushes.

The second home was a brick three bedroom ranch style, used by the ranch foreman. There were also two barns, one that was gray, beaten and weathered with rusty tin covering its roof, the other barn new, with shiny paint and bright red metal corrugated metal roofing. In between them were two towering red silos.

Across and down the road a half-mile away was Warner's Ozark Sorghum, that seemed to be in full operation; however, it was still two months to go till sorghum would be ready to mill.

Yakira had changed into faded pink jeans and a three button pink top with a white-collar and of course her bright pink tennis shoes. Meanwhile, Ryder went to Weston's Garage and rented a light gray Ford Sedan. The number one rule for stake outs is being invisible, and with a Jaguar in an area where it is more common to see a Ford tractor, this made more sense. He parked the car just down the road from the mill, and through binoculars he watched as three men in white overalls loaded a crate of sorghum into a white van with blacked out windows. The crates were six feet long, two feet wide and two feet high. They slid it into the van and went back into the mill. He handed the binoculars to Yakira.

"I don't know any of them." She said as she focused the binoculars on another man. He was standing on the other side of a light blue and white 1979 Ford F150 pickup with the door open, he was putting something behind the seat. He closed the door, and he walked around the pickup.

"I know who this guy is." She said handing the binoculars back to Ryder. "That is O'Malley. I have seen him in my gun shop before; he tried to sell me a hot rifle."

Ryder focused the binoculars and saw a tall man, wearing a blue plaid shirt that fit him in length, but gapped around his chest. His hair was closely cropped, and partly hidden with a Pennington Seed and Grain cap. His jeans were faded and well-worn, as were the tan lace up work boots that were on his feet. The man stepped up on to the running board and got in the pickup behind the wheel and drove off, heading back up to the ranch. Another crate was placed in the van and the men slammed the van doors shut.

"Holy crap!" Ryder said as he watched one of the men turn where he could see the man's face. "That's Agent Chris." He laid the binoculars down in between the seats. He turned to Yakira. "One of Alex's agents." He picked up the binoculars again and watched as the van drove away.

Ryder fired up the dull colored Ford and drove up to the mill and they got out. He looked around, making sure there was no one else there. The mill consisted of one white building 110 feet long and thirty feet wide. The loading door was open and they entered. The lights were on, revealing the equipment inside, a huge press, with its massive cast iron wheels turned by the large woven belt that ran from one end to other. It was here that the cane stalks were squeezed of their life juices, it would then continue down a shoot to a large brass flat top cooker heated by a large steam-powered wood fed furnace. Ryder remembered when his grandfather worked here, and he would come to see him. The heat from the furnace was nearly unbearable, and he watched as his grandfather sweated, taking his red bandana handkerchief and wiping his brow, before using a long stick with a cotton mop like head to move around the syrup and skim the foam from the top of the golden sweet syrup. Another thing he remembered was his grandfather giving him a piece of cane to chew; it was so wonderful and sweet. Ryder picked up a piece of cane; it was dry and brittle. He rubbed his hands over the huge gears; they were grease free and covered with dirt.

"This place hasn't been used in years." Ryder said as he looked for Yakira. She was in the shipping department; there were shelves from the floor up to the roof, holding bright metal cans with red and white labels that read 'Warner's Ozark Gold Sorghum.' On the table was one of the large crates. On top of the lid was a label that read "Warner's Full of Grace Foundation." Beside it was an empty tape dispenser that once held a roll of green colored tape. Ryder lifted the lid of the crate and tapped on the bottom. It had a false bottom."

Meanwhile Yakira grabbed a can from the shelf and set it on a large wooden table. She looked around for something, finding a flat head screwdriver she pried one of the lids open and looked inside. "Is this Black heroin?" Ryder put his finger into the dark-gold liquid. He sniffed, and then tasted it.

"Sorghum," he said as he spit it out, "about a couple years old by the taste."

She began to open up another can but Ryder stopped her."You may be right, but it isn't in the cans." He said. "It is going under a false bottom in those crates." She stood up and glanced over at the crate on the rolling conveyor belt. Something on the floor that was bright and shiny caught her eye. She bent down and picked it up.

"Look what I found." She said, softly at first, then repeating louder. "Look what I found!" It was Annalisa's ring. "That means she was here." She handed it to Ryder. He examined it: there was a small piece of skin dangling from it. He reached into his jacket and produced a small plastic zip top bag from the roll that he always carried and placed the ring inside, zipped the bag up and placed it back into his pocket.

"Come on We have to get out of here before someone shows up."

Chapter 14

Switching back to the Jaguar, they returned to the ranch, looking for Speaker Warner. It appeared that no one was around, only the high-pitched whistle of a red tailed hawk that soared across the barnyard, circling before landing at the peak of the old weathered barn. The doors of the barn were wide open, exposing the faded green combine that was covered with a blanket of dust. Beside it was a row of large round hay bales. At the top in the loft were smaller bales of hay, as a gentle breeze drifted over across the barn yard, Ryder was met with a fresh sweet smell that was drifting from the old barn. The hawk's tail twisted back and forth and as they walked towards the newer barn, and he let out another whistle.

Ryder stood up and looked at the barn, it was better than most of the homes around the county, a two story with everlasting white vinyl siding with glossy red trim and roof, a cement floor and an upper story that featured six pane swing out windows on the front and the back. Sitting outside the main doors of the barn was a brand new shiny green John Deer tractor with a front loader scoop. Ryder ran his fingers over the scratches in the bottom of the bucket; they were deep, down to the naked metal.

There were two sets of tracks that ran from the driveway back to the barn, made when it was muddy, just after the rain. He kneeled down and put his finger in the tracks that were heading to the barn, they reach the middle joint of his index finger, but the ones coming out were at least six inches deep. He may have spent most of his adult life in the city, but Ryder was farm born and raised, once bare feet touch the cool grass of the country summer, it is something that can't be removed. When Ryder saw a keypad electronic lock on the barn door he found it odd, no farmer would do that.

"Do you know Warner's birthday?" Ryder asked, standing in front of the lock.

"April 17th. Why?"

Ryder pushed the button 0417 then enter. The screen flashed 'Code incorrect.' Ryder looked down at the ground, there were several foot prints. Some of athletic shoes, others of work boots, but it was one set that garnered interest, they belong to a woman wearing high heels. He spanned his hand over the print, size seven he guessed. He followed the footprints around the side of the barn and they stopped in front of a multiple pane window. Thick black plastic was taped to the inside, so he couldn't see in. He ran his finger over the glass, the panes were covered in dust, except one that was in the middle near the lock, and it was clean.

"What size shoe did Annalisa wear?"

"Seven, why?" Yakira said as she walked over to him and looked down at the prints.

"What are you doing?" A man said as he approached them. It was O'Malley, the ranch foreman. Ryder casually let his gaze drop down to the man's boots.

"Is Speaker Warner here?"

No! "And this is private property. I am going to call the sheriff if you don't get out of here."

"I think that would be a good idea." Ryder said as he stood up and stared at a man who was standing ten feet away. "Then you can explain why your boots are stained with blood."

"What blood?" Shawn asked in disbelief as he lifted his foot up, revealing the splattered tan boots. "I was castrating pigs! Who are you?"

"My name is Ryder."

"You are the detective from Kansas City I heard about, the one that won the lottery." He glanced over at Yakira. "Sorry to hear about your sister. She was a lovely lady. Place hasn't been the same since she left." He turned back to Ryder. "But I didn't murder her."

"I didn't say you did."

"We know that Warner did." Yakira spoke up.

"What? That is insane."

"Speaker Warner, the night of the murder he said he was here with you. Is that true?" Now this was a complete lie, and Ryder knew it, but it wasn't just the answer he wanted, it was how the man would react.

"No, that is not true. He left here around four to meet Susan in town. He told me he had to go to Springfield for some kind of interview." Ryder watched the man; he looked directly into his eyes, he did not waver, nor did he move.

"Could he have been working at his office in town?"

"No, absolutely not! If he works late he has my wife Dawn bring his supper to him. She was here all night too." His tone became firm, as if he was determined that Ryder believe him. "We were both here together. Watching TV."

"What did you watch?"

"I don't know. I don't remember."

"What about the night after the murder, did you go anywhere?"

"No, I don't think so." Shawn answered with a shake of his head, dropping his gaze down from Ryder's eyes.

"You didn't give a sandwich to Susan to give to Yakira's aunt at the funeral home?"

"Now that you mention it, I do remember that." Shawn said pulling out a white handkerchief from his pocket and wiping the sweat from the back of his neck.

"Was that your idea to do that?"

"No. No, it wasn't me!" Shawn insisted. "It was Speaker Warner; he thought it would be a nice gesture."

Ryder glanced over at the keypad on the door. "I have never seen a key pad lock on a barn before."

"You saw the price of hay lately? Somebody tried to break in just a few days ago. We had to replace the glass."

Ryder looked back down at the tracks in front of the barn. "Guess you been doing a lot of haying?" Ryder said as he turned and looked at the man. "Putting it all up in the barn?"

"Yeah, a lot."

"Big round bales, right?" Ryder pumped him for information.

"That and hay for the horse upstairs. I thought you were investigating a murder; what do these questions have to do with that?"

"Nothing." Ryder said, jotting all the information down in his notebook. "I am just an old farm boy and miss those days of bucking hay. Kids don't have to do that anymore. I think they are really missing out on something, don't you agree? You said Warner is not here where can we find him?"

"I think I have answered enough questions." Shawn said as he pulled the cap back down on his head. "I have to get back to work." He turned away from them and added. "You found your way in. You can find your way out."

"Well then, I guess I will just sit here and watch for him."

Shawn, stopped, turned and walked back. "When he is not here he likes to stay at the Hotel at Roaring River in the Dogwood Suite.'"

"He lied." Ryder said as he slammed the car door shut.

"About what?"

"The hay." Ryder fired the car up. "Anyone knows you don't put up wet hay. And those tracks were made when it was muddy. If he was putting hay into the barn the tracks would be deeper coming in, not going out." He looked out the windshield and pointed towards the old barn. "See all the loose hay in front of it? There isn't one sign of hay in front of the new barn. Whatever is that barn, it isn't hay."

So where to now?"

"After we make a few phone calls." Ryder said with a small grin, turning to her. "We're going to go question a certain congressman."

Chapter 15

Once again Ryder found himself walking across the interwoven pattern of bricks in front of the Inn at Roaring River, pulling open the doors, and once inside he removed his sunglasses. His eyes scanned across the lobby with the skill of an assassin, hunting for his target, hidden somewhere among the rustic furnishings. From the shadow box coffee table, with the stuffed and mounted fish and arrangement of flies and lures, that greeted the visitors as they passed by, to the old metal minnow buckets attached to the ceiling, intertwined with white Christmas twinkle lights that adorned a nearby hallway. The ceiling over the lobby opened into a great dome highlighted with wooden beams spread out like a giant spider web, speckled with lights that shone down on the stone pillars that guarded each doorway.

Ryder continued to scan the room, from the frosted glass divider wall to the Riverside conference room. He could hear a voice, a voice that could only come from a politician, a voice full of deception and deceit. Ryder's sights locked on him and he moved in. Warner was snuggled down in an overstuffed leather chair that was next to the fireplace.

"Mr. Ryder and dear sister Yakira." The speaker said haughtily as he looked up to them. "To what do I owe this pleasure?" He raised a glass of red wine in a toast. Across from him, sitting on a matching love seat, was a thin framed blonde haired woman, U.S. Congresswoman Lydia Custer from Louisiana and her husband Mark James, the typical power playing couple, dressed in the latest fashions, dripping with jewelry, stinking of French perfume and aftershave. Seated on the leather sofa that faced the fireplace was Special Agent Alexander, county prosecutor Price, and next to him the political county leader: Chad Shrum.

"Well, isn't this cozy." Ryder said with a sneer as he looked at each of them, stopping at Chad, a slightly plump man with a salt and pepper beard and hair to match. "Three little politicians sitting in a row. My oh my how the lies must grow."

"Ryder, we are civil human beings here." Chad said.

"You know of me?"

"Everyone knows of you. You could join us, if you like."

"No." Ryder said, turning and looking at Alex, who sat there with her legs crossed, revealing her long smooth legs that peeking out from under her dark gray skirt. "Unlike my friend here, I keep track of the company I keep."

"And what do you mean by that, Mr. Ryder?" Congresswoman Custer asked, pulling her gold rimmed eyeglasses down on her sloped nose and shifting her gaze up to him, the strong chemical smell of her perfume drifting up, making him cough.

"Simple, ma'am. If you step in a pile of dog poop, it doesn't matter if it is Chihuahua or Great Dane, it still smells the same. Republican, Democrat, you are both the same. You both stink."

"What are you here for?" Mark asked.

"Murder!"

Warner lifted the wine glass to his lips and downed the last swallow of the bitter liquid. "Oh, yes." He drew out with an arrogant tone. "You are still looking into that?" He looked down into his empty glass and pouted. He turned to Alex and said "Honey, be a sweet dear and get me some more wine." He handed the glass to her and she got up and took the glass. "Anyone else want anything? Oh well, we will have her go get it when she returns."

"She is a trained F.B.I. agent, she isn't your servant." Ryder said, annoyed, watching as she walked over to the restaurant.

"She is a government servant and I work for the government. So she serves me. Who do you serve Mr. Ryder?"

"The truth." Ryder said before he leaned down on the arm of the chair, his fingers dug into the soft glove leather and he said in a soft tone "Now we can do this here in front of everybody, or we can do it in private, in there." Ryder pointed to the conference room. "It is your choice Mr. Speaker, but it is going to happen."

Ryder pointed the way and held the door open and they entered the sealed glass room. There were several round tables with chairs all around each table. Warner and Yakira walked to the table in the middle and he sat down as Ryder closed the door.

"This is a real nice place." Warner said as he glanced around the room. "We have our meetings here. But we usually have something to eat." He turned back to Yakira and said with a grin. "Be a good little sister and go and get me a pork sandwich out of the restaurant

"I didn't know pigs ate their own." She said with a tilt of her head, as her frustration grew.

"So what do you want to ask me?"

"Where were you when Annalisa was murdered?"

"Again with this!" Speaker Warner said heatedly. "I told you Mr. Ryder, I was at KYTV station in Springfield. I was there until a little after midnight."

"Talking to a reporter in Phoenix, Arizona, right? For their ten o'clock news?"

"Yes, because they are in Mountain Time one hour behind us. So eleven would be ten o'clock there."

You know, I hate the change over from daylight saving time." Ryder said. "I always get confused. Do you set the clock ahead or is it back. How about you, Mr. Speaker?"

"No, anyone with any intelligence knows it is spring forward and fall back."

"However, if we lived in Arizona we wouldn't have that problem. They don't have Daylight saving time there. They have standard time all year-long. However, when we have daylight saving time, which we are still in, they are not one hour behind, they are two. So to talk to a reporter at ten in Arizona it would have to be midnight here. You just said you left at midnight."

"Well it might have been later than that."

"Even stranger, dear brother Scott." Yakira said in a mocking tone. "When I called the news station in Phoenix, they told me that while they talked to you for their ten o'clock report that it was prerecorded at five p.m. their time." She sat down across from him. "That is seven o'clock here."

97

Ryder turned a chair around so he could face Speaker Warner. "Do you remember a woman named Jo Anna Jones? She is the make artist at KY3 TV station."

"No."

"Funny thing, she remembers you. In fact, she put on your make up a little after six p.m. she also remembers that you got a phone call around seven and then you made a call shortly after that, and then you left around seven thirty and didn't come back till around eleven that night. She said you were nervous and sweaty; she had to redo your entire make up. She also said you changed clothes."

"She is lying."

Ryder reached into his jacket pocket and pulled out his phone and brought up a video. "These things are amazing anymore. "This is the report that was done for Phoenix." Ryder scooted over beside the speaker and placed his arm around the man and showed him the phone. "If you notice you are wearing a slate gray jacket and bright red tie. And down here in the corner it reads previously recorded." Ryder took the phone and pulled up another video and played it. Once again he placed his arm around the speaker. "This is the report that was done in Springfield for the ten o'clock report. Notice now you are wearing a dark charcoal jacket." Ryder stopped the video and leaned back. "What happened to the other jacket?"

"So I changed my jacket. There is no crime against that."

"So you could show us that jacket?"

"I could." He said, standing up and pulling his jacket down with a jerk. "But I won't."

"Is that because you got her blood on it?"

He straightened his tied and looked at Ryder. "Get this through your head. I am the freaking Speaker of the House, and now with all the caring votes for the man who lost his wife I am a shoe in to become the next president. Let my worthless son rot in prison and I will show I am tough on crime and have all the votes wrapped up." He headed towards the door.

"Why did you break into Annalisa's casket?" Ryder asked and Speaker Warner stopped. "Did you find it?"

"And what would that be Mr. Ryder?!"

"A flash drive that contains information you want."

"Silly person, don't fall for the lies that are told to you by ludicrous ones." Speaker Warner pulled the door opened and glanced over Yakira and added."Like the child you are running around with." He stepped out of the room. Anger was trembling, shaking as a massive earthquake in Yakira, building up from her brightly colored shoes, up through her legs, souring her stomach. Her teeth clenched and her hands shook as she watched him take the glass of wine from Alex. He had just taken a sip of the wine when she dashed out the door, leaping out; she landed on his back, forcing him down to the floor. Using her hands she slammed his head down into the carpeted floor. He pushed her over, tossing her off. She leaped on to him again, Ryder quickly darted out of the room and he scooped Yakira up, wrapping his arms around her tightly. He lifted her straight up, her arms and legs flailed about as he twisted about, pulling her away from the speaker, who Mark and Alex had helped to his feet.

"Let me go!" Yakira yelled. "I want to kill him. I want to kill him!"

"All right, that is enough." Price said. "I want this woman arrested."

Yakira was twisting and turning, making it hard for Ryder to hold on to her. He sat down on the floor but kept his arms wrapped around her. "It was just a family disagreement. " She said, forcing a mock grin. "Right, dear brother-in-law? You don't want me to give the twelve reasons, do you?"

Speaker Warner held a napkin up to his bleeding lip. "It is like she said, 'just a family disagreement'. Everyone is on edge. No need for anyone to be arrested." Ryder let Yakira go and she turned and walked outside.

"Let's get you cleaned up, sir." Price said as he helped the speaker over to the restroom.

"This is what you are defending?" Ryder asked as he looked at Alex.

"Rick, you don't understand."

"Enlighten me."

"I can't."

"Just what I thought," Ryder's mouth drew up in disappointment. "You sold your soul for a shiny badge and more money."

"I am not like you; I have to work for a living."

Ryder reached into his inside jacket pocket and pulled out a leather wallet. "You need money!" He opened up his checkbook. "Would a million do it for you?"

"This isn't just about money." She reached up and grabbed his hand that held the checkbook and pushed it down. "This isn't even about murder. There is a lot more here."

"Like what?"

"I can't tell you now." She wrapped her arms around him, kissed him on the cheek, and whispered in his ear. "Meet me in my room tonight at midnight." She released him. "My room is at the end of the hall. I will explain everything then. And come alone."

Chapter 16

By the time Ryder had caught up with Yakira she was already outside in the parking lot, stepping right out in front of a car that was leaving. The driver honked the horn and slid the car to a stop, just before hitting her. She just looked at the driver and continued on to the Jaguar, slamming the door shut as she got in. Ryder stood there a few feet away watching her as she was screaming and yelling to herself, pounding on the door panel of the car. He continued on to the car and got in the driver's seat and she turned away from him, looking out the window as he drove out of the parking lot.

The Jaguar had just begun the ascent up the hill, out into the valley; she reached over and flipped on the radio. A news report was on. *"Senator Dan Goodman expressed his outrage yesterday on the rash of missing weapons from US Military bases across the country he has asked the FBI to look into a group called black…"*

She reached over and changed the station to music, and the opening notes of Queen's *'Somebody to Love'* started to play. He glanced over at her singing alone, acting as if she were playing piano, and using the car's dash as her keyboard. He reached over and turned the sound down and said "Is that what you really want?"

"Somebody to love?" She asked innocently. "Of course. Doesn't everybody?" She reached back over and turned the sound back up, and began to sing even louder, drowning out the radio. She was barely keeping tune, especially as she tried to match the singer's high parts.

"No." Ryder said, turning the radio down again. "About wanting to kill Speaker Warner."

"Oh." She said with revulsion and cranked up the volume again, even louder. "Sing with me." Tilting her head back and swaying to the beat she sang at the top of her lungs.

"What are the twelve reasons?"

Her song slowly drifted till she was silent, she reached over and turned the radio off. She turned away from him and stared out the window. The thick foliage stood on both sides of the highway, protecting peering eyes from looking down into the valley. The only sound was the purr of the engine as the Jaguar wound its way up out of the park.

"I hate that man." She finally said, breaking her silence.

"Because of what he did to Annalisa?" That was the only reason he could think of that would draw this much, but her stillness told him there was more than just that, and when she spoke it confirmed it.

"Yes. " She turned back. "But also what he did to me."

Ryder's head twisted back and forth from her to the road. He was trying to see her reaction, but still guide the Jaguar through the hard twisting curves. Not wanting to talk she reached over and turned on the radio and heard Night Ranger's '*Sister Christian*'. She began singing with it. The tears running down her cheeks, she mumbled and he barely heard her. "If you are supposed to be my big brother, why didn't you stop him?" She looked out the side window once again. She turned back to him and said firmly. "Why didn't you stop him?" The tears were streaming down her face. "I was only twelve years old. "

Ryder slammed down on the brakes and the antilock brakes kicked in, causing the steering wheel to shake violently. He guided the car off the highway on to a side road, and he parked under a shade tree that was right at the intersection. Shoving the gear shifter into park he turned to her. Her hands were shielding her face as she sobbed out loud. "All I wanted was that beautiful dress." She spoke, her hands still clasped over her face. I was going to wear it for my *Bat Mitzvah*", a celebration that observed a young Jewish girl making the transition from Child to woman. She lowered her hands and turned to him and sniffed. "He said he would buy it for me. He was my brother-in-law, he was family. Then he said okay, but also bought this swim suit. He told me I looked so pretty that we should take some photos. At first it was in my dress, I felt like a beauty queen, then in the swim suit. Then he told me, you know what real women wear, nothing." She hung her head down and her hair fell down along the sides, swinging as a pendulum of humiliation.

Ryder reached up and pulled his sunglasses off and laid them on the instrument panel and he said softly. "Oh for the love of…"

"He made me pose in all sorts of nasty ways." She said in a shuddering breath as she lifted her head and looked at him, her bright eyes glistening with her tears, even though they were swollen and red. "He brought his friends in to watch. Oh, Ricky." She unhooked her seat belt and fell over onto him, burying her face into his shoulder.

Ryder opened up his arms, and she slid herself across the console, getting closer to him. He placed one of his hands behind her head; his hand clenched into a fist then unfolded as he carefully stroked her hair.

"If I had known…. I could…" He had no words to say, none that he knew were right. He tenderly pushed her back and using his thumbs he wiped the tears from her eyes and rubbed them over his eyes and said. "Your tears are my tears. I don't cry. You don't cry. But if we weep, we weep together." He placed his hands under her chin and tenderly lifted her head. He lowered his face closer to hers, their lips almost touching; he turned and kissed her on the cheek. He leaned back in his seat and grabbed his sunglasses off the dash then slipped them back on and said: "How about a Texan burger?"

"You read my mind." She said as slid back into her seat. He reached into his jacket pocket, producing something a homicide detective always carried, a white handkerchief, be it picking up evidence so you don't get fingerprints on it, or times like this, to wipe away tears.

The gas gauge was reading nearly empty in the Jaguar so the first stop had to be a local convenience store. Yakira went inside to wash her face, as he filled the tank, finding the automatic pay option at the pumps was down, he had to go inside to pay. Ryder laid the money down on the counter and looked up at the TV that was hanging on the wall behind the counter. A blonde woman news reporter from FOX news was speaking.

"Federal authorities are still investigating the murder of Speaker Warner's wife Annalisa. While they have no suspect in custody at this time, they do have several persons of interests and they are actively in the process of gathering evidence and questioning witnesses. Department of Justice spokesperson Marcella Bradley has stated "that this case will be wrapped up soon."

"Which means they have no idea what they are doing?"

Why do you say that?" The owner, a heavy-set woman named Joanie White, asked.

"It is an old police trick." He said, remembering how his department did the same thing in the Kansas City Butcher case. "If you have one person of interest, it means you just don't have the evidence yet, but you know who did it. But if you have 'several persons of interest' you have no idea who did it. And all you are trying to do is spook the one that did do it, to make them do something that will give them away."

"You sound like a cop."

"Used to be." Ryder said as she handed him back his change. Ryder's lips curled up into a small smile as he added. "Kind of like being an alcoholic, once you are one you can stop being one, but always are one."

"Well, it is too bad Annalisa got murdered. She was good peoples." Joanie said as she closed the register drawer. "God may get me for this, and I may have to ask for forgiveness, but I wish it was that damn L.J."

"God will forgive you, Joanie." Ryder heard a man say from behind him. He turned and saw a small man. He was a foot shorter than Ryder, his bony frame stooped over, and leaning on a twisted cherry wood cane. His hair and beard were gray and long, his clothes dirty and ripped. The old man took a stumbling step toward Ryder and looked up at him. "You that there detective that everyone has been talking about? The one that won all the money?" He took another step towards Ryder. "What would it mean to you...?" He said hungrily as he stared at the money in Ryder's hand, licking his lips; as if he were a hungry dog waiting do his trick so he could have the treat. "...to know that I might have saw that kid with the woman that was murdered."

Ryder stood staring at the man, it was not always a good idea to pay for information as people would gladly lie for cash, but he was not building a legal case, that was up to the police; he was just trying to get to the truth. He turned back to Joanie and pulled out a hundred-dollar bill from his wallet. "Give me change for that, ten ones and the rest in tens and twenties. She counted the change back and he turned back to the man. "If it is something I ready know." He held up one single dollar bill. "If it is good information," He held up one single twenty. "If it is great information," Ryder held up the entire amount in his hand. "Maybe even more." The man's eyes devoured the bills.

"Oh just tell the man, Jack." Joanie said just as Yakira returned from the restroom.

"What do you have?" Ryder said as he reached up and pulled his sunglasses off and laid them gently down on the counter behind him.

"She was his stepmother." The man said and Ryder peeled off a dollar and handed it to him. "She was at the baseball park, where the old city pool used to be. And they got into an argument." Ryder peeled off a ten and handed it to him.

"When was this?"

"It was Saturday."

What was the argument about?"

"Money." Jack said, waiting for a bill to come his way. Ryder peeled off another dollar bill and handed it to him. "The word is that the old man was no longer going to bail the kid out." Ryder peeled off two more dollars and handed it to him.

"You want this?" Ryder asked, holding up the rest of the money, then he placed it down on the counter and the old man reached for it, but Ryder grabbed his arm and warned him. "Not till you give it all to me."

"He was trying to get money out of her. He said 'he knew a secret', one that if she didn't come up with some money he was going to tell whole damn world. That it would ruin her and her family, the old man and…" he paused and stroked his long beard with his hand, and Ryder noticed that he had two fingers missing, only his ring finger, the pinkie and thumb remained.

"And who else?"

"And you."

"Me?" Ryder asked as he pulled out the notebook and began writing in it. "He mentioned me by name?"

"Na but he told her to get the money from that pal of hers that won the lottery because it would destroy him too."

"How did she react to this? What did she say?"

"She told him to leave her alone, that there was no secret.' He pushed her up against her car and showed her a paper he was holding. She fell down on the ground, and began to cry. He told her get the money by Monday or he would make her pay with her life."

"How much money?"

"Two hundred and fifty thousand."

"Why that amount?"

"Don't know fer sur buts he has a gambling problem; bets on everything. Talk is that he's in for big bucks with a hood in Little Rock."

"What happened next?"

"He got in his old man's truck and drove away."

"Is that all?"

"Nah, I seens em again Monday night. She was in a fancy red sports car. She told him she 'couldn't get the money. Wanted to give him the car.' "

"What time was that?"

"Six." The old man said still gazing at the money lying on the counter, wondering when he was going to get it. "He warned her again that he was going to tell the secret. She got this mean nasty look on her face. She pulled a gun on him."

"What kind of gun?"

"I dudn't know. Sort of looked like those on those detective shows back in the 1960's.Yous knows like Mannix. But it was bright."

"Smith and Wesson 32 special custom revolver, brightly plated, with mother of pearl grips and a small little rose stamped into the trigger guard." Yakira said as she walked up behind Ryder.

"How do you know that?" Ryder asked turning his head to her.

"That is the one I gave her."

"He said he would kill her if she didn't git the money. Then…" the old man laughed out loud. "The she lowered the gun, kicked him in the nuts, and left." He laughed again. "It wasa kinda funny seeing him rolling around on the ground. And that is all I know."

Chapter 17

3:55 p.m. afternoon: The restaurant was just opening. Ryder was surprised that even being the only ones there at the restaurant they were met with warm and friendly smiles. They knew exactly where to seat them: third booth up, from the left. Ryder sat down and Yakira sat across from him.

"If it isn't my two favorite customers." Kathy said gleefully, her green eyes shining as much as her smile as she set down two glasses in front of them. Sweet tea with a half-twist of lemon. "The Knight and the Princess."

"I beg your pardon?" Ryder asked, not understanding her comment.

She turned back to Yakira to explain. "The way he rode out of here the other day to your rescue, He is a knight." She grinned slightly, but not showing her teeth, and added. "Don't you agree?" A warm flush came over Yakira's face. She lifted the menu up to hide it. She turned back to Ryder and continued. "All you need is your bright charger."

Kathy grabbed the menu from her, then from Ryder, and ordered for them. "Texan Burgers for two." She kneeled down beside the booth and added, "Tell you what I will do. I will leave off the onions and bring you a 'love bird plate.' " She stood up. "French fries to share."

"We're just friends." Ryder said.

"Too bad, because you two make a cute couple. Do I leave the onions off or not?"

"Leave them off." Yakira said, taking a sip of her tea.

Shortly Kathy returned with two plates that held the sandwiches. "Texan burgers with dill pickles." She said setting the plates down in front of them. She quickly returned. "And a lovebird plate." She set down a large order of French fries on a plate in between them.

Yakira picked up the salt shaker and salted her dill pickles. Ryder sat there dumb founded, just staring at her. "What?" She asked, looking up at him and setting the shaker down. "Okay, so I'm crazy! I like salt on my pickles." He didn't say a word, just picked up the shaker and salted his pickles. "You too?" Yakira laughed. "I have never met anybody else who does that".

"Annalisa would always give me a strange look and say 'why would anyone want to salt something that is already salty? I would tell her...."

"Because it makes it taste better." They both said together, and laughed.

"Maybe I chose the wrong sister."

"Maybe so." She said so low in tone that he didn't hear her. She offered a small smile as she looked at him, before dropping her gaze down to the table.

"What? Did you say something?"

"No—I just said that—that I usually get these to go." She stumbled over her words, and again felt that warm glow over her face, and this time there was nothing to hide behind. She quickly took a drink of iced tea, hoping it would cool her embarrassment. "Kind of nice to eat it here."

"I have to ask you something."

"Really?" She replied, again nervously taking a drink of tea as if she were a teenager out on their very first date.

"It was clear that L.J. was blacking mailing her. Do you know what the secret could have been?"

"Oh, that?" She said, sounding disappointed. "I don't know for sure." She picked up her burger and took a bite. "Maybe it is what Scott was involved in. If she was involved..."

"You are forgetting." Ryder said as he took a sip of tea. Ryder reached into his inside jacket pocket and pulled out the notebook he had been writing in. He flipped through the pages. "Susan said. 'That she held up the flash drive that was Monday night. Jack said the argument was on a Friday. He flipped back a few more pages. She made a purchase at Wal-Mart for a USB flash drive Saturday morning. She wasn't seen again till eleven o'clock Saturday night when she filled the car with gas at a station just off I-44 in Joplin."

"So?"

"You have to think like a detective." He said as they both reached for a French fry at the same time, and their hands touched. She smiled and pulled her hand back and again took another sip of tea. "She didn't have the flash drive when L.J. threatened her. But she did have it Monday to confront Warner. Whatever was on that drive it was not the secret L.J. threatened her with, it was something else. Do you know of anything? Something that your family may be hiding." He munched on a fry.

Yakira took a drink of tea. "Well, there is one secret I know about. Annalisa is…" Catching herself she quickly corrected herself. "…she was adopted."

"What? I didn't know that."

"How do you know?"

"I overheard mom and dad talking one day; they were arguing about the yearly payment."

"Whoa, Whoa! What about this payment?"

"My parents had been taking out $5000.00 every year." The first one was given to Dr. Curtis when she was born. Then it started again when she was five years old, the last one was when she turned eighteen."

"No doctor charged that much back then." Ryder stroked his chin with his hand, he didn't like what his mind was coming up with but it was the only solution that made sense to the puzzle. "An illegal adoption, but Doctor Curtis died a long time ago back when we were just kids, in fact I was five at the time, how could he blackmail your parents after that?

"It was a woman on the phone."

"How do you know? Did you hear her?"

"No, but mom called her a *shiska*. You do know what that means?"

"Oh, boy!" Ryder said, rubbing his temples and looking down at the table. "You just added more suspects."

At that time Kathy walked up carrying a pitcher of sweet tea. "Well, here comes the cheapskate!" She said as she glared across the restaurant. Ryder looked from his meal and watched a pudgy man with a round clean-shaven face, except for the small patch under his lower lip. His dark colored hair was buzz cut. Ripped jeans and a black t-shirt with a yellow yield sign turned upside down with the words 'Yield to No One' on it. His arms covered in tattoos. "The congressman's *dear wonderful son*." Ryder could hear the sarcasm in her voice.

"Is that L.J.?"

"Mr. *Big Spender* himself." Again her disdain showed through. "You know what I get for a tip from him?" She turned to Ryder, curling her lips into a sneer. "A nickel." Ryder looked over at the man. He was complaining the fork was dirty, and it was not. That the lights were too dim, although they weren't, making one of the waitresses read the menu to him. Complaining about the prices, and then ordering a hamburger, which he always did, only to be told it was from the child's menu. Ryder's eyes followed him like the crosshairs of a rifle scope as he walked over towards the other side of the dining room.

"What is back there?"

"Our restrooms."

"I think I better wash up." Ryder said with a smile as he stood up. He followed the waitress out of the room and back to the men's room at the end. He pushed opened the door; L.J. was in the stall wadding up paper towels and throwing them into the toilet, trying to make it overflow. He looked up and saw Ryder, who was standing in front of the door.

"Who are you, freak? " L.J. demanded, turning around and facing him.

"Someone looking for answers."

"You are that detective dude that the old man told me about." L.J. smirked and stepped towards him. He beamed with a grungy smile. "You gonna get out of my way? Or do I have to mess you up?" Ryder didn't say a word; he just stood slowly flexing his fingers. He wasn't worried about this punk. One, he was taller and outweighed him, and what weight L.J. had was mostly fat, not the muscle tone that Ryder had. While Ryder played football, this guy sat under the bleachers hiding his beer in a soda cup, then getting arrested and having daddy bail him out, besides, under his coat was the Glock. He tried to step around Ryder, but Ryder moved over in front of him. "I am leaving, man."

"Not till you answer some questions."

"I am warning you, dude!" L.J. reached into his pocket and produced a switch blade. With a flick the blade flung open. "I'll cut you."

"Are you really that stupid?"

L.J. held the knife up and jabbed it at him. Ryder stepped out-of-the-way. Grabbing L.J.'s hand that held the knife; he twisted it around and brought L.J.'s arm down over his leg. L.J. cried out and dropped the knife on the tile floor. Ryder kicked the knife across the room and then twisted L.J.'s arm around behind his back. With his other hand Ryder grabbed the back of LJ's head and forced him over to the sink and pushed his face down onto the counter.

"Now are you going to answer my questions or do we have to continue this?"

"You know where you can go you son-of-a—!"

Ryder turned on the water and began to let the sink fill up. You shoved his face down into the water, and then lifted his head back up. "You ready to talk now?"

"Go to hell!" L.J. said as he coughed and looked up at Ryder. Ryder spun the man around and threw him on the floor. L.J. quickly got to his feet and bum rushed at him. Ryder bent down and drove his shoulder into L.J.'s gut; he quickly rose and tossed L.J. to the floor.

"Got any more left or are you ready to talk?" Ryder said, leaning on the sink cabinet. "Or do I let Yakira come in here and do what her big sister did to you, and I don't think she needs a gun to do it."

"I should have taken that gun away from her and made her eat it." L.J. was huffing like a steam engine trying to pull up a steep hill. "I am going to kill you and that dirty Jew girlfriend of yours out there."

"What did you call her?" Ryder asked through clenched teeth.

"You heard me, pig! A dirty filthy Jew!" Ryder hated this phase, meaning that one was unclean, unworthy of the love of God, he had gotten in so many fights over this in school when someone would call Annalisa that. He grabbed L.J. by the arm and spun him around, twisting L.J.s arm around behind his back. With his other arm he wrapped it around L.J.'s neck placing him in a choke hold and began to squeeze.

L.J. gasped for air. "You ever call her that again. I will break your freaking neck." Ryder lifted back then released him, throwing L.J. to the floor one more time. L.J. sat rubbing his neck, his eyes piercing into Ryder.

"I am going to sue you for police brutality."

"Only one problem with that." Ryder said as he bent down, grabbing L.J.'s shirt and picking him up off the floor. "I am not a cop." He grinned mockingly. "I am just somebody looking for the answers." He slammed L.J. back against the wall. "Why did you kill Annalisa?"

"I didn't kill her!"

"You were blackmailing her!"

"Who?"

"Don't give me that." Ryder pushed on LJ's face, making his head twist around. "You know I am talking about Annalisa. What did you have on her?"

"Believe me. Of all people. You don't want to know."

Ryder spun him around, pushed his back up against the wall. "What are you talking about?"

"Secrets, and the one that has been kept from you." Ryder released him. L.J. leaned against the wall. He placed his hands behind his head, revealing the flaming skull tattoo on his forearm, on the forehead of the skull was a rising sun. "Besides, it's none of your business, pig! I got it covered; the old man is going to take care of me." L.J. walked over and picked up the knife, folded the blade and put it back into his pocket. "Even if I did kill her. I wouldn't see a day in jail. "

113

Ryder grinned. "You really are dumb, aren't you? Haven't you heard the news?" Ryder asked as he saw L.J.'s face twist in puzzlement. "You daddy has decided that votes are more important than you are. He isn't going to help you anymore. He will get more votes if you go to jail."

"You lying pig!"

"Go ask him."

With that L.J. fumed out of the bathroom and Ryder followed after him. Ryder stood in the doorway of the hall and looked out across the dining hall, even before he saw them he could feel that every eye there was on him. He reached into the pocket of his jacket and slipped on his sunglasses. He adjusted them and then walked forward.

"Just typical!" He heard Kathy complain. "He skips out of here without paying." Ryder reached into his pocket and pulled out a hundred dollar bill. "That is for our meal." He and pulled out another hundred. "And that is for the wet biscuit." He turned to her and grinned. "Maybe that will make up for his nickel tips."

"What did you find out?" Yakira asked, walking up to him. He didn't answer her. He just walked towards the front door and she followed after him. Outside L.J. got into a new dusty gray Ford pickup and sped away, squealing the tires. "Ricky, are you okay?" Yakira said as he glanced down, there fluttering on the pavement was a butterfly, next to the Jaguar. He bent down and gently scooped it up in his hands and with tender care he stroked the beautiful insect, making sure it's bright white wings were not broken.

"I am fine." He said, without any feeling as the creature crawled up on his finger, and he held it up close to his face. He remembered what his mother had told him when he was a child. 'A white butterfly is an angel waiting for you to tell your secret prayer to it, then it flies away to tell God. The butterfly fluttered its wings and he held his hand up over his head.

"What did he say?"

"Nothing." He said watching as the butterfly take flight and fly away. He turned to her and said. "Let's go back to Cassville; there is somebody I need to meet."

114

Chapter 18

'Give with good will, and good things will come'. Ryder's uncle Tony had always told him. He hoped that was true, as there were more questions now than there were answers about Annalisa's murder. It had seemed so simple coming down from Kansas City; it was Speaker of the House Scott Jacob Warner who had murdered Annalisa. The motive was simple, she was going to divorce him, and it would have ruined him politically, and obliterated his chances for being president. Now there was L.J., what was the secret that he held over her? Was it about being adopted? It seemed if that were it that would not destroy lives. What about the adoption? The Rosen family had made payments to someone for eighteen years, why did it stop then? What about the gun? That question was about to get answered. Ryder wheeled the Jaguar into a parking spot in front the Sheriff's office.

It was a large white structure, looking more as if were an old house with large pillar posts on the front porch. It was located next to the jail. He walked over to the other side of the car and opened the door for Yakira, holding it open.

"What are we doing here?" She asked as she got out.

"To ask somebody some questions." Again Ryder's tone was low and harsh.

"Who?"

"The sheriff himself."

"About what?"

"A gun." Ryder replied frankly.

Ryder stepped up on the front porch and pulled the front door open, they walked into the department and Ryder reached up and pulled his sunglasses off. Deputy Thompson was behind the counter sitting in a chair, devouring a slice of supreme pizza. "Ryder!" He said, wiping his mouth as he stood up. "What are you doing here?"

"Come to see your boss. Where is he?"

The sheriff, hearing Ryder's voice, came out of his office. "Ryder?" He questioned, puzzled as to why he would want to see him "You want to see me? What about?"

"That fancy gun of yours. Could we see it?"

"Sure. It is in my desk. Come on back."

Ryder and Yakira walked back to the office, it was typical cop, typical small county budget with low dollar furniture, that had seen one too many terms of use, swivel chairs that squeaked and moaned as the sheriff sat down behind the desk. Hard uncomfortable chairs in front of the desk that caused Ryder to feel the Glock bite into his side as he sat down, making him want to tell everything he knew. Drawers that groaned and grabbed as they were opened, bumped as they were closed.

Sheriff Hart placed the weapon on top of a pile of papers on the desk and Yakira picked it up. She immediately flipped open the swing out cylinder to check if it was loaded. It was empty. She flipped it back into place. "What is this all about?" The sheriff asked, watching Yakira flip the weapon over to inspect to the trigger guard.

"This is my gun! See the mark?" She said as she pointed to the rose shaped mark on the trigger guard.

"What!" the Sheriff said in amazement.

"You said you bought this gun at a pawn shop, Sheriff. When was that?" Ryder asked.

"It was Tuesday Morning. At Tuland Pawn at Hilltop. You can check if like." He leaned forward and looked at Yakira. "I didn't know it was yours. I always check to see if a gun has been stolen. You didn't report it stolen." He turned to Ryder.

"I gave it to Annalisa." Yakira said. "She was scared somebody was trying to hurt her.

"Who?"

"We are not sure," Ryder said as he stood up. "We will be taking the gun, sheriff."

"No problem."

"And I will be checking with this pawn shop. Who should I see?"

"Leon, the owner." The sheriff stood up and escorted them out of his office, when suddenly he stopped. "Oh I just remembered. Leon went out of town. He won't be back until just before the opening of deer season. I will give him a call and see what I can find out. Maybe he can tell us who sold it to him." He continued to talk as he escorted them past the counter and towards the door. "May take a few days; he went to see his brother in California. But I will let you know when I do." Ryder stopped on the front porch and turned back to the sheriff, who ran his fingers through his hair. "This could be the big break we are looking for. You want me to tell your pal the F.B.I. lady?"

Ryder stepped off the porch and towards the car. He opened the passenger door for the Jaguar and held it for Yakira. "I will let her know when I see her."

Yakira got in and Ryder went over to the other side. "So what now? Back to the lake house?"

"No, I told you. I have to meet someone later tonight."

"Alex! Right?" Her tone was almost angry.

"She knows something, maybe she can help put this all together. I thought we would go to the gun shop and wait there."

"Why can't we just wait at the park?" She almost seemed to be pleading with him.

"No, the shop. There is something I need to pick up there."

The shop was one of the older buildings in town, with weathered wood siding, and shingles, a faded sign that had so many different names painted across it, no wonder it was peeling now. The tile floor has lost its luster long ago, the roof leaked, as did the front window, during a hard rain storm. The layout consisted of four different rooms, the main store at the front, and an office, bathroom and an unused store-room at the back. The front divided into separate sections; guns; fishing supplies; boating, and other sporting goods which included Cassville Wildcats, Exeter Tigers, and other local school clothing apparel. Business had been good, but over the last six months it had fallen off considerably, to the point that she was not able to pay her bills. She hated to go to her store, for she feared what would be waiting for her in the mail.

Ryder pulled the car in behind the shop and parked it, she didn't wait for him to open the door; she was the first out. She glance over at the darken store, knowing what was waiting for them, more darkness because they electricity had been turned off, because she couldn't pay the bill. She didn't want him to know. She turned and looked away from the store as he approached the back steps. A warm breeze made her hair flap like the flags of a used car lot; she brushed it back out of her face, before turning back and faced the store again. Suddenly the security light came on, revealing several boxes sitting there.

"What? " She asked, confused, as there was power to the store again. She stepped up and unlocked the door, reaching in, she turned on the light. The security alarm was flashing. She pushed in the number code: 5772. She walked further into the shop and turned on more lights. She turned back to him, standing in the open doorway.

"I thought I might set up a crime lab here in the back room. I would gladly pay you rent. I have already ordered stuff, computers, evidence collection kit. That is the stuff outside."

"You know, don't you?" She said, interrupting him. "That the shop is having trouble."

"Why didn't you tell me? I have all this money."

"I couldn't ask you for a loan." She said as she walked into the small office and turned on the light, then walked behind the small desk, crowded with piles of catalogs and unopened mail.

"What loan? I would give it to you."

"There you go again." She said with a half grin as she sat down behind the desk. "You're the knight and I am the princess, and you are coming to the rescue." She leaned back and the old wooden office chair squeaked. "All my life you have been there to pull me out of every stupid thing I have done." She leaned forward and the chair squeaked again as he stood in front of the desk, looking down at her.

"I'll have a quarter million wired to your account tomorrow. I take care of my little sister. "

"Yeah, okay!" She protested, holding her hand up for him to stop. She stood up and walked around the front of the desk and sat down on the corner and crossed her legs. "But I don't want you to look at me that way anymore. Can't you see I am not that little girl anymore? I know I may not look like it, but I am a woman. *So no more little sister*!" She made her last words demanding.

"Okay then, we are partners. Okay?" He held his hand to her.

"Partners fifty/fifty."

"Now I am going to get that stuff inside."

Ryder had carried the boxes inside and started unpacking them. "Oh shoot! They forget the fuming chamber." All of sudden he heard Yakira curse and storm out of the office. "What is wrong?"

"Nothing." She said, heading for the back door. "I am just tired; can't we just go to the lake house?"

"I have to meet Alex. Take your truck. I had the tank filled."

"You will lock up?" She asked as she walked out the back door and walked over to her pickup: a 1977 Chevy C10 short bed pickup, painted gray and pink metallic, with pin striping separating the two colors. She fired it up and the side pipes roared to life. She seemed sad, she must be missing Annalisa, Ryder reasoned. He watched her drive away, and then went back inside, there lying on the floor was a rolled up envelope. He bent down and picked it up and read the address on the return: it was Speaker Warner.

Chapter 19

The clock on the dash read 11:52 as the Jaguar descended down the steep hill into the darkness of the park, navigating the hard turn to the right, just before crossing the bridge, a pickup raced in from a side road that led to the park office, it was a two-tone late 1970's Chevrolet four-wheel-drive, it fishtailed and the rear of it slammed into the side of the bridge, breaking the driver's side tail light.

Ryder slammed down hard on the brakes and jerked the steering wheel hard to the left. The Jaguar slid to a stop sideways in the highway. Ryder watched as the pickup turned to F- highway and headed out of the park. Ryder straightened the Jaguar and continued on to the inn. The restaurant was already closed; the lobby was dimly lit, only by the lamps on the end tables. There was no one at the check in counter, and it seemed he was all alone. Passing under the minnow buckets and the dim glow of the Christmas lights, used for the cabin feel of decor, he turned left and went down the hall.

It was a long hallway, lit only by the warm white glow of fish-shaped sconces mounted on the walls. Alex's room was located at the end of the hallway on the right, next to the Dogwood Suite where Speaker Warner was staying. He knocked on Alex's door, there was no answer. He knocked again; it was then that he noticed that the door to Warner's room was slightly ajar and blocked with something, a large bath towel. There was a large dark-colored spot staining it, he had seen that stain enough in his life, not to have to guess, he knew what it was-it was blood.

He reached under his coat and slipped the Glock from its holster. He was so glad that he had listened to Captain Grosstree who had told him 'a gun may be a cop's best friend, but light is a very good friend.' Luckily he had a tactical light mounted to the bottom of the pistol. The entire room was covered in a sheet of darkness, but the bright blue beam of light pulled that sheet back and Ryder entered the room.

Gripping the guns with both hands he shined the light around while he called out. "Mr. Speaker. Congressman Warner! It is Rick Ryder." All the while the beam moved over the room. The bed was messed up. The sheets were pulled back, the pillows sunk in and the bedspread had slid off on to the floor. The carpet squished under his feet and the sound of running water was coming from the bathroom. He continued moving slowly, deeper into the room, letting the beam of light and the barrel of the pistol lead the way. As he got further into the room, he nearly tripped over a leather briefcase on the floor. Ryder kneeled down, and reaching into his pocket for a pen, lifted the briefcase up with the pen through the handle and saw that the locks had broken, and that there was a single Benjamin left inside. He lowered the case back down onto the floor.

The strong smell of fish invaded his nostrils, it was one he knew. It was caviar, just after he had won the money one of the first things he bought was a bottle of French wine and caviar. *Fish eggs are highly over rated.* He shone the light down into the trash can and saw a small empty jar and an empty sleeve that had contained club crackers. It was then that he caught sight of a half-drunk bottle of white wine lying on its side, spilling out its contents onto the floor. There was a spot of blood on the end of the bottle and more staining the carpet, as droplets of blood led toward the bathroom door, near the front of the room. Ryder kneeled down to examine the glasses next to the bottle, one with lipstick on it. He looked carefully at the glass, wondering if it was the same shade that Yakira wore. His mind was racing with what could have happened here, that Warner forced himself on her.

Suddenly out of the corner of his eye Ryder caught movement. The bathroom door was opening. He quickly drew the Glock up and aimed it at the door as he stood up. Taking slow steady steps, making sure the Glock was going there before him; it was instinct, having been drilled into him by the instructors. He whipped around to step into the bathroom.

Water was pouring over the edge of the bathtub and flooding the floor, and he could feel it soaking through his shoes, into his socks and onto his feet. The white shower curtain was pulled over the tub, and stained with spots of blood. He pulled the curtain back, and dropped the gun down, as his finger gripped around the trigger. He gasped, and then cursed.

Speaker of the House Scott Warner was dead. Face down in the tub, covered with murky red water. A yellow Ethernet cable sawed into his neck. Ryder pulled him out of the water by his collar. Glassy- eyed and warm to the touch, he hadn't been dead that long.

He shoved the Glock back down into it holster, and quickly left the bathroom. Grabbing up a plastic grocery bag he saw lying on the floor he placed the wine glass with the lipstick on it in the bag, along with the wine bottle and left the room.

By this time the water had spilled out into the hall, he couldn't go back the way he came, his shoes would leave tracks. At the end of the hall were two double doors that led out into the service area. He reached down and slipped off his shoes and pulled off his socks. He pushed the double doors open. Straight ahead were the stairs leading down to the lower floor and more rooms, to his left was another hallway that led to an outside door.

Turned over in the middle of the floor was a maid service rack with towels and other items used to service the room, including trash bags scattered all over the floor. He took a towel and dried his feet until they were bone dry. Using the towel he dried his wet footprints off the tile. Taking a trash bag he shoved the shoes, socks, and the wet towel down into the bag. Using another towel, he placed it on the floor and stepped on it, using sliding steps he made his way down towards the stairs, this was a public area that many people used, one of the first things he was taught was you don't search for prints here, too many people used it. Even bare footprints would not be unusual. He shoved the other towel into the bag and quickly but quietly made his way down the flight of stairs to the bottom floor. He had only taken a couple of steps when he felt something under his foot. He looked down; it was a bracelet. He picked it up and quickly recognized it, was Annalisa's, the one that Yakira had been wearing. Slipping the bracelet down into the pocket of his jacket he continued on the stairs to the bottom floor, using his hip he pushed the exit door open. Lights were on in a couple of rooms. So instead of taking the sidewalk along the back of the building and having a guest see him, he ran out across the lawn, and then sneaked back to the wooden steps that led down to the highway. Halfway down his knee was hurting him. He sat down on the bench seat to rub it, the stillness broke with the screaming yelp of a siren; with each wail it let out it grew a little closer. He moaned through the pain as he pushed himself up, and forced himself down the stairs.

The glow of flashing lights cut through the darkness, painting out across the rocky hills and the tops of the trees as a deputy sheriff's cruiser was heading down the hill into the park. He took off running across the highway; he could feel the warmness of pavement on his bare feet. He had just made it across the highway and slid down the side of the bank as the headlights of the cruiser spanned out over the highway. He ducked down as it raced by in a flash, turning and heading up into the parking lot.

Ryder climbed back up the bank and onto the edge of the road, he could see the red and blue beams flashing up high into the nighttime sky, it reminded him of when the 'Old Settlers Reunion' would come to the fairgrounds with all the rides and they would use these big searchlights that they would shine up in the sky, and he could see it at the farm. Suddenly, his mind was shattered back to reality as another siren was approaching; by its wail he could tell it was an ambulance. It was fourth down and ten, and with only a few seconds to go on the clock, they were behind four points, it was time for a quarterback run. "*Hike.*" Ryder said in his mind and then took off running down the road back towards the hotel. His leg was hurting badly, but he didn't stop.

The siren was growing closer and another in the distance could be heard. He took a deep breath and fought though the pain, his toes digging into the grass as he climbed the hill to the parking lot. He took another deep breath and dash out across the parking lot. He had just reached the Jaguar when the ambulance pulled up into the driveway of the hotel. He ducked down beside the car, and watched as the paramedics got out, retrieved their first aid kit and went inside. The other siren was growing louder, and closer. He could tell by the sound it was a cruiser, his job would be to seal off the parking lot. He had to get out before that cruiser arrived and not be seen.

He fired the car up and backed it out of the parking place, leaving the headlights off he guided the car out of the parking lot and down the highway. Once again the flashing lights painted along the tree tops. He quickly turned onto F- highway, and didn't turn on the headlights till the highway made a hard turn to the left and he left the park. He could hear the scream of other sirens filling the air. Barry County was about to have its biggest murder case ever.

It was around one clock Thursday morning when Ryder drove up to the lake house, and parked behind Yakira's truck, the bed had a fresh scrape in the paint on the driver's side and the tail light was broken. He picked the trash bags up off the floor of the car and headed inside.

The lights were still on in the great room and the sliding glass door that led out onto the deck was wide open. He started to close it when he heard a sob from out on the deck.

"Yakira." He said softly and tenderly as he stepped outside.

"Oh, Ricky." She blubbered as she got up from the chaise, where she had been curled up on her side. She ran to him and wrapped her arms around him. "I am in so much trouble." She buried her face in his chest. He could feel her tears soaking into his shirt. He placed his hand on the back of her head and stroked her hair.

He placed his hands down on her shoulders and pushed her away from him. He lifted her arm up. "Where is your bracelet?"

"I must have lost it." She said, rubbing her arm where the missing bracelet should have been, there was a small scratch on her wrist where the lobster claw clasp broke.

"Guess what I found." He said, pulling the bracelet from his pocket.

"Where did you find it?"

"Where you lost it. The hotel at Roaring River."

She shrieked and placed her hands over her face as she sat down on the deck chair. "I didn't mean for it to happen." She bowed her head down. "I didn't." She looked up at him. "I really didn't."

"It is okay." He said confidently and sat down beside her and she put her head on his shoulder. "I don't care if it costs me every dime I have. I will make sure you don't go to prison for this."

"Prison! They can put me in prison for this?" She pulled away from him, sounding even more baffled. "For what!"

"When you murdered Warner."

"WHAT!" She turned back around in shock. "You think I—I ..." She stumbled over her words, as if she was a drunken coed. Her breath came in short spurts as she stood up and walked back inside the house and flopped

124

down on the black leather love seat that faced the glass doors. "He's dead?" She asked, bewildered, as she looked up at him, closing the sliding glass door behind him. Now in the light he could see her eyes were red and swollen from crying. "And you think I did it?"

"You were there. You nearly took the nose of the Jag off."

"That was you?" She panted. "Okay, I was there." She said, standing up and walking around and placed her hands on the back of the loveseat.

"Why did you go there?"

"I got a notice that the mortgage for the gun shop had been bought by another company- Warner Finance." She said, digging her fingers into the leather. "He was demanding payment with penalty in full. I went to see him and talk him out of it, but…"

He picked up a box of tissues from the end table and handed the box to her. She pulled out a couple and dabbed her eyes. So you didn't—he didn't try to…."

"Oh Sweetie, I didn't even see him. I started up the stairs and heard a woman scream and she ran by, she was naked, holding up only a towel in front of her. I got scared and ran away; my bracelet must have gotten caught.

"Who was the woman?"

"It was Susan Glenn."

Chapter 20

Morning came much too quickly for either of them, and coffee wasn't doing it, it just wasn't the boost he needed. It was on the morning after his first all night stakeout, that Captain Grosstree showed him the nitro boost. He pulled a couple of cans of coke out of the cabinet, room temperature was a must, and then a couple of Hershey milk chocolate bars from the refrigerator. He popped open one of the cans and handed it to Yakira, and then a chocolate bar. "Don't know if this is kosher, but it will wake you up."

"You are kidding, right?"

"Guarantee it." He said, popping open the other can after eating the other chocolate bar. He downed the rest of the coke and burped. "Do you have a fish tank at the store?"

"A what?" She baffled as to what he would need this to get finger prints.

"An aquarium."

"No, what do you want one for?" She said, as she, too, down her coke and burped.

"So we can get fingerprints off this." He opened up the trash bag and carefully lifted out the glass using his handkerchief.

"You can do that?"

"Sure! With Superglue®."

"I can tell you whose prints are on that glass without that." She said, looking at the lip print on the glass. She looked up at him and grinned. "Why did you take that glass?"

"I needed proof that…"

"No you didn't." Her smile grew wider as she realized what he had done. "You took that because you thought I was there. You took that because…" She reached up and stroked his face, he felt the softness of her fingers as he looked into her eyes, they seemed to capture the morning light and sparkle. "…you thought it was me." She grinned even more. "You were trying to protect me." She walked over to the sliding glass doors and pulled them open, and stepped out on the deck to soak up the morning air, it was crisp and clear, the sounds of a morning dove cooing on the other side of the lake was heard. "It is not mine." She turned back to him. "That is Passion Fruit Red."

"How do you know that?"

"I may not wear that much makeup, but growing up with a beauty queen as a sister I got to know it." She walked back to him. "Trust me; there were only two women wearing that shade, Susan Glenn and your pal, Alex."

"What motive would Alex have for killing Warner?" He said wrapping the glass up in a paper towel and placing it back in the sack.

"Are you kidding? The way he was treating her? You know what kind of man he is." She walked over and pulled the door closed. "Your little trick isn't helping. Can we make some coffee?"

"Just give it a little time." He said, heading for the front door. "But we will get some hot tea when we get into town. We need to talk to your friend at the hospital."

"Tracy? " She asked as she followed him outside and to the car."Why?"

He held the door open for her. "Because you have a little tummy ache?"

The Cassville hospital had gone through many changes during its life, from being right out small town USA, a small white building, known for its country doctors and medicine, but with each addition it lost a little country charm and gained its city's pre-eminence, complete with a first class trauma unit and emergency room.

Basically Annalisa died from a drug overdose, just not by her hand. Ryder had a homicide case in Kansas City that was similar to this; it was found that the drug had come from the hospital. While Yakira had a friend who worked here as a nurse in the E.R., Ryder knew he couldn't just walk in and demand answers to his question. First he no longer wore a badge, second he wasn't sure who might be involved and he couldn't tip off anyone, although Yakira assured him that her friend Tracy would never be involved. He had to have a way to get in without them drawing attention. So he decided to do what he did with the case in Kansas City, go under cover. Who is the one person that is not noticed at a hospital? A patient, a woman patient.

Outside in the parking lot, Yakira looked in the mirror and slipped a long blonde wing over her head, tucking her dark locks under the wig. She slipped large black frame glasses over her eyes. She blinked and weaved back and forth in the seat.

"Can you see?"

"Barely." She said, turning trying to focus her eyes on him." But I don't think I am going to blink again. That stuff has kicked in."

"You know what to do?"

"Yes, pain on right side, just to the side of my belly button."

He handed her a cup of hot tea. "Here you go." She took a drink of the fairly hot liquid. "Keep it in your mouth till they are about ready to take your temperature. She nodded her head and they headed for the door to the Emergency Room.

As they entered, Yakira bent over holding her stomach, moaning as if she were in pain. "What is the problem?" The nurse behind the desk said.

"Pain in the stomach on the right side. She has been throwing up and running a fever."

"Is the pain severe?"

"MMM." Yakira moaned out, still trying to hold the hot liquid in her mouth.

"Name?"

"Mildred Jones. She doesn't have insurance. I am going to pay cash." Ryder said as he helped her back through the door and into the E.R. "Just in hang in there, baby. Swallow up the pain." With those words Yakira swallowed the tea. She sat down in a chair as the nurse took her temperature and it read 103, the plan worked perfectly. Too low, it wouldn't have been a concern, too high, they would either see her as faking it, or worse, would have drawn the doctor's attention too quickly.

"Where does it hurt?" The nurse asked. Yakira pointed to her tummy just to the right and below her belly button. The nurse pressed down and Yakira moaned louder. "Let's get her back to one of the cubicles." They transferred her to a wheel chair. "Tracy's got one for you. Severe abdominal pains. Possible ruptured appendix."

Yakira twisted her head around. This was person she wanted to see, her friend Tracy. She was fifteen years Yakira's senior, with darkening blonde hair in a pixie cut. Her face was beginning to weather with age, but her sweet calming smile never seem to change, which is probably good as it was always the best medicine that she could give. It was her hobby that allowed her and Yakira to connect, skeet shooting; she came into the shop and bought a new twelve gauge.

Tracy pushed the wheelchair into cubicle number three and pulled the curtain back in place. She walked over and pulled open a drawer and produced an examination gown and laid it on the table. "Take everything off except your underpants and put this on; the doctor will be right with you."

"You really think that is necessary?"

"Yakira?" Tracy asked turning around surprised. "What are you doing in that blonde wig?"

"We need a favor." Yakira said reaching up and pushing the wig off her head and removing the glasses. "A big favor."

"Then why not just ask me?"

"Because we don't know who we can trust." Ryder said.

"Oh Tracy, this is my friend Rick Ryder. This is Tracy Katz."

"Trust?" Asked a puzzled Tracy.

"Annalisa was not murdered they way everyone thinks." Yakira said.

"What! How?"

"She was given an overdose." Ryder said. "A drug you don't find on the streets but one you find in a hospital."

"You think I had something to do it!" She asked raising her voice than quickly lowering it to avoid being heard. "I didn't have anything to with it. I was here working I had a double shift that day."

"Tracy we don't think you had anything to do with it." Yakira said grabbing Tracy's wrist. "We need your help."

"What do you want from me?"

"We want you to take a look in your drug cabinet. See if there is anything missing?" Ryder asked.

"What are you looking for?" "Amytal Sodium, said Ryder. What is it used for?"

"Hypnotic, for the short-term treatment of insomnia, and of course a sedative. I don't know if I could check that would be in the pharmacy."

"Please Tracy, can you try? I have to find out who killed my sister."

Ryder reached into his pocket, producing his wallet, and pulled out a hundred-dollar bill. "Could Ben here help you make up your mind?"

Tracy looked over at the bill and shook her head. "No, I won't do it for money. If someone killed Annalisa that way, then…" She turned and looked at Yakira and said. "I will do it for you. You are my friend." Tracy pulled the curtain back, and then turned back to them. "I will try to stall the doctor."

"Oh! One other thing." Ryder said, making Tracy stop and glance over her shoulder. "Don't let anybody know. And also check on Sodium Pentothal."

Yakira grabbed an IV stand and rolled it around. She looked down at his feet. Since his leather loafers were ruined last night, he was now wearing the red athletic sneakers with wide white stripes; the only other choice was boots, not one of his favorite footwear.

Ryder was deep in thought as he stood in the doorway of the cubical gazing across the room to where another nurse was starting an IV, he watched as the nurse carefully wiped the man's arm and then carefully inserted the needle into his skin. "That other nurse didn't know what she was doing; kept jabbing me. I am going to have bad bruises," the man said. Ryder drew back into the cubicle.

"What are you thinking about?"

"Two people," he turned back to her, two injections, two people. If someone who was giving her Sodium Pentothal wanted to kill her, all they would have to do was increase the amount. It was someone else who gave her the Amtyal."

Tracy stepped in and pulled the curtain back. The pale look on her face told Ryder everything he needed to know. A vial of Amtyal, 5 grams, is missing."

"What about Sodium Pentothal is any missing?"

"No." Tracy said as Ryder jotted down information in his notebook. She looked at him. "You don't seem surprised."

"It just confirms what I thought." He looked up from the notebook. "Who would have access to that drug?"

"Mainly the pharmacist. Tech in there. I could get you a list if you want."

"That would be good. Now where can I get fish tank?"

"Where everybody gets everything in this town. Wal-Mart®

****

After buying a 30 gallon fish tank, complete with cover, a roll of aluminum foil, a few tubes of Superglue ® a heating pad, and a roll of clear packing tape, from the local discount store, they drove back to the gun shop. Ryder unpacked everything out of the bags from the discount store and put everything to the side except the main tank and the cover, which he placed up on a counter top, close to an electrical outlet. After placing the heating pad under the tank, he made a small square container out of the aluminum foil by folding it up on the edges. He squeezed a tube of Superglue ® on the foil and carefully placed it in the tank. Next to the foil he placed a bowl of hot water, then using the paper towel he carefully set the wine glass in the tank. Lastly he covered the tank up and turned on the heating pad.

. It was like magic as she watched the prints appear on the glass. He removed the cover on the tank, standing back as the fumes escaped from it. He reached in and carefully lifted the glass out. He dipped the fine tip brush into the fingerprinting powder from his evidence collection kit, and lightly dusted the prints on the glass. He took the tape, and holding it in both hands, he pulled off a strip. Using his thumbs he guided the tape down onto the print and he quickly lifted the tape along with the print. He took the tape and cleanly placed it down on an index card.

"Can I learn to do that?" She asked, moving over closer to him.

"Okay, dip the tip of the brush into the powder." He said, standing behind her and putting his arms around her to guide her hands. "Okay, now tap the brush on the paper. You don't want too much powder." As he moved closer to her, she leaned back onto his chest. "Put the brush in your fingers like this." He placed her index finger and thumb on the handle of the brush. "Pick up the glass. Now twist the brush lightly over the prints in circles. Don't put too much pressure on it. Okay, now blow the excess powder off the glass."

"Like this?" She asked, blowing a puff of air over the glass.

"Now we are going to lift it." He pulled the inch wide tape out and let her take a hold of it. "Pull the tape out some more. Hold the ends up. Now carefully put the tape down on the print. Now in one quick motion, pull the tape up." He grabbed an index card. "Carefully put the tape down on the card. Don't get any wrinkles. Great job."

"I have a question?" She said. "Why do we have to put the powder on the prints we can already see?"

"So we can run them through the FAFIS." Ryder scanned the prints into the computer and accessed the K.C. Department account. He was shocked by the return:

"Alexander, Isabelle, age 44. Address: 14500 Rosewood Apartments B, Springfield, MO. No known arrest record. Special Agent Department of Justice, F.B.I. Springfield, Mo Division.

132

Chapter 21

It was back to Roaring River State Park. Susan was nowhere to be found. She hadn't checked out of the inn, but after giving the desk clerk a couple of fifties she reported that she had seen her early yesterday evening, and that she was heading down the hall, around six o'clock, she was carrying a bottle of wine and a small plastic sack. Another fifty to the maid allowed him and Yakira into Susan's room, which was down stairs. A quick search revealed the bed had not been slept in and there was no sign of the sack or the bottle of wine. He realized one thing; he had these items. Things were not making sense, if Susan brought the wine, why was it that Alex's fingerprints were on the glass? As they walked back upstairs and back towards the check in desk Ryder saw Alex walking toward the restaurant; he knew what he had to do. "So- we question Alex now?" Yakira asked. He turned back to her and said-

"No, I question her."

"But we are a team, aren't we?"

"Yes." He said as he turned and watched as Alex was escorted inside to a booth. He turned back to Yakira. "We are partners—but this time I have to do it on my own."

"Go take a walk down by the river. Take a drive. It is best that I do this alone."

Ryder went into to the restaurant. Alex was sitting in a booth staring out the window, watching as a pair of eagles soared over the valley, dipping down and with a flap of the wings soaring back up, circling over the tree-lined hills, keen eyes staring down at the forest floor for the smallest movement. "Need some company?" He asked.

"Always." She said with a grin as she turned to him. He sat down across from her. "You know how I hate to eat alone." The server came over and set down two glasses of water. He looked up at her and said. "Bring the lady a club sandwich. No fries. Chips. To drink, a diet coke, with very little ice. For me just bring me a sweet tea with a half twist of lemon."

"You remembered." She said with an even larger grin, taking a sip of the water and the grin quickly faded as she added. "But you are not here for a walk down memory lane, are you?"

"I have some questions." He said as the server set the drinks down in front of them.

"Are you accusing me of killing Annalisa?" She said, as she slowly twisted the glass around in her fingers.

"Should I?"

"What motive would I have?" She looked down as she twirled the glass of soda in her hands, and she softly said. "You?" She looked back up at him."As you said the night it was over, feelings come and then go."

"I found your prints on a glass in the Speaker's room."

He leaned back in the booth, and pulled the notepad from his jacket pocket. "It isn't what it looks like, Rick. He didn't have glasses so he had me go get them. That is why they are on there."

"Explain the lipstick." He said as he lifted up her glass of water and looking at the lipstick print on the glass, it was the same shade that was on the wineglass.

"Okay." She said, dropping her gaze back down and twirling the glass in her fingers. "He invited me in, saying he wanted to talk about possibly giving me a promotion. He poured me a glass of wine. And told me when he became president I could be the head of the F.B.I." She lifted her gaze. "He then told me what he wanted in return for that by trying to put his hand up my skirt. I took the bottle and busted his damn head open. He bled like a stuck pig. But he was alive when I left."

"Belle, "Ryder said tenderly.

"You have called me that since…" She said with a small grin as she pushed her hair back over her ear. She reached over and put her hand on top of his. He could feel the smooth skin of her palm and the warmness of her touch as she let her fingers slide down in between his, snaking around his index finger and lifting his hand up towards her lips. "…maybe we could go back to my room." He quickly pulled his hand back.

"You are too smart for that. You wouldn't fall for his cheap lies. What did you have on him? What are you checking out on him?" His questions came like the rapid fire of a machine gun spreading out a spew of bullets, hoping that one would be answered. "Was it something to do with the sorghum mill? You didn't care about Annalisa, why would you investigate her murder? What were you going to tell me last night?"

She leaned back and lifted the glass to her lips, taking a sip as she glared over the table at him. "That's the way it is going to be? All business! No fun!" She set the glass back down on the table and added as she stood up. "Not here. Let's go for a walk."

Ryder paid for their drinks, leaving a good size tip, and told them to hold the meal till they got back. Most of the trails in the park were an adventure but the newest one, Springhouse trail, was just across the parking lot of the inn. It was just a short trail less than a half-mile in length that led out into the woods and circle back to the starting point. They walked on the trail till they could no longer see the hotel to the point that the trail began to circle around. At this point they walked off the trail, climbing up the hill and deeper into the woods. They plowing through the layers of the old decaying leaves that had fallen from autumns of the past, frightening the squirrels, making them scamper up large oak trees. A white tail doe stopped, raised her head, and sniffed the air, before running away.

They came to a gully that was partly filled with leaves and rocks; along the edge was a large fallen tree. He removed his jacket and folded it up, putting down on the trunk, and invited her to take a seat. Dressed in her usual hue, a light colored pant suit, she sat down on his jacket and he sat down beside her. He didn't ask her a question, he just turned to her.

"First off, my whole case is gone because your little girl friend killed my number one suspect."

"She didn't kill anybody!" Ryder said. "What were you investigating him for?"

"You remember when we were spending all those nights together looking for the Kansas City Butcher?' She leaned her head over on his shoulder.

"What were you investigating him for?" Ryder repeated his question, raising his tone, showing her he didn't want to go down memory lane.

"You're all business." She said, sounding disillusioned, and lifted her head from his shoulder. "All right Detective Ryder, I am investigating the theft of weapons from military bases."

"Like Fort Leonard Wood?"

"That was just the last of them but we got a break there; we caught somebody. Sergeant Frank Larkin, responsible for the garbage detail."

"Garbage?"

"Government cutbacks, garbage is now sent out to public dumps; no one wants to check smelly garbage... "

"So he put the weapons in the garbage?"

"O'Malley would wait for the truck to leave and he would dig the boxes out, clean them up, and take them to Warner's ranch." She stood up, taking a couple of steps away.

"What does this have to do with Annalisa?"

"I believe that she stumbled on to what they were doing." He stood up and walked over behind her. "I think she copied the information on the Speaker's private laptop." She turned around to him.

"What happen to the laptop?"

"The jerkass shredded the hard drive. There is no way we can retrieve the information. She had the information; I had to have it."

"Oh my god, it was you!" He jerked his sunglasses from his face and rubbed his fingers over his eyes as he lowered his head. He sighed heavily and looked back up at her. "You were the one that drugged her."

"I had to." She said as he turned away from her and slipped the sunglasses back over his eyes.

"You killed her." He said soberly as he gazed up at the trees and the sunlight that was illuminating the leaves as if they were precious jewels, ready to be stolen.

"I didn't kill her!" She walked back to him and stopped in front of him. "I wanted the truth out of her. I had to have it."

"Why?" He asked as walked over and picked up his jacket and threw it over his shoulder. "Let me guess: you can't tell me." He turned his head to her and continued. "It is classified." He took a couple of steps away from her.

"She even pointed that blasted gun at me. I took it away from her and placed it on the table in the garage." He swallowed hard as he stood there listening to her. "I made sure everything was going right with her. I used a low dose, slow drip, I needed her awake. I even gave her oxygen when she needed it." He turned and faced her as she continued to explain. "She was coming out of it, she was doing great. I went to get her ice chips because I knew her throat would be dry. But her blasted ice maker wasn't working. It was just before eight o'clock; I went to town to get the ice and something to ease her stomach and when I came back I found her slumped over, someone had beaten the hell out of her. I untied her, she was bleeding all over, and it even got on my shoes. We had the same size feet so I just switched shoes with her." She walked over closer to him.   "I tried everything. I gave her CPR; I gave her mouth to mouth. She was just gone. When I heard the coroner say that it was a drug that killed her, I freaked out. I couldn't let anyone know. So I had to make sure the report read that someone strangled her."

"Did it work? Did you get anything out of her?"

"All I got was that the weapons were in the barn. I checked it out, but…" She paused for just brief moment. "…they are gone. I couldn't let it be known that the Pentothal killed her."

"It was Amytal that killed her, not the Pentothal."

"What? I didn't use that. I needed her alive. You believe me, don't you? Rick?" He didn't reply to her, he just turned and walked back down the same way they had come. "Ryder. Ryder! "She screamed but he just kept walking. As he walked out of the woods he slipped the jacket back on and saw Yakira sitting on the side wall that over looked the wooded area. As soon as he emerged from the woods, she leaped down and raced over to him, grabbing his arm.

"You got to see this!" She insisted, pulling him in towards the car in the parking lot. "I found someone! You have to talk to this guy." She led him back to the Jaguar. He got into the driver's seat, the seat had been pushed all the way up, and the steering wheel was rubbing his chest. He wanted to readjust the steering wheel but she was so ecstatic about getting over across the road, that she insisted he had to leave right away; he could adjust the seat later. It was difficult but he managed to drive the car across the highway and up to the camp kitchen.

"Come on!" She said, pulling on his hand with the insistence of a young child dragging their parent to the toy section of the store. "He is over here." She led him across the grass, to a picnic table where a man was sitting.

"You got to hear this!" Yakira said excitedly. The man stood. He was heavy-set and burly, with a scraggly overgrowth of whiskers on his chin and cheeks, which lacked another couple of weeks to go to be a good beard. His hair was covered with a light beige cap with the Roaring River logo, a jumping Rainbow trout on it. His t-shirt was dark colored with Branson, Mo on the front, his hairy legs were revealed under his short pants that came to his knees, his feet covered in Reeboks.

"Love your Jag." He said pointing towards the car parked at the edge of the road revealing his nails; they were well cared for. These things all told Ryder one thing- this man was not a local, he was a tourist enjoying the sights around the area, most likely a professional, who was kicking back and was camping here.

"Tell him what you told me." Yakira said eagerly.

"I saw the Ferrari that they found the dead woman in."

"You saw it here?"

"No, in town." The man explained. "I was wondering could I get a photo with the Jag? I've always wanted one, but I have seven girls I am putting through private school. A photo is as close as I am going to get."

"Tell you what, Mr.?" Ryder held out his hand to the man.

"Rogers. Dr. Ray Rogers." The man replied, shaking Ryder's hand.

"You tell me what you know about the Ferrari and you can drive the Jag."

"I had to go to town. The girls decided they wanted to roast hot dogs and make s'mores; we had already had dinner, but I can't refuse them."

"What time was that?"

"I don't know. It was already dark, maybe after nine or ten. Really don't look at a watch here. Anyway, that is when I saw it."

"The Ferrari?" Ryder had to make sure it was his car.

"Yes."

'Who was driving it?"

"Nobody! It was on a trailer." Dr. Rogers said. "Every time instead of following the road I turn right. I think it is because at home that is the way we go home so I get on to highway 248. It isn't till I get out a few miles that I realize it; I always turn around at the house that has a circle drive in front of it. There was a pickup with a trailer; they were putting the Ferrari on the trailer."

"Who was?"

"I couldn't tell. I had never seen any of them before."

"Could you recognize them if you saw them again?"

"No, it was way too dark."

"What color was the truck?" Ryder asked anxiously. This was one of the most solid leads they had yet.

"Don't know."

"What kind of Ferrari was it?"

"458 Italia Spider painted *Rosso Sclderia* with gold wheels."

"Come on! Most people would have just said red." Ryder insisted. "You know that paint color yet you can't tell me what the pickup was. You are a car guy; what was the pick up?"

"It was a late model Ford XL, 2-door, maybe white, might have been gray, and the lights change the color. Dr Rogers paused, and then asked. "Can I drive it now?" Ryder knew there was more to the story, something that Dr. Rogers was not telling him.

It was only a short drive, up to highway 86 and back, but as they topped 'Suicide Hill', Ryder felt his stomach go up to his ribs, and back down into his lap as the car settled back down on its suspension. He looked over at Dr. Rogers; he was grinning as if he was a young lad riding a merry-go-round for the first time. His fingers gripped around the leather steering wheel, waiting for what was coming around the next curve. As the Jaguar twisted around the final turn and back down into the park, Ryder knew now was the time to ask.

"Are you sure you didn't see anything else?"

"Well…" Dr Rogers paused after he brought the Jaguar to a stop in front of the park store. "There is one other thing I might need to tell you. The reason I left…" He seemed nervous, as if he was afraid to say anything.

"I am just looking for the truth, that's all."

"You will keep my name out of it?"

"Just the truth." Asking he almost felt like a TV detective nestled in the gritty screen of a black white rerun.

"I lied. I didn't leave right away. I watched two men carrying something wrapped in a blanket out of the garage. You are sure you will keep my name out of it?" Ryder nodded. "They put it in the Ferrari."

"What was it?"

"I didn't know at first. But…" Dr. Rogers paused again. "I shouldn't be telling you this. Are you sure you won't use my name?"

"You have my word."

He opened the door and got out of the car. He looked around to see if anyone was watching. The he looked back into the car and said. "I saw a hand fall out. It was a body."

Chapter 22

What Dr. Rogers said coincided with what Alex had told but it put a different spin on what had happened to Annalisa. First off, she wasn't murdered at Roaring River; she had been murdered somewhere else and moved there. *But why? Where was this place?* Since Yakira knew exactly where this place was, he let her drive. Back towards town and then turn right on highway 248 and follow the highway. The circle driveway gave it away.

"This was Annalisa's house." Yakira said as they drove in and parked in front. "She moved here because she couldn't take it anymore, she would just live her life alone."

"What?"

"It was something I couldn't tell you. She said you couldn't know that she was available, because she could never be available; not to you."

"What does that mean?"

"I don't know. I think she was beginning to lose her mind. "

Ryder gazed out the windshield at the house. The yard was huge, at least three single lots long, beautiful and green, with rose bushes, tall oak trees, and black walnut trees and a line of pine and cedar trees in the back yard. The house wasn't as grand as the compound at the ranch, but it wasn't your typical ranch style house either. Constructed of red brick it was nearly a hundred feet long and thirty feet wide, with a fireplace in the center and one on the end.

"Do you have a key to this place?" He said as he stepped out of the car.

"No, but I know where it is." She said as she shut the car door. "It is around back." They went around to the back yard, with a beautiful view of a meadow with a gentle rolling hill that turned into a small wooded area. It was strangely still, not a single bird could be heard, nor traffic going by on the highway.

Yakira spotting an area in the yard that appeared to have had trash burned there, broken glasses jars and blacken tin cans, one of which was crushed at the top and sitting at the far edge of the burn pattern. She bent down and picked up the crushed can and under her shoe she pressed the can open, picked the can up and dumped out a small metal box, inside of it was a key, the key to the front door. She unlocked the door, but it wouldn't open; something was blocking it. Ryder pressed his shoulder up on the door and pushed hard. The place had been trashed; someone had been looking for something.

The large living room was dominated by a see-through fireplace at the corner of the wall that separated the living room and the family room, with French doors that led out onto the deck. The living room was furnished with comfortable black leather club chairs with maple end tables beside them and a black leather ottoman; there was also a large dark red upholstered sofa facing the fireplace. In front of the sofa was an antique trunk that had been restored, this served as a coffee table.   The living room flowed into the dining room with a rectangular shaped maple dining table and six chairs surrounding it; in the corner was a large maple hutch with antique red and white English transfer ware china and gleaming crystal inside it.   A sloping cathedral ceiling was over the living room, kitchen, breakfast nook, and family room area, which reached a peak height of 16 feet in the center.

Everywhere Ryder looked there was destruction. Annalisa was a neat freak, everything had its place, once she used something she would put it right back in its place. This was not normal. He couldn't take a step without stepping on something. Furniture turned upside down, the fine fabric and leather sliced opened, the stuffing pulled out and thrown on the walnut hardwood floors, particles of dust floated in the air, catching the angling rays of the sun that was shining through the skylight in the family room. All the drawers from the end tables were pulled out, their contents spilled out onto the floor.

In the kitchen the copper pots and pans were pulled out of the chestnut cabinets, every jar of spice emptied on the pale quartz countertops. The strong smell of cloves and cinnamon made him cough and burned his nose. It was like a sign from heaven, the sunlight was gleaming down from a skylight onto the ivory-painted wooden table right on to a white envelope. He picked up the envelope and inside was three hundred dollars, all in tens and twenties. This showed him one thing for sure: it was not a robbery. Piled in front of the freezer door of the side by side were packages of meat and ice cream cartons that were defrosted and spilling out onto the floor. He pushed the food to the side and opened the door and there were no ice trays. He pressed down on the wire bar on the ice dispenser; it made no sound whatsoever. It meant one thing: Alex was telling the truth.

"All her jewelry is here." He heard Yakira say from the other end of the house. He walked through the breakfast nook, stepping over the broken plates, and through the family room, the large screen TV, the DVR, the sound system, it was all here. He walked down the hall past the common bath and into the master bedroom at the back corner of the house.

The master bedroom was large; 20 feet long and seventeen feet wide. The sloping ceiling theme was carried on into the dressing area, with a vaulted ceiling that was sixteen feet on one side and eight feet high on the other. As he entered he passed by the closet, her purses were cut open and her shoes, sneakers, loafers, sandals and flats were thrown all around the room as well as all her clothes.

The button tufted cream-colored linen headboard was torn apart, the mattress slit open on the sides. The drawers of the nightstands and dresser were emptied. Just as Yakira had said, Annalisa's jewelry was spread out on the top of the dresser. Pearls, gold bracelets, ruby earrings and an emerald and diamond necklace were all here, and another $150.00 in cash.

The sunshine was gleaming through another skylight over the huge jetted tub in the master bath; all the towels and wash cloths were strung out on the white marble floor. The shampoos, body washes, and conditioners had been emptied into two amber and turquoise swirled hand-blown glass sinks. Across the hall were two more rooms. Another bedroom, it too was trashed. And the back room was being used for an office. Ryder pushed the door open.

Unlike the other rooms in the house this room was simply furnished, and all business. The walls were painted dove gray and all that was in the room was a simple walnut desk with a desktop computer and two filing cabinets, but no swivel chair, all the contents of the files were spread out across the floor.

"What does all this mean?" Yakira asked, kneeling down to pick up some of the papers. She stood up and let the papers fall back on the floor.

"Someone was looking for something?"

"Alex?"

"No, this isn't the way she works." Ryder said, closing the door behind them, glaring at the mess that was from one end of the house to the other."She

143

wouldn't have wanted anyone to know that she was looking." He took a giant step forward over a pile of broken bottles in the hall. "It was someone desperate to find something." Ryder's head swivel as he took it all in, the smell of rotting meat mixed with the broken bottle of perfume. "We haven't found it yet."

"What's that?"

"The place she was murdered." He glanced down the hall past the laundry room, to a single wooden door painted white. "We have searched every room except the garage."

Twisting the door knob there was that tightness in his chest; he knew what this room meant. Even hidden in the darkness, he knew what he would find. When Yakira flipped on the light, he caught sight of the large handmade work bench on the other side of the garage. The only thing on it was a large red tool box. Then his eyes saw what his mind felt. A padded office chair laying on its side near the garage door and flies were buzzing around a dark spot on the floor, the cushion of the chair was also spotted, he didn't have to test it, just by the putrid smell he knew it was blood, human; there was no other smell like it, the true smell of death, and without a doubt it was Annalisa's. Unlike at the river, he felt her here. This was where she had been murdered.

It didn't make sense to alert the authorities; the official report was that she was strangled to death; any other injuries that occurred during the accident were not going to change that. It was how the bureaucratic system worked, Annalisa was just a spouse of a member of congress, and now with the death of that member, she would just become a foot note in the history of all this. Ryder had the answers, the speaker was involved in shady illegal things, and now he just hoped Thom had the question to his answers.

Back in the Jaguar Ryder pushed the seat back and lowered it, it felt more comfortable.

"So where are we going?"

"You are going to your mom and dad's. Me, I am going to see Double T." He added, almost in an afterthought, "You ever saw an autopsy?"

"Saw them on TV. On Quincy reruns." She said and he turned and gave her a doubting look. "What?" She asked anxiously. He turned back and rested one hand on the steering wheel as he guided the Jaguar down the paved strip of highway. He didn't say anything for a little while, and then she asked worried. "Is it that bad?"

"There is an old saying. Homicide detectives are not born, they are made at their first autopsy."

As they entered the city limits Yakira was not sure how she was going to handle this, as he kept telling her stories of how these big macho cops would just fall on the floor, or run for the door, sometimes tossing their shield down behind them, to take a job selling sunglasses from a booth at the mall. As they turned onto Main Street and headed towards downtown, she felt even more nervous. "So what was your first time like?"

"My first time?" He said with a naughty grin. "Oh! It was in the park under the stars. Very magical." A warm glow flowed over her face which she tried to hide with her hands as he added "But it was over way too soon. What about you, where was your first? " He laughed as her face flushed a dull red. She reached up and pulled her hair down over her face to hide her embarrassment.

"Well, there hasn't been a first." Her face glowed even warmer as she pushed her hair back and fanned herself. She repositioned the air conditioning vent on to her face. "Wow, it is hot in here." She reached over and clicked the fan up on high on the air conditioning control. He tilted his vent over to her as they approached Main Street, and yielded to the traffic, he tried hard to keep in a laugh that was building up inside of him, as she wouldn't dare look at him. She seemed to gather her nerve back up and said. "I meant your first autopsy."

"Oh, that. That wasn't so magical and lasted much too long." He said, repositioning himself in his seat as if the memory of it made him uncomfortable. He let his eyes drifted up to the rear view mirror, when he noticed a county cruiser had turned from out from a street and was following them. Waiting on another side street was another cruiser; it had plenty of time to turn out into the street, why wasn't it moving? Ryder looked down at the speedometer, it was right on 25 mph, the speed limit. He looked back at the cruiser following them, he pressed on the accelerator and the Jaguar leaped forward, quickly rising up to 37 mph. He looked back, waiting for the light bar to flash, knowing he was going over the 10 mph grace mark. There. He backed off the accelerator and slowed to a crawl of 10 mph; the cruiser also slowed and then moved up closer to the rear of Jaguar.

"It is Brian." He said as he watched the headlights on the cruiser flash three short times three long, and three short. "SOS!"

"What?"

He was using Morse code trying to warn him. Ryder caught sight of two city black and whites turned out and followed behind them. Ryder turned the signal light on; each cruiser behind did the same as if they were all playing Simon says.

"We have trouble." He said, his eyes still glaring up at the mirror as he passed his turn and the cruisers continued following. Except the city cruisers which turned east on a side street. "

"What is it?" Yakira asked as she turned and looked back out the rear window. Ryder turned off Main Street; there turned sideways and blocking the street in front of them were two city cruisers, the red and blue lights flashing, the officers standing behind their vehicles, guns drawn.

.Ryder slammed down on the brakes, and the Jaguar slide to stop as the county cruisers behind slide around sideways blocking the street behind them. The officers got of their cars and drew their weapons, including Deputy Thompson, who did it begrudgingly, aiming his service weapon at the back window of the Jaguar. "Ryder, you know the drill." He said.

Yes Ryder knew the drill; he had ordered it many times. However, he had never had to follow it. He reached over and rolled down the windows. He turned to her and said "I want you to slowly put both of your hands out the windows."

"Why?'

"Just do what I do and nothing else." He said as he reached out the window with both hands and opened the car door from the outside. He then stepped outside, raising his hands. "I have a weapon that I have a permit to carry. I am removing it now." He reached over with his left, keeping his right hand up, and slipped the Glock out of the holster and placed it on the roof of the car. Raising both hands again he took a couple of large steps away from the car before kneeling down in the street interlocking his fingers behind his head. Ryder saw a man approaching them: it was Sheriff Hart.

"Put your weapons down." The sheriff ordered. The officers didn't respond and the sheriff repeated his order as he continued to move towards Ryder.

"You keep those weapons pointed on them!" He heard Prosecutor Price shout from behind him; he turned and saw the prosecutor walking up behind him. "You keep those guns drawn. If he moves, you shoot him."

"You may be the county prosecutor, but I am the sheriff. And this is my county." Sheriff Hart said. He shouted out his order this time. "Lower those weapons! Now!" The officers lowered their weapons. "Besides, he is not the one under arrest." He turned to Ryder. "You can stand up now."

Ryder rose to his feet and lowered his hands. "Hart. What the hell is going here? And what do you mean I am not the one?" Ryder turned and watched as two female officers pushed Yakira face down on the hood of the Jaguar. They quickly searched her and read her rights and hand cuff her hands behind her back.

Ryder turned to Price. "I am arresting your little girlfriend here."

"She didn't kill Annalisa."

"She is being arrested for the murder of Speaker of the House Congressman Scott Warner." Price grinned devilishly as he looked over at Yakira, as they escorted her back to a squad car. "I got witnesses that heard her threaten to kill him. I was there." Price laughed and slapped Ryder on the back. "I may even call you as a witness."

"Icicles will be hanging off the devil's nose before that happens, Price."

"Don't worry, honey!" Ryder shouted. As the officers pushed her head down, to help her into the back seat of the squad car, she looked over at him, he didn't know what it was, but there was a tickling cold feeling inside of his chest when the officer closed the door.

"Let's just say I didn't want it to happen this way." Sheriff Hart said as he walked up beside Ryder. Ryder turned to him and he continued. "I wanted it so she could have turned herself in. I don't care if she threatened to kill him, I just don't believe she did it. Any more than she could have given her sister that fatal dose."

"I really don't care who killed Annalisa right now." Ryder said, turning around and glaring at Prosecutor Price. "I am switching gears. I am going to find out who killed Warner." He walked over to Price and added in low mean tone. "And when I do I am going to shove it down your throat and hope you choke on it." They stood there face to face, as they did years ago up on another battlefield, rival schools, rival quarterbacks.

"Hurts to lose, doesn't it Ryder."

Ryder grabbed the prosecutor by the collar of his jacket and slammed him up against the side of the Jaguar. "Price, it took you three times to pass the bar, but you better have every "I" dotted and every "t" crossed. I am hiring the best team of attorneys and they are going to come for you" Ryder pulled Price up to his face and away from the car. "You think it was bad that you lost a stupid football game." He pushed the prosecutor backwards towards the county cruiser. "And after that, you better pray to God to save your soul, because, little baby bear; this wildcat is going for your throat."

Chapter 23

Ryder got in the car and drove back up to the funeral home. All the way there it just didn't seem right, that empty seat next to him, it felt as if part of him was missing. He could swear he could still smell her perfume, it wasn't the sickening chemical smell that other women wore, and it was just the light aroma of honeysuckle.

Death had been all around him all of his life. It just seemed that anyone he dared to love would somehow end up here, and he would just find himself hurting and vowing to never let it happen again. He walked through the back doorway. He stepped into the elevator and pushed the down button and it began its decent into the basement.

That creepiness that he had felt when he was just a little boy, seeing his grandfather lying up there in the box, was returning, all these tall strange people dressed in black, flowers in their lapels, escorting him forward, that first icy cold touch of death as he reached up and touched his grandfather's hand, there was nothing else that he had ever felt again that was as cold as that. That was until the doors opened and that cold of colds was blowing down on his neck from the air vents in the ceiling, there again was the cold breath of death.

"Good evening." Thom said with a joking creepy tone. "Welcome to my laboratory." Then he laughed like a mad man. He looked at Ryder and moved over to him, hunched over and dragging his foot behind him as if he was Igor. He reached up and grabbed the sheet that was covering the congressman. "He is….." He stood and in his normal tone he said. "Dead. Now we are going to find out how he died." He was lying face up on the metal table, stripped naked except for a delicate piece of tissue paper that was modestly placed over his groin. The body was a pale shade of gray, rigor mortis had set in, and his eyes were closed and flattened due to the loss of fluid. "You have the first question." He said, still in a joking manner, looking at Ryder.

"Time of death?"

"That is a tough one." The M.E. said in a normal tone. "The tub was filled with hot water, which really messes with body temp. However—." He pointed to the corpse's legs, they looked bruised and there were small cuts and scrapes on them plus there was a bump on his head. "The pooling of the blood in the lower extremities, the color of the skin. I would say death occurred between 9pm and when was he found?"

"I found him around midnight."

"Then it shall be."

"But he was warm when I touched him."

"Still could be the hot water." Thom said. "Next question."

"Cause of death?"

"It wasn't the hit on the head, and it was not due to strangulation."

"But he has the blood necklace." Ryder said pointing to the red marks on the man's neck.

"Sorry, but you didn't give your answer in the form of a question. And you lose your turn." Thom joked.

"Thom, enough with the stupid jokes!" Ryder grabbed Thom's wrist. "They arrested Yakira for his murder." He released him. "We have to prove she didn't do it."

"What! When?"

"Just a few minutes ago."

"I was wondering where she was. She has been like your shadow lately. Price has lost his freaking mind if he thinks I am going to stand still for this. His eyes narrowed as he continued. "I can't tell you who killed him but I can tell how it was done." Thom picked up a pair of forceps off the metal tray and a metal ruler.

Using the forceps he pushed the skin back and measured the gashes that were on the sides of Warner's neck. They were 3/8 of an inch wide and deep enough that it sliced into the flesh.

"See these lacerations?" Thom asked and Ryder leaned over and looked at the deep cuts into dead man's neck. Thom picked up a scalpel and sliced into the corpse's neck on both sides and folded the skin back. "Just as I thought, right through to the External Carotid Artery and the External Jugular. This sucker bled to death because someone sliced his throat."

"Double T, I have never seen cuts like that. What kind of knife did that?"

"Not a knife, my dear friend." Thom said as he took a step back and picked up Ethernet cable that was lying on his desk at the back of the room."This."

"Ethernet cable?" Ryder questioned, it was soft and covered in rubber. "How can that happen? It is not sharp."

"Give me your wrist." Ryder held his arm out and Thom wrapped the cable around his bare wrist and started sawing back and forth with the cable. Ryder cursed, pulling his arm back.

"Son-of-…!" Ryder pulled his arm back and rubbed his wrist noticing a red mark around his wrist where the cable had been. "That hurt."

"You can saw into frozen meat with one of these things." Thom tossed the cable back onto the desk. The motive behind this murder is pure passion. Well, more pure rage!" His remarks didn't clear Yakira, in fact they inched that lethal needle closer to her arm.

"So how does that clear Yakira?" Ryder asked.

"It doesn't. That will be up to you to do it."

****

The next day was spent seeing attorney after attorney, the best in the state, creating the ultimate all star team, coming from Kansas City, St. Louis and Springfield, all at the top of their class. The next day was spent in court and hearing the undesirable news that Yakira would be held without bail till her trial.

Alex was no help; she just seemed to be furious with Yakira, not believing him that she was not guilty, telling him over and over again that "there was more to this, but she just couldn't tell him and that he couldn't understand. That this was much more than just murder."

Yet another day had begun. He begged his friend Judge Vic Weber, to overrule and give her bail, which he would pay whatever it was, but he was instructed that he couldn't, since Judge Weber knew Yakira personally he had to dismiss himself from the case. "Besides, it was the speaker of the house that was murdered." Judge Weber told him. "It was a federal matter."

He had just stepped out of Judge Weber's chambers and into the main lobby of the courthouse. It seemed like a grand castle made of Carthage stone; voices and footsteps would echo off the hard marble inside. The bathrooms were in the basement, accessible by going down a large flight of cement steps, it was creepy down there. When he was a kid, he was scared to go down there and use the bathroom, because his uncle Tony had told him that that was where they came with the prisoners before they marched them out to be hung. Truth was, there was only one hanging in the county, and it was more of a lynching.

"They will hang you if you go down there." He heard a voice say from behind him. He turned around and saw a stocky built man, with a reddish complexion, straight-as-a-board red hair, and a speckling of freckles on his face, framing baby blue eyes, it just seemed natural that an Irish brogue would spill from his mouth. It seemed odd when it came out as pure Ozark hillbilly. It was his uncle Tony, Father Anthony Delany, his mother's only brother. "Remember when I told you that?" Ryder looked at the man dressed in a long black cassock and white cleric collar.

"Is that the thing that a priest should tell a kid?"

"No, but it what is what an uncle would do." Father Antony said with a mocking grin as he playfully punched his nephew in the shoulder.

"They arrested Yakira for the congressman's murder." Ryder said as he headed for the exit, walking past the names of those who served in World War I and II, painted on a large sign attached to the wall, right inside the west side doors. He would always stop and look at his grandfather Lawrence Delany's name.

"I know I just came from seeing her."

"But she is Jewish, Uncle Tony." Ryder said, pushing the door open and walking down the steps. "Why would you go see her?"

"She is one of God's children, is she not? If she needs comfort, I should be there to give it to her. I was there the day she was born. Besides, she is like family." Father Anthony said as they walked along the sidewalk and back to the Jaguar. "What about you? You need comfort?"

"I need answers, Uncle Tony." Ryder said, grabbing the door handle. "And prayer doesn't give that to me." He jerked the door open and looked out across the roof of the Jaguar, as he pulled the sunglasses from his inside jacket pocket and slipped them on.

"One of these days you are going to find out that may be all you have left."

"Get in uncle, I will buy you lunch." Ryder said as he slid down into the driver's seat, and slammed the door shut. He glanced over at the father and cocked his head sideways. "Hurry up! The offer is only going once. Your favorite place." Father Anthony opened the door and got inside, pulling the seat belt up in place.

"Honeysuckle." He said inhaling as Ryder backed the car out onto the town square.

"I hadn't noticed." Ryder said as they drove by the stores, the car's image reflecting in the glass of the stores line up on the south side of the square.

"Yeah, right." Father Delany said, disbelieving, as Ryder turned back on the main street and headed south. He glanced over at Ryder. "When are you going to go see her? She has been asking for you."

"I can't do it. I can't see her in there."

"Why not? She needs you. That little girl loves you. And you.."

The stoplight at the Y-intersection turned red and he brought the car to a stop; he turned and looked at his uncle. "I don't want to hear that." He turned and looked back out the windshield as his finger's gripped the rim tighter. He swallowed hard, letting his right hand slip down to the console.

"Because you might have feelings for her too?"

"I can help her better by finding out who killed Warner. I can get her out of there." The light turned green and he pressed down on the gas and the car moved forward. "My gift is playing this game."

"What game?"

"Murder. It is a game. Two sides play; those who commit it and those who solve it." Ryder wheeled the car into the left turn lane in front of the Sonic drive-in; as he wheeled the car into the drive he said. "I play to win."

He pulled up to empty spot and pushed the button and waited over the voice to ask for his order. "Give me. A Super Sonic with mustard, fries, and a diet coke. And also a grilled cheese and a Dr. Upper."

"What?" The confused teenager working there replied.

"Take a Dr. Pepper, fill it three-quarters of the way up and then fill it the rest of the way with 7 Up. And go very easy on the ice."

"Stomach upset?" Father Delany asked.

"A little." Ryder said turning to him. "I haven't had much to eat in the last couple of days."

"Mmm huh?" The good father drew out in a disbelieving tone.

"What is that supposed to mean?"

"Nothing." His uncle said in with blameless reply as he pulled on his collar.

"And what does that mean?'

"That girl you saw as a little sister isn't anymore, is she?"

The waitress was barely seventeen, fresh faced with long chestnut hair flowing down on her shoulders, a class ring on her hand; she was graduating this year. Ryder handed the sonic burger and diet coke to his uncle. She handed him the other drink and asked. "I never heard of a Dr. Upper before. What does it taste like?" She handed him the sandwich.

"It has a little lemon lime taste to it." Father Anthony said, leaning forward so he could see out the driver's side window. "It is great when your tummy is

154

upset. Like during finals, big games, or…" Father Anthony's face grew into a large grin as he continued. "On a first date."

"Really?" She asked in amazement.

"It does sound better than a root beer suicide."

Ryder had just taken a sip of the drink; He set the cup down. "Root Beer suicide?" There was only one person he knew who drank that. Susan! "That person who ordered that drink; are they still here?"

"Yes, she is right over…" She started to point again; he grabbed her hand.

"Just tell me, but don't point."

"White Mustang convertible across and to the right."

White Mustang base model, with the top up the driver was certainly looking out-of-place, wearing a large brimmed cream colored hat, the brim pulled down over her face and large sunglasses that hid her eyes, most of her face was covered, but that witch like nose wasn't, it was Susan all right. Ryder and his uncle sat eating their lunch as Ryder watched Susan. She was finishing up her meal.

Ryder fired the Jaguar up and drove around the Sonic, not daring to look at her as he drove past. He crossed Main, down First Street, back around behind and parked up beside a convenience store on the other side of the street. He parked where Susan could not see him, the building hiding the car, but where he could see her.

"Uncle Tony, I want you get out and call Sheriff Hart and tell him I found Susan." He watched as Susan fired up the Mustang and drove north on Main. "Tell him I am following her." Father Anthony got out and as the Mustang passed by, Ryder watched the Mustang turned right at the stop light and headed east on highway 112. He quickly put the Jaguar in gear and drove out onto Main Street, following her, keeping enough distance between them and the Mustang, not letting her know that he was following her, even allowing a Ford station wagon between them. Susan was going right at the speed limit; she did not want any possibility of gaining the attention of a cop.

Blood Necklace

The left turn signal on the station wagon began to flash, however, it was what was coming down the other side of the road, that made him cuss and slam his fist into the steering wheel, it was a slow-moving John Deer tractor and behind it a line of angry drivers. But not as angry as he was getting as he looked up into the rearview mirror and saw a line of cars building up behind him. He cursed again and beat the steering wheel with both hands. He could not go around the wagon without alerting Susan, who would run. By the time traffic cleared, Susan would get too far ahead. There were many county roads she could turn on. He had to face it: she got away.

He pulled out his phone and dialed his old department in Kansas City. "Natasha." He said, talking to the dispatcher. "I need a big favor. Can you run a plate for me? The number is 231 Edward Adam William Missouri plate." The plate traced back to an Abbie and Vivian Cates at 1422 F.R. 2220 Cassville, Mo. To a 2001 Mustang."

The address was on the Cassville prairie. Down the old two lane highway that led to the Corinth church, turning left by a large house, and following the road as it cut in between neatly laid out fields, some already harvested, now lying bare, sleeping, waiting for the spring to come and become expectant with new crops. Other fields were waiting to give birth to the harvest, while others were being turned over, the fresh soil exposed to the bright blue sky. The road made a hard bend to the right, and in that instant became farm road 2220.

It was a strange feeling, any tourist who had come to drop in a line at Roaring River, or took a quick dip in Table Rock, would go back and tell their friends that the Ozarks were full of green hills that locals called the Ozark Mountains, they would have never dreamed that there would be flat land this close. Field after field, as farm touches farm. Old worn out farm machinery resting along the triple woven barbed wire fence, like an old man that sits out on his front porch and waves at all the vehicles driving by, longing wistfully for his grandchildren that he knew were on their way to see "the old gentleman farmer," long since retired.

Soon the paved road ended and it became dirt. A dust cloud flew out from behind the tires of the Jaguar, and Ryder was reminded of the days when he lived on a dirt road. He and Annalisa in the back of the old dark red Chevrolet C10 pickup, his mom speeding back from town because she didn't want the ice cream she had bought in town to melt. Pass by a large acreage of woods. The road just stopped, and became nothing more than just a dusty driveway. And sitting in the middle of it, up next to the garage was the white Mustang.

He got out of the Jaguar and removed his sunglasses as he scanned over the area. It was a farmhouse, single story with cherry colored wood slats and a gray metal roof. The sharp shriek of a meadowlark, and repeat of a mockingbird broke the silence, the smell of cut and baled fescue drifted over to him as he walked around the edge of the house. He heard voices from around back of the house. He slipped his sunglasses back on and followed the sounds.

In the back yard was a gazebo, it was small, just big enough for a small round table, four chairs, and a propane gas grill and made of redwood planks with cedar shake shingles on the roof. There were four people sitting in the chairs, including Susan, who saw him and began to run. "Susan!" Ryder shouted. "You can either talk to me, or we can call the sheriff and you can talk to him."

"Actually, I am already here." He heard Sheriff Hart say and saw him stand up in the gazebo. Ryder slowly pulled off his sunglasses and stared at the man. Ryder stepped up on to the gazebo floor. Besides the sheriff and Susan, there was an older farmer and his wife there. It was Susan's aunt and uncle. "She was just telling me what happened. The Cates' son Ben used to work with me in San Diego. They called me."

Susan, who had lost her disguise, now sat with arms crossed in front of her chest, keeping her head down, only rolling her eyes up to gaze at Ryder, then quickly dropping them back down.

"Vivian, I think we all could use some more iced tea." The sheriff said. "Maybe you can help, Abe."

"What?" He asked, confused.

"You old poop!" Vivian said as she reached down and grabbed his shirt and pulled him up. "He is saying he wants us to get out of here."

"Well why the hockey puck didn't he just say so?" He grumbled as they stepped down from the gazebo and went into the house. The sheriff turned to Susan, who lifted her head up. "So tell us what happened."

"Scott wanted to go over some notes on his speech about setting up a scholarship in Annalisa's name, and he asked me to work late."

She was lying and Ryder knew it, but he also knew how to fish, you had to wait till the fish took the bait to set the hook, pull too soon and you would lose the catch, pull too late the fish would just take the bait, and all that is left is a clean hook. He had to let her take it. "Did you have wine and caviar at this meeting?" Ryder asked.

"Of course not…" she hesitated before saying "I mean, he did!"

"But you didn't touch it?" Ryder said, seating himself in the chair across from her.

"I never drink on the job."

Time to set the hook. "How often do you get undressed on the job?" Ryder asked as he pulled out the notebook from his jacket.

"What?" She asked, not offended that he would ask this, but instead startled. The hook was set, now was the time reel her in. "I never!"

"I have a witness that places you running out of the hotel wearing very little." He paused for the information to sink in.

"I was getting ready to take a shower."

"You have a habit of taking a shower in a man's hotel room? Especially when your room is in the same hotel?"

"That is where I was."

"Then why is it that the staff hasn't replaced the towel in your room for four days?" He had he reeled in now it was time to place her in the net.

"Okay!" She broke down, placing her head down on the table. "I admit it!" She lifted her head up. "We have been having an affair for the past year." She looked over Ryder "Annalisa wouldn't let him touch her. What else was a man supposed to do?"

"Remain loyal." Ryder said.

"It wasn't like that." Susan pleaded. "It wasn't that we were cheating. He didn't love her anymore. She was just the icing to get the votes. He loved me. He was going to be with me. He was going to get rid of her."

"Rid of her? How? *Murder*?" His question was more of a demand as he stood up and glared at Susan. She was numbed by the question, she just sat there. "Answer me!" He shot back. "Did he murder her?"

"No! I mean—I don't know." Confused, she placed her hands on her cheeks. "

"I think she has answered enough questions." The sheriff interrupted. "She needs to be read her rights."

"She isn't under arrest. She can leave anytime she wants." Ryder said.

"I really think it would be best if..."

"I don't know anything about it." Susan interrupted the sheriff. "I didn't have anything to do with her death. And neither did Scott!"

"He had means, motive and opportunity."

"He was at the station."

"He left just before seven. She was murdered at around eight. He had time."

"But he didn't....."

"Records show he got a call from an unregistered cell phone before seven. Shortly after that he made a call to his son L.J. what did he say?"

"I don't know."

"You do know!" Ryder said moving closer to her, looking deep into her eyes. "There is not a place he went that that you didn't go. If someone talked to him you were there and you heard it .What did he say?"

"He told him to get it cleaned up. And to tear the place apart and find it or else."

159

"What did he mean get it cleaned up?"

"I am not sure, but since Annalisa was…." Susan paused and swallowed hard. "I just figured that it was about her. He told L.J. if he took care of his problem then he would take care of his." Ryder leaned back and she continued, "You have to believe me; I didn't have anything to do with her death. I wanted her out of the way so that Scott and I could be together, but I didn't want her dead." She curled her lips under her teeth and said. "He said Annalisa was no longer a problem."

Ideally in questioning this would have been when another officer would take over the questioning, throwing the suspect. However, it seemed that the sheriff, being a customs agent, didn't understand. He just had to continue. "You were there. You know who killed Speaker Warner, don't you."

"I don't know for sure."

"Who?" His question more of a demand.

"He showed up around ten o'clock screaming and yelling. He—well—we were in bed together. He started banging on the door, screaming about if he was not going to pay."

Ryder leaned over, placing his hands on the table and moving to where he was almost nose to nose with Susan and he asked. "Who was it?"

"I can't tell you! He will kill me."

Ryder placed his hand down on her shoulder. ""Who was it!"

"It was, L.J."

Chapter 24

Sheriff Hart put out an A.P.B. on London James Warner age 29 distinguishing skull tattoos on wrist, a suspect in the murder of his father Speaker of the House Scott Warner. Consider armed and dangerous.

Even with the A.P.B. it seemed that he was nowhere to be found. It wasn't as if anybody wasn't looking, as everyone was out looking including Ryder himself. It might have been the people like Yakira, who hated L.J. and of course it might have been the three-hundred-thousand dollar reward that Ryder offered for him, there was a stipulation, to get the reward, he had to be alive.

Ryder was outside the cell unit of the Barry county jail. According to regulations, he handed his side arm over and the sack that contained the burger and drink was checked by Lee Ann Thompson, the attendant. She was the wife of Deputy Brian Thompson. "Rick." She said handing him back the sack. "It is nothing personal. I believe she is innocent. I just have to do my job."

"I know, Lee Ann." He said, dismayed, as he took the sack back.

She buzzed him in and he walked back to the very back of the jail to a small eight by eight foot cell, where Yakira was being held. The concrete walls were painted a dull lifeless gray, and there was only a small cot, sink and stainless steel stool inside. There was no TV or radio and just a single over head lamp for light. All part of Sheriff Hart's new decorating plan. Yakira was wearing a white with black striped one piece jump suit, the legs and arms were rolled up so that it would fit her, and it hung loose and baggy on her, on her feet were sandals, that barely stayed on. She had showered and her hair hung down like the strands of a worn dirty string mop. Her face was washed clean, and that sparkle in her eyes like the stars in the daylight seemed to be hidden away. Standing in front of the cell door was his uncle, Father Anthony, holding a small brown paper sack. He walked up to the cell door and she offered no smile.

"*Shalom*, Darling." Ryder said without much emotion. It was odd to Ryder, any other time when he looked through the bars; it was at someone he thought to be guilty, that he felt good about himself for ridding the world of another soulless sin of society. He didn't think of those that were left helpless looking in, now it was he who was the helpless one.

Shalom." She replied with just as much lack of emotion.

"Kathy sent you a burger and iced tea." Ryder said, handing the sack and drink through the bars. "Told me to tell you 'they believe in you and that they are praying for you.' How are you doing?"

"I am doing." She said, taking the sack and drink and sitting down on the cot, taking the burger out of the sack.

"Do not give up hope, child." Father Anthony said. "God is still in control. Remember like Paul did; pray for courage."

"Uncle Tony, she is Jewish. She doesn't know who the saints are."

"Ricky, I am not stupid." She said, gazing up from her lap as she took a bite of the sandwich. "I have heard the tales of Yeshua and the saints."Tears puddle in her eyes as she took a bite of the burger, through the mouthful she mumbled out. "Right now I believe in all things if they will just get me out of here."

"When we find L.J. you will."

"Would you like me to pray for you before I leave?" Father Anthony asked he placed his hand up on the bars.

She placed the burger down on the sack that was lying on the cot and walked over to the bars. She looked up at Ryder and sobbed "I want you to pray for me."

He bowed his head and started mumbling out words. "Lord you are Holy…" but he stopped, lifted his head, and said. "I can't."

"Please, for me."

"They would just be empty words." He turned and walked away.

"Forgive him." Father Anthony said as he placed his hands on hers. "He doesn't know what he is doing." He opened up the sack. "Stopped by the house and got this for you." He pulled out a prayer shawl, white with pink stripes, fringes on both ends. He slipped it through the bars to her; she unfolded it and draped it over her head. "Now may I offer a prayer for you?" She nodded and he offered the *Birkhat HaGomel-*

"Blessed are thou Lord our God, King of the universe, Who bestows good to sinners, even as He has bestowed to me every good.

She replied back in Hebrew. *'Mi shegmalkha kol tuv,hu, yigmalkla kol tuv."* She leaned her head against the bars, and said. " *Selah"*

"Amen." Father Delany said. " God who has bestowed upon you every goodness..." He paused. "And may His Son bestow His love on you too." He stepped back from the bars and said. *"Shalom,* Yakira."

"And Peace is with you, Father." She watched as he took a couple of steps away. "Uncle Tony." He turned back to her. "If I don't get out of here. Promise me you will look after him." She placed her hand upon the bars.

He walked back to the cell "I always have but…" He placed his hand on hers. "Someone else needs to do it now. You are going to get out of here tomorrow."

"How do you know that?"

Father Anthony stepped back and smiled and pointed straight up. "He told me so. Just have faith."

Meanwhile Ryder was just exiting the jail section, placing his weapon back in the holster. He didn't say a thing to anyone, he just walked out and got into the car and drove back to the lake house. .

If the seat in the car felt empty, the house was worse, everywhere he looked there was something that was her. From the twin set of dishes in the drainer, gun magazines lying on the coffee table, her bed still lying in a mess, the sheets twisted and pulled up from the bottom, smelling of her perfume, to a load of clothes that she had washed but failed to dry. He removed the clothes from the washer and opened the dryer door, and he saw his old Wildcat jersey, the one that she had worn as a nightshirt.

"She's gotten to you, hasn't she?" He heard someone say. He turned and saw Father Anthony standing in the doorway that led to the kitchen. "Thought you might like some company." He walked down the hall towards Ryder, taking the jersey and folding it up and placing it in the basket on the dryer. "Brought some catfish, just caught them a week ago down at Twin Coves. How about that and some fried taters and onions?"

"Not really hungry." Ryder said as he moved past him in the hall and headed into the great room. He pushed the sliding glass door open and stepped out onto the deck. The sunset was an orange reddish glow spilling out over the waters of the lake. It almost gave Ryder hope, just a small miniscule amount, for a moment, just a brief moment; he didn't feel alone in the world , but just as quickly as the glow faded so did his hopes. Father Anthony walked up behind him. "If you don't want anything to eat, maybe something to drink?"

Ryder looking over his shoulder and saw the father was holding a brown bottle. "This means I should just accept it and give up?" Ryder turned around and took the bottle. "Every time we have done this it was because I needed to accept something. Something bad, this means I should give up on her? "

"Men talk things over with a nice cold bottle of beer." The father said, tilting back the bottle and taking a drink.

"It is root beer, Tony." Ryder said as he let his gaze drift over to his uncle. His gaze drifted back to the lake and he heard a big bass leap up and grabbed an insect flying over the surface of the water, then land back with a large splash. "When I was kid I thought it was beer." He took a swig of the brown colored liquid. "The night mom died. This is what we did. When Annalisa turned me down we drank it. When my knee went out from under me you brought root beer to me in the hospital. It just seems that every time we have a beer together it is the end of something. " Ryder leaned up and turned to his uncle. "Are you telling me that this is end of Yakira?"

"No, just that there is something that root beer can't handle."

"Prayer again, Uncle Tony?" Ryder asked as he took a large swig of the pop and it fizzed in his mouth, and he swished it around before swallowing it, as he leaned back down on the rail again. "Because it doesn't work."   Ryder took another drink; he could taste the sweetness as he swallowed. "I prayed every day to heal mom but he still took her. Prayer doesn't work."

"Each thing that happens to us is for a reason, our hurts just as our joys guide our life forward."

"Yakira is locked away. She looked helpless. Being so little and so short that the first thing she does when she get in the car is push the…" Ryder stopped speaking. Suddenly the one thing that had been bugging him about the crime scene photos came to him. "Forward!" Ryder shouted. "It is the seat."

"What are you talking about?"

Ryder began searching his jacket. "Where is my phone?"

"I put it on the charger in the living room."

"Your prayer might have been actually worth something." Ryder said as he picked up his phone off the charger and began scanning through the photos of Annalisa's file. "Forward." He said as he tapped on the photo of the interior of the Ferrari. "It is the seat! It is all the way forward." Come on unk! We are heading to the sheriff's department."

Chapter 25

Ryder parked the Jaguar in front of the sheriff office and walked in with Father Anthony following behind him. "Brian!" Ryder said with excitement as he saw Deputy Thompson behind the counter. "Tell me you didn't print the seat adjustment in the Ferrari."

"Okay. We didn't print it." He said, sounding confused as his wife Lee Ann came up from behind the counter, handing her husband a cup of black coffee. "What are you talking about?"

"My Ferrari. When you started printing it. You started with the steering wheel, and door handle, when you didn't find any you stopped, thinking it had been wiped clean, right?"

"Yes, it was clear the car had been wiped clean."

"So why wouldn't you do the seat adjustment?"

"Most likely we would have just found Annalisa's prints. We knew she was driving it. Most anyone else wouldn't have touched it."

"Almost everyone else." Ryder looked over at Lee Ann. "How tall are you?"

"Five foot ten."

"The same height as Annalisa. You have the car here?"

"It is in the impound garage."

"I brought a print kit." Ryder said lifting up a small toolbox.

Deputy Thompson led them out the door and down the street to a neighboring building. He unlocked the pad lock on a large garage door. "We have to keep it in here." He turned on the light, revealing the bent and twisted remains of the wounded Italian beast. Ryder grabbed the door and pulled it open. He was instantly met with a strong musty smell as mold was beginning to form on the leather seats from being wet. He glared down at the adjustment button; it showed no signs of finger print dust.

Ryder kneeled down and opened the kit. He picked up a small bottle of light gray colored dust and a small brush. He dipped the fine tip brush into the powder, and lightly dusted the prints on the button, slightly rolling the brush in his fingers, and a clear thumb print appeared. Ryder held his hand out and Deputy Thompson handed him the fingerprint tape. Ryder holding it in both hands, carefully placed it over the print, and with a quickly steady movement he lifted the print from the button and placed it on an index car.

"Looks like a woman's print." Ryder said as he held the card up, noticing it was small.

"Like I said. It is probably Annalisa's." Deputy Thompson said.

"You know, the other day Yakira drove my car. When I got back in I could barely move, but I was still able to drive. However, just to move my car from the street she had to move the seat forward, because she couldn't reach the pedals." He looked over at Lee Ann again. "Like I said, you are the same height as Annalisa was. Get in." He stood, holding the door open. Lee Ann sat down in the seat, her knees were bent up under the steering wheel and her chin rested on the leather rim. "Comfortable?" She shook her head. "You think you could drive like that all the way from Kansas City?"

"No way!"

"So what does this prove?" Lee Ann asked as she got out of the car.

"The last person to drive this car was not Annalisa. It was someone shorter."

Deputy Thompson ran the fingerprint first through their own data base and it showed no match. "Run it through the F.B.I. system." Ryder said. He ran it again and a match showed up. Ryder leaned forward and read the name. "That, I wasn't expecting."

****

It was a name he didn't he didn't even think of, and until this time had only heard once, in questioning another suspect. Although it didn't make sense, what motive would Dawn O'Malley, the wife of Shawn have to murder Annalisa? *Did she catch Annalisa downloading the information from Warner's computer? No, it couldn't be that.* "Ryder reasoned. *Was it something more*

167

personal? All these questions would have to wait till tomorrow. He needed sleep, but he just tossed and turned and all he could do was see Yakira's face as she was pushed into the police car, and then her behind the bars. He would get up and walk outside and stare up at the stars that were partly hidden behind a thin veil of clouds. It was around three when he drifted off; only to be awakened a few minutes after sunrise by the phone.

L.J. had been caught by The Springfield P.D. trying board a jet to Phoenix, where he had a connecting flight that would lead him out of the country. He was being transferred back to Barry County later today. He got up, showered, shaved, and dressed in what he always did: a nice suit, minus of course the tie, he had worn the hangman's noose for years and didn't miss it. He made breakfast, even having bacon since Yakira wasn't here, but as he placed it on the table and not seeing her there, he just made a sandwich, wrapping the bacon and egg in the toast and heading out the door. Ryder made one stop, before heading back into town: Weston's Garage.

There were two reasons he had to stop here. One was to pick up a silver Ford sedan, and the other because the owner Gene Weston was working on a special project for Ryder, restoring a one of kind classic 1971 Charger Killer Bee. Built as a show car it was to be a continuation of the 'winged warriors'- the Charger Daytona and the Road Runner Superbird. It still featured the aerodynamic nose, but with a grille was more like the production model, instead of a screen, and Plexiglas covers over the headlights, instead of the flip up headlights. In the fenders, just behind the front wheel wells were twin side air vents, used to exhaust the hot air from the powerful 440 cubic inch engine. At the back was still the crowning achievement of this steed: the high wing spoiler, now with two horizontal blades, the lower one was thinner and featured a cut out that allowed the trunk lid to open.

Ryder stepped into the garage and pulled his sunglasses off as he gazed over the dull primer gray Dodge sitting proudly in the middle bay of the three bay garage. A middle aged man with thinning red hair swept over in a desperate attempt to cover the ever creeping baldness that was taking over was busy working under the hood, installing a twin four barrel intake on the engine. Ryder could see him through the open cut out for the shaker hood scoop.

"Where are the keys to the Ford?" Ryder asked as the man stood and looked at Ryder, his hazel eyes blinked as if they were an Aladdin's lamp sending out

Morse code to another ship. He wiped his hands on a towel that was hanging out of the pocket of his blue coverall's as he took a step away from the Dodge.

"They are over there on the desk." He said pointing across the garage to a small metal desk pushed up against the wall, where he did all his paperwork. Ryder walked over and picked up the key that was attached to a yellow key fob. "I thought we might go over some color choices." Gene wiped his hands before he stuffed the rag back into his pocket. "You haven't picked one out yet."

"Pick one for me, Gene." Ryder said as headed back out of the garage. Ryder slipped on his sunglasses before turning back to the man "Find one that suits me."

Gene followed Ryder outside and over to where a line of used cars set. Ryder opened the door of the fifteen year old Ford. "Are you sure you want to trust me?" Gene said, his eyes quickly blinking three times.

"Sure."

"Well, I was thinking orange and pink."

"That would be great." Ryder said as he sat down in the seat of the Ford; he started it up and backed out of the row. He slammed on the brakes and the passenger window rolled down. "Orange and pink?" Ryder asked, his tone showing the disgust of the combination.

Gene laughed, showing his gold capped front tooth."Had to see if you were still listening." He walked over to the Ford and leaned down on the door. "Don't worry, I will make you proud. I will pick out something nice and subtle." Gene laughed again as he stood up and Ryder drove away.

After picking up his uncle once again, he had parked down the road from the Warner Ranch."Can you tell me again why you have this car?" Father Anthony asked as he looked over at Ryder behind the steering wheel, gazing through binoculars at the foreman's house.

"Because no one notices a light colored sedan." Ryder said putting the binoculars down and turning to his uncle.

"Then why not my car?"

"A full size white sedan..." Ryder picked up the binoculars and refocused on the ranch. "Looks too much like a police car; might spook her". His eyes followed as a thin small woman, not even five foot in height walked out of the house and got into a late-model gold Buick sedan. It was Dawn O'Malley. She had never been arrested, or in trouble with the police at all. In fact, if she had not worked for the public school system as a cook, there would have not been a match to her fingerprints in the system and Ryder would still be searching, wondering who the print belong to.

She pulled out of the driveway. Ryder fired up the Ford sedan and followed behind her just far enough back that she wouldn't notice him, but not so far that he could lose her. They headed south through a maze of twists and turns, ending up on Business highway 37 and he followed her towards town.

"I just can't believe that Dawn would be mixed up in this." Father Anthony said. "She is a good woman. She is always at mass."

"Just because someone goes to church doesn't make them good, Uncle Tony."

"I know, but she never misses. Except since...."

"Annalisa's murder?" Ryder asked, glancing over at him.

"Yes." Father Anthony said starting straight ahead out the windshield as the gold colored Buick's right hand tail light flipped on. "You really think she is capable of murder?"

"Everyone is."

"Even me?" He asked, turning to his nephew as the Buick slowed and turned on the side street that led to the Barry- Lawrence county library.

"Everyone." Ryder said as he turned to his uncle. "If they reach a certain point where they see there is no other way." Ryder wheeled the Ford up the hill and stopped as he watched the Buick pull up into a parking space in front of the red brick building. Ryder pulled the Ford in behind the Buick, blocking it from leaving.

Ryder and Father Anthony walked into the library and saw Dawn sitting at a table about halfway across the library, near the non-fiction section. She was plain-looking, and had premed black hair. Sitting next to her was a man dressed in a polo shirt and jeans. He couldn't see the man's face as he had his back to him, but there was something very familiar about him. Suddenly this was taking another turn, could she be cheating on her husband?

Ryder grabbed a book on sports cars and he and the father sat down at another table. He flipped through the pages of the book as he watched the couple, it seemed that they were talking, while she touched the man's hand it was more sisterly than a stolen glance. Finding the picture of the car he had been looking for, Ryder stood up and walked over to the table Dawn was sitting at.

"Ever drive a car like this, Ms. O'Malley?" Ryder said in a low voice, laying the book down in front of her. It was the same model as his Ferrari, even the same color, and with the gold wheels. She glanced over at the man and back to Ryder. Ryder glanced over at the man. It was the county prosecutor. "Price! What the hell are you doing here?"

"I could ask you the same question?"

""I can ask a better question: 'Why did this woman's thumb print show up on the adjustment rail on my Ferrari?

"What!" Price said loudly as he stood up, making the librarian glare at him that only meant to hush. He lowered his tone. "I told you to wipe that car clean."

"Oh dear Mother Mary who are full of grace." Ryder heard Dawn say as she performed a cross over her chest and bowed her head. "Oh God, please forgive me."

"He will, Dawn." Father Anthony said tenderly as he walked over to them. "But you have to tell the truth."

"What do you know about this, Price?"

"Maybe we should talk about this outside." Price said.

"After you." . Ryder said pointing the way. They all walked outside, down the sidewalk, across the parking lot and stood under the shade of a group of pine trees.

"Okay Price, what are you doing here? No more crap! Or I am making a call to Judge Weber and telling him you are tampering with evidence in an ongoing case."

"Stop it!" Dawn shouted as she grabbed Ryder's arm. "He didn't have anything to do with it. He was just trying to protect me."

"Protect you? Why?" Ryder asked as he looked at her.

"She's my sister, Ryder." Price said as a cool breeze sweep across them. "The only one I have. I couldn't let her go to jail."

"You murdered Annalisa?" Ryder asked.

Dawn turned and looked up at her brother and then over to Father Anthony before turning back to her brother. "I have to tell him."

"Dawn, shut up!" Price stepped between her and Ryder, grabbing her arm, and trying to pull her away. "I told you, we can…"

"No! No more lies." Dawn turned to Father Anthony dropping down to her knees on the ground. "Father, please forgive me for I have sinned."

"Dawn, I can give you absolution." Father Anthony reached down and helped the woman to her feet. "But if you have committed a crime. You must take your punishment."

"Dawn, stop this!" Price said, pushing Father Anthony away. "You are going to be in trouble."

She buried her face in her hands. "I didn't kill her, but I did help to move her. I had to. He was going to blame it on Shawn."

"Who?" Again his tone was harsh and demanding.

"L.J." She said, lifting her head. "If I dared to refuse him he would make it look like Shawn killed her."

"Ryder, you don't understand how powerful Warner was in this county. He got the sheriff elected. He got…"

"You elected?" Ryder turned to Dawn. "Did he kill Annalisa?"

"I don't know." She said, her voice breaking. "She was already dead when I got there." Her hand shook as she reached up to wipe a tear away. "She was just lying on the garage floor. L.J. took the cord and wrapped it around her neck. He said we would place her in the sports car and crash it into the river. No one would know; it would look like an accident." She sucked in her breath and continued. "They put her in the car. He told me to drive it up on the trailer but, I couldn't—.

"You couldn't reach the pedals. So you moved the seat forward." Ryder said, pulling his sunglasses down.

"Yes.

"Did you lift her?"

"No, but--."

"Shawn did?"

"He had to." Dawn sobbed, "Years ago when he was just a kid Shawn was drunk and he hit a kid on a bicycle. Scott covered it up, but--."

"He has been blackmailing him ever since."

She dropped her head down and nodded. 'But he didn't kill her." She lifted her head again. "You have to believe me."

"What about L.J.?"

"I—don't know.   —but—." She tripped over own words, remembering back to the night of the murder. She dropped her gaze down to the ground once again, as if she were looking for a small granule of courage that she could use to spit out the rest of the story. She lifted her head once again. "Before he left the ranch that night he was screaming about—about how he had to stop her. Something about, something she took. " She inhaled and swallowed hard before adding. "When we arrived his shirt was covered in blood."

"Where is the shirt?" Ryder asked.

"He threw it away, but—."

"You kept it." Ryder said and she nodded, dropping her gaze down once again. "Where is it?"

"Our pickup." She looked back up at him. "It is behind the seat. The pickup is at Weston's Garage."

Chapter 26

It had been over a week that Yakira had been locked up and now it seemed that another was slipping down from the sky. Today was Friday; in another hour it would be the beginning of the Sabbath for her. Father Anthony made sure that she could have the things she needed to worship. The sun had dropped down over the hill as they pulled into the driveway of Weston's Garage, just outside of town.

"Gene!" Ryder shouted as the man was getting ready to go home, luckily his home was right next to the garage. He turned and walked back to the garage.

"Ryder! I got a guy in California making the hood scoop." He quickly blinked eyes and continued. "They never put a shaker hood scoop on a Charger; had to be custom made, it kind of looks like a 440 six pack scoop."

"Where is O'Malley's truck?" Ryder asked as he tossed the keys to the Ford back to him.

"Who? What?"

"Shawn O'Malley's. Where is his truck?"

His question seemed to make Gene's chubby face and pale coloring grow even paler. "You are here for what I found." Thinking he meant the bloody shirt, Ryder nodded.

"It is around back in the lot." Gene said, leading the way around the side of the garage to a holding lot. The lot was surrounded by a twelve-foot high chain link fence with barbed wire at the top. The double gate was locked with a chain and pad lock. Gene unlocked the gates and pushed them back. Inside the lot were the cars he was working on, or were for sale or rent. They passed by Ryder's Jaguar and 1968 light blue Camaro RS and 1976 Mercury Montego coupe. Behind the garage; backed up next to the fence was a light blue and white 1979 Ford F150.

"When I saw it." Gene said. "I didn't know what to do. Or who to call." He pulled the door opened and pulled the seat back. "I didn't touch it." Ryder stepped up and looked into the truck, his chin dropped down in shock.

"Oh, for the love of Mary." He said with shock as he reached up and removed his sunglasses. There, lying on the floor was a rifle; wrapped in dark-colored cloth. Ryder looked around in the truck, finding an old shop rag he reached in and picked up the weapon. As he held it up the cloth unwrapped, it was the t-shirt. "Gene, you have some paper sacks around here?"

"There is a bunch inside."

"Get me three of them and some masking tape."

Gene went inside the garage and returned with three large brown paper sacks. Ryder used the cloth to pick up the t-shirt and place it in one sack. He folded it down and taped it shut and handed it to Father Delany. Using the cloth he picked up the rifle and again held it up.

"AR-15, right?" Gene asked, looking at the rifle.

"No, this is an M-16. If I am guessing right, one stolen from Fort Leonard Wood." He gripped the rifle by the barrel. As his uncle held the sack open, Ryder slipped the rifle down into the sack; using the other sack to cover the barrel and using the masking tape he sealed the two sacks together. Pulling out his pen from his pocket he wrote on the sack, where the rifle was found. He handed it to Gene. "Hold on to this." Ryder reached into his jacket and pulled out the notebook, wrote a number on the paper and pulled it out and gave it to Gene. "I want you to call this number. She is an F.B.I. agent; tell her what you found." Ryder and the father walked over to the Jaguar, Ryder opened the door and the interior light spilled out onto the gravel parking lot. "And talk to no one else but her." Ryder and father Anthony got into the Jaguar and sped away.

Now it would make sense that he should have taken the shirt to the S.D. for testing, and all the detective in him, told him that was the right thing to do, however it was the man in him that told him trust only your gut, and his gut was telling him to have Thom test it.

The lights were still on at the funeral home, which meant that he was still there. Knowing that Thom always kept the back door unlocked, Ryder and Father Delany walked in. Immediately Ryder heard the muffled sounds of rock music, it was coming from the basement. Instead of taking the elevator, this time he took the stairs, at the bottom Ryder stopped and a grin broke across his face as he saw Thom dancing, embracing himself as he sang along to Journey's *'Lovin Touchin Squeezin'*. A body lay on the table, covered with a sheet. He had his back to him and Ryder walked up and grabbed the man's shoulder. Thom screamed out "Oh sweet Jesus, help me now!"

Thom turned around. "Ryder you son of a…" He looked over at the father. "Sorry, father. Did you come for last rites?"

"Were they Catholic?"

"Not them father, me."

"But you are Baptist, my son."

"I will take whatever I can get with that crazy idiot nephew of yours around. I need it." Thom looked at Ryder and at the sack that he was carrying. "What are you doing here, anyway?"

"I need something tested." He handed Thom the sack. "I need you to type that blood for me?"

"Whose shirt is this?"

"L.J.'s"

"And whose blood are you looking for?" Thom paused. "Let me guess: Annalisa's."

"She had a rare type. AB negative."

Thom took the shirt and using a scalpel he scraped a little from the dark spot on the black t-shirt and placed it on a glass slide. Using a couple of drops of distilled water, he let it set for a moment. Using an eye dropper he sucked up the reddish colored liquid, and placed it on a testing card. "AB Negative."

"Got him!" Ryder said pumping his fist in the air. He scooped the shirt up and placed it back in the bag and turned, ready to walk back over to the elevator.

"Ryder, wait one freaking minute! Yes, she had a rare type but she wasn't the only one who had that type."

"It is mine too." Ryder said.

"It is also L.J.'s"

****

Darkness already covered the town for three hours when he pulled the car into an empty parking place in front of the jail; as soon as he opened the door he met Sheriff Hart.

"L.J. is here." The sheriff said with a sour tone. We have been working on him all day. He ran his own attorney off." The sheriff walked behind the counter and poured himself a cup of coffee and added a packet of sweetener, stirring it with a spoon, he turned back to Ryder. "You're a big city cop, maybe you should try."

"Go ahead; I am going to see Yakira." Father Anthony said. "And tell her what is going on."

"Here, hang on to this for me." Ryder said, handing his uncle his phone, I am expecting a call. He turned back to the sheriff. "I may have the one thing that can break him." Ryder said, holding up the sack. He handed it to the sheriff. "Run a DNA test on this."

"That will take a few days." The sheriff replied. "What are you looking for?"

"Proof that is Annalisa's. He got her blood on his shirt, just like everybody else that was around." Ryder handed over his weapon. "He doesn't know we haven't yet tested it." The sheriff escorted Ryder back to the interrogation room. Ryder pulled the door open and stepped inside; there was something comforting about it, like going back to a place that he knew well, like visiting with a favorite cousin.

The room small was simple with a table in the middle of the room and three chairs, two on one side and one on the other. Deputy Thompson was already in the in the room on one side of the table and L.J. on the other. There was a video camera on a tripod in the corner of the room.

"Well, sending in the big guns?" L.J. laughed and leaned back in his chair on two legs till he saw who it was. "You!" He said hesitantly and lowered the

178

chair back down on the floor. "You told me you were not a cop. You can't question me."

"There is no rule that says it has to be a law enforcement agent to question a suspect." Ryder said as he removed his jacket and placed it on the back of the empty chair.

L.J. glared over at Ryder and leaned back once again in his chair. "I have rights, man. You can't touch me." Ryder didn't say a thing, he just lifted his foot under the table and kicked the leg of the chair, and L.J. hit the floor.

Ryder got up and reached down and grabbed L.J.'s t-shirt, twisting it in his fingers, exposing a belly button ring. Ryder pulled him to his feet. "Did your mother tell you that you should not lean back in a chair?" Ryder released him, bent down and up righted the chair. "You might get hurt." He added as he pushed L.J. back into the chair.

"You bastard! You ripped my shirt." L.J. fumed as he tried to smooth down his ripped t-shirt. He looked over at Deputy Thompson. "I am going to sue you, the county, the…" L.J.'s tone slowed and he looked over at Ryder and laughed mockingly. "Oh no! I'm not going to fall for that good cop bad cop stuff. "He leaned back, placing his hands back behind his head. "I am not saying a thing. And you don't have anything on me."

"You are wrong! You were blackmailing Annalisa. Your old man cut you off. She wouldn't pay. You wrapped the Ethernet cable around her neck and squeezed the life out of her."

"No! I didn't kill her!"

"Your father ordered you to kill Annalisa!" Ryder slammed his fist down on the table and shouted. "Admit it!"

"Suck it, old man!"

"We can make a deal L.J. that can save you from the needle." Deputy Thompson said.

"Go to hell and die! You can take your deal and shove it!" He looked over at Ryder. "All you care about is getting that little girl friend out of jail. The little dirty Jewish girl." L.J. grinned devilishly and leaned over the table towards him "You have children with that thing. "He paused and laughed before adding. They'll be born dirty sons of...." Ryder pushed the table forward, it slammed into L.J.'s chest knocking him over, and he hit the floor again.

"You worthless piece of garbage." Ryder said as he grabbed L.J. by the shirt and slammed him up against the wall, pressing his palm against L.J.'s chin, pushing his head sideways. "I told you to never call her that again."

"What's the matter; you don't want little dirty children?" L.J. said. Ryder spun him around in front of him and wrapped his arm around L.J. and he started applying pressure.

"Ryder, Ryder, Rick!" Deputy Thompson said as he raced over, grabbing Ryder's arm. "Let him go. Let him go! He is not worth it." Ryder released the choke hold and L.J. fell to the floor. "You are too close to this. Take a break."

Ryder grabbed up his jacket and slung it over his shoulder as stomped towards the door, slamming it shut as he walked out of the room and over in front of the monitor where Father Anthony was standing and watching. Ryder watched as Deputy Thompson again tried to get L.J. to talk.

"I am going to kill him!" Ryder bristled gripping his fingers tightly into a fist, picturing in his mind L.J.'s neck in his grip. "I am going to break his freaking damn neck!"

"You are going about this the wrong way." Father Anthony said, still looking at the monitor. "You can't fight hate with hate." He turned to Ryder. "Fight it with love."

"You expect me to show love to *that*?" Ryder asked, confused, as he pointed towards L.J. in the room.

"People are born into sin, but they are not born into evil. It is always a choice."

"Why does it sound like you swallowed a bible?" All his life his uncle would say these things.

"Comes with the collar." Father Anthony smiled and brought his hand up to his neck. "Something caused him to be the way he is; find out what it is and use it."

Ryder couldn't believe it, he had let L.J. get to him, it was the first thing that Captain Grosstree had taught him, it could never get personal. He slipped his jacket back on and walked back into the room; He sat down in the chair and faced L.J. again.

"Back for more? Want to beat me some more? Well I can take it!"

"Must have been tough on you losing your mother so young." Ryder said, placing his right elbow up on the table, resting his chin lightly in his fingers. "I lost my mother when I was twelve; I thought my whole life ended. And my old man, he is worthless. I haven't seen him in twenty years. You know what? I don't care."

"Nobody could be as bad as my old man."

"Yeah, when I was born." Ryder said leaning forward a little. "My father was with another woman. When my mother died he was with her. Then he left her for another woman."

"Just one? That is laughable, man." L.J. drew an imaginary picture on top of the table, not looking at Ryder. "My old man got everything he ever wanted, money, women, power." He lifted up his head. "You know what I was to him?" Ryder let him continue. "I was nothing but a political tool that was trotted out every two years for pictures. Had to make sure I was wearing the right thing, saying the right things. So I started dressing like this; all of sudden he didn't want me. I thought that was what I wanted but—I hated that SOB!"

"No you didn't. You loved him."

"You are crazy! I hated him."

"In fact, you love him more than anything. All you wanted was his love. And if he told you to do something you did it, just because he needed you." Ryder leaned back in the chair. "L.J., I found your shirt. The one you tried to get rid of. The one soaked with the blood. The DNA proves it is not yours. It is time you tell the truth."

181

"What?" He asked, befuddled.

"Someone saw you trying to get rid of it. They took it and gave it to me. Confess made it will go easier on you."

"Okay! I admit it!" L.J. said. "I killed the old man!" Ryder was stunned; he dropped his arm down on the table and looked over at Deputy Thompson, there was confusion on his face also. He turned back to L.J. who continued his confession. "After all I did for him. I cleaned up his damn mess! He promised me he would help me. And he cut me out." He laughed mockingly. "Can you believe it? He was going to let them kill me, just because he could get more votes that way." L.J .shook his head in disgust as he continued. "That is all he ever cared about—votes. That is why he married Annalisa; she was the pretty prop he could escort out." His tone change quickly to rage. "He told me I wasn't going to get a dime anymore then he got up and went to the bathroom saying he was going to take a dump and that it would be worth more than I was. I saw the Ethernet cable in his briefcase. I grabbed it, and it felt so good wrapping it around his neck. I wanted to *cut his damn blasted head off!*" He shouted, and then he calmed again and continued." I tossed him into the bathtub; thought the water would wash everything away. But I noticed he got blood all over my shirt."

L.J. laid his hands out on the table, revealing the marks that the cable left on his palms. "It was that bitch Susan that saw me, wasn't it? Why did she give it to you for?"

"She didn't. I found your shirt with Annalisa's blood on it. The one you were wearing the night you murdered her."

"I told you man, I didn't kill her. I just cleaned up the damn mess. She was already dead when I got there she was lying beside a pool of her own blood."

"How did you know to go over to her house?"

"The old man called me and said clean it up. That is when he promised me the money. But I didn't kill her. And I don't know who did. I wouldn't have done that, she was nice to me."

"You were blackmailing her."

"I had to have the money, man, those guys in Little Rock were going to kill me if I didn't."

Deputy Thompson stood up and took the handcuffs from his belt and placed L.J. under arrest, snapping the cuffs around his wrists. Ryder sat there, he had done one thing right, and he had proved that Yakira didn't kill the speaker of the house, yet he was back to square one on Annalisa. Deputy Thompson escorted L.J. over towards the door; L.J. spoke up.

"Don't you want to know what the secret is?"

"What secret is that?" Ryder asked turning his head and looking over his shoulder at the man.

"The one that she knew but you didn't."

"That she was adopted?" Ryder asked as he stood up and faced him.

That is what you think it is!" L.J. grinned as he struggled to turn and face Ryder. "Don't you know the road to hell is paved with good intentions?"

"And what does that mean?"

"You may have good intentions in figuring this out, but when you do, you are going to open the gates to your own private hell" L.J. turned back and took a step out of the room. He glanced back over his shoulder. "Want to know more, go ask your mother."

Ryder walked into the outer room; rubbing his aching neck, he yawned and rubbed his hands over his eyes. He looked over at Father Anthony.

"You did it."

"We did it." Ryder said, knowing it was his uncle's suggestion that broke L.J.

"Well, praise the Lord!"

"You're starting to sound like a Baptist there, Uncle Tony."

"Well, I am a man of many talents." Father Anthony turned to the sheriff. "So let's get her out of there."

"Can't just yet." The sheriff drew out "We will get the confession written up and get L.J. to sign it. And get Judge Weber to sign a release."

"Or we can get him to sign it right now." Ryder said walking toward the front door.

"Ryder, it is one o'clock in the morning. I am not waking a judge up."

Ryder yawned and rubbed his face again. "He still lives down at Eagle Rock, doesn't he? A phone he cannot answer. Me banging on his door he can't say no to." Ryder turned and looked at Father Anthony. "Uncle Tony, you go tell her parents what happened and get her some clothes and get her ready. I will be back in an hour with the order. Or the judge himself."

"Oh, by the way, Alex called, said to tell you she had picked up the package and was going to have the lab print it. And that the serial number did check back to a weapon stolen from Fort Leonard Wood."

"What is this about Leonard Wood?" The sheriff asked.

"We found a stolen M-16 in O'Malley's pickup and turned it over to Alex."

"The F.B.I. agent?" She's working that case? I thought it was about Annalisa's murder."

"Yeah, it seems the good congressman was running guns, along with O'Malley and others. With the rifle she has now, she is going to be able to get a warrant to search the place."

"Wow! Gun runners right here in my county".

"I got to get going." Ryder said with a grin that felt good to smile. "I have a judge to wake up."

Judge Weber lived two miles east of Eagle Rock. The sky had clouded over and the moon was hidden, leaving a dark night surrounding Ryder as he pushed the Jaguar hard through the twisting turns through Roaring River and F highway.

On highway 86 he was all alone on the road, not a glimmer of a headlight, and most of the homes he passed by were encased in darkness, their occupants fast asleep, dreaming, something so wonderful that the dreamer doesn't awake, others nightmares that just don't seem to end.

The rearview mirror caught the flash of headlights coming up from behind him. He raised his eyes to the mirror, the lights were getting brighter and brighter and they were coming up fast. Ryder's hands gripped the leather rim of the steering wheel; he was approaching the Eagle Rock Bridge. The vehicle started to pass. He could see by the height of the headlight beams that this wasn't a car, it wasn't a pickup truck or…They passed under a security light and he saw it was a van, a white Dodge van with blacked out windows. The van was to the side of him.

Bam! It slammed into the side of the Jaguar, causing the car to fishtail all over the pavement. Ryder fought the steering wheel hard, trying to keep the car straight. He pressed down on the gas. The car jumped forward, leaving the van behind. Sudden the van swung back, clipping the back end of the car. The Jaguar twisted and turned hard to the left, Ryder turned the wheel hard to the right, turning into the skid. BAM! The van hit again. Then he flew off the highway, into a field, the nose plowed into the dirt and the car flipped.

Ryder sat there, looking through the blurry world of a busted windshield. Something warm and wet was running down his forehead. He touched it, it was blood. Steam was rising up out of the crumpled hood; he could make out a dark figure coming towards him. They stopped beside the car and said.

"The case is over. L.J. will confess to both murders." The figure turned and walked back to the van. He reached for his phone and remembered his uncle still had it. He looked back at the highway; there were beams of headlights and someone was coming towards him. Then everything went black.

Chapter 27

There was a bright shining light. First in his right-eye then in the left eye, then as quickly as it appeared it vanished. It took a couple of seconds for his eyes to refocus to realize he was staring straight up into the bright lights of a florescent light in the ceiling. The bleep, bleep sound of an EKG machine made him turn his head. He saw a man standing there, pleasant appearing with a clean shaven head and face. He shoved a pen light into his breast pocket.

"You are at Mercy Hospital in Cassville. "I am Dr. Crowley. Could you tell me your full name?"

"Detective first class Richard Thomas Allen Ryder Homicide Division Kansas City Metro Division. Badge number 10798." He said it as a matter of repetition, as he had said it so many times.

"How do you feel?"

"As if I had head butted a Brahma bull driving a U-Haul hauling moonshine." He felt a sharp jab in his right arm, and turned and saw a nurse. She had placed a rubber tube around his upper arm to make the veins pop and she had jabbed a large needle into his vein and was drawing blood. He knew why she was doing it, he had cracked up a car; they were testing to see if he was sober. It was Tracy and she had just had her hair colored. "Tracy, are you a vision of loveliness." He said.

"Well, aren't you the charmer." She replied back, patting his face and smiling even more. "I can see why Yakira has been talking about you so much."

"You are a lucky man." The doctor said as he cleaned the wound on Ryder's forehead. "If the sheriff hadn't seen that van following you out of town, and followed along you might not have made it.

"He is a good guy." Tracy said. "He helps with the drug stealing; he comes each week and checks it and makes sure nothing is missing."

"Going to be a little stick." Dr Crowley said as he jabbed the needle into Ryder's forehead. Why was it they always said that, when it was never true. Just once he would like to hear it will hurt like…. his fingers grabbed the sheet of the bed as the doctor jammed the needle into the flesh, numbing the side of his face. Fourteen stitches, X-rays, CAT scan and headache that wouldn't quit and he was back in his E.R. cubical, the bright light was shining down on him and shone through his eye lids when he closed his eyes. He took in a deep calming breath and he could smell honeysuckle. His eyes opened and he looked around the room.

"She is here." Tracy said.

"How…?

"When you didn't go see the judge. Your uncle called him. He personally came in and got her free. He said to tell you he would see you on the golf course next week. If that makes any sense?"

It made perfect sense; he wanted Ryder to be his partner in a golf tournament. Ryder didn't want to do it, but now he had to go. "Perfect sense."

Tracy left the cubicle, and Ryder laid back and closed his eyes once again." He heard the curtain open; at first in his mind he envisioned Yakira standing there all dressed in pink, it made him at ease, even if he dared to say it. For it seemed every time he dared to do it, something always came crashing down, spoiling it all. Yes, for that moment he was happy. He turned and looked down and there were a pair of red high heel shoes. Then the sickening smell of a strong perfume, made that image shatter.

"Maureen." He said, disheartened, as she walked up to the side of his bed.

"I am here to take care of you, son."

"You are not my mother."

"I am the best one qualified, as I used to be a nurse." She said as she tried to pat her hand on his bandaged head and he pulled away from her.

"Leave me alone." His tone was harsh and he squinted, making the stitches pull in his forehead. She began yammering; he remembered L.J. confessing to his father's murder, but not to Annalisa's. No matter how hard he had tried he just couldn't get L.J. to confess to her murder. What difference did it make? In Missouri a first degree murder was going to get him the death penalty. If it was feds that prosecuted him it would be death. Why wouldn't he confess to

Annalisa's murder? Then Ryder remembered the last thing that L.J. told him. He turned and saw Maureen over across the room; she is holding a wash basin. He didn't know why it was, but L.J.'s words came back to him.

"What do you know about a secret?" Ryder asked, his head throbbing.

"I don't have any." She said as she dropped the pan to the floor, spilling the water. She picked up the pan and grabbed a towel and began mopping up the water.

"L.J. confessed that he was blackmailing Annalisa, about a secret that will destroy the family." Ryder pushed himself up in the bed; his face was still numbed and his words were slurring slightly. "He told me to ask you." Ryder paused to watch her reaction as she dropped the pan again. As she stood up, he asked "Does it have something to do with Annalisa being adopted?"

"What! L.J. knows this?" Then she quickly tossed the towel on the floor, before she turned and pulled the curtain to the cubicle back. "I will get somebody in here to clean that up. I have to go. The little Rosen girl can take care of you." Her words came as fast as her steps that he could hear on the hard surface of the floor as she walked away.

"How come you know? She was adopted?"

"Rebekah told me one day. I have to go! I am just going to let Yakira take care of you." She turned and quickly left. Ryder lay back on the cot and closed his eyes as he felt the bandage that was on his forehead just above his left eye. He closed his eyes again.

"They can give you something for that headache." He heard Father Anthony say. Ryder opened his eyes and saw his uncle standing at the foot of the cot.

"Yeah, how do you get her to take it?" Ryder joked as he placed his hand over his eyes to shield them from the bright lights overhead. "I am so tired of this place."

"The hospital or the world?"

"Both." Ryder grabbed the rail of the bed and pulled himself up. "I can do something about getting out of one of them, though." He swung his legs around, and stood up. He could feel the coldness of the floor on his bare feet.

He was wearing nothing but a hospital gown. His clothes were folded, lying on a counter across the room, except the jacket that was hung up. He took a couple of unsteady steps.

"Don't you think it is time you quit this? Someone tried to kill you tonight."

"Wouldn't be the first time, Uncle Tony." Ryder grabbed up his clothes and sat down in a chair and began to get dressed. "Won't be the last time…" He looked up and gave him a half grin. "…well, unless they succeeded. Then I guess I won't have any worries then." Ryder stood up as he slipped his pants on. He looked at the empty holster lying under his shirt and picked it up. "Where is my service weapon?"

"They have it locked up at nurse's desk." Father Anthony said as he sat down on the cot. "You just can't give up; it is a game to you, isn't it?" Ryder didn't reply, he just continued to get dressed. Ryder sat down in the chair and slipped his shoes on.

"It is like a puzzle. And I have to put it back together."

"I remember buying you a puzzle for your tenth birthday. You spent all the rest of the day trying to put it together, but there was one piece missing. I went and bought you the same exact puzzle. Instead of just using the missing pieces, you had to put the new puzzle together." Father Anthony dropped his gaze to the holster that was clutched in Ryder's hands.

"A puzzle has to be solved." He slipped his shirt on, it was still unbuttoned and he wobbled on his feet. "Otherwise, someone gets away with murder."

"What about her?"

"Who?" Ryder, said, then realizing he meant Yakira. "Oh, her."

"Why do you think she is doing it?"

"To find out who murdered her sister?"

"Bull!" Father Anthony shouted back. "It is because she thinks it will make you happy."

Ryder held his hand up to his aching head, and fell down onto the chair. "She is a misguided kid." He said, as he hung his head down.

"Think again. Why don't you open your eyes and see who she really is." Father Anthony's word made him raise his head and look at him. "She is not that little girl anymore". Ryder took in a deep breath as he grabbed his jacket and slung it over his shoulder, and Father Anthony continued. "She is a woman."

"I know she is a woman, Uncle Tony."

"No, you don't. Open your eyes and see. Let your heart decide what you feel."

"What if I don't feel anything?"

"Then walk away. But let her know. The worst thing you can do to a woman is keep her guessing. Tell her." Father Anthony said as he stood up and walked over to his nephew and placed his hand on Ryder's shoulder. "I saw you how you reacted when L.J. said what he said about her. That was the same way you reacted when someone would say something against Annalisa."

"Why is it that someone who has never been married knows so much about women?"

"I am an observer. Sometimes the observer knows more than the one being observed." Father Anthony said before turning and walking out of the ER. Ryder stood there, his world in a slow spin in more ways than one as he steadied himself, holding on to the cot. He inhaled. *Honeysuckle.*

****

The next few hours were hazy, murky memories that didn't make sense at all. He swore that he must have been in heaven lying on a soft pink cloud, all the while a beautiful dark-haired angel sat next to him, taking care of him, wiping the sweat from his brow, while the bright light shined down upon him from a bright blue sky and some woman kept waking him up, asking him simple questions, such as his name, age. "Who is Yakira? Are you hungry? You want something to eat?"

190

"Shalom, sweetie. You ok?" He heard a voice say and his eyes opened. The vision was blurry, just of dark hair and a pretty face, it was the angel. Above was a bright light, he blinked a couple of times, and rubbed his eyes, and refocused them. It was a low hanging chandelier, suspended from a ceiling painted like the sky. He was lying in a white iron bed covered with bright pink sheets. "You want something to eat? Are you hungry?" He nodded and turned as he watched a woman walk from beside the bed and over to the door. She was wearing a flowing white sundress, that struck her about 3 inches above her knees. Pale pink eyelet lace made up the empire-waist bodice of the scoop-necked dress and it had a lace hem of white eyelet that swirled with her movement, as her bare feet, with pink polished toenails, strolled across the walnut hardwood floor. "Mom, he says he is hungry!" She shouted out the door. She turned and walked back to a white wicker chair with ice pink cushions that she pulled up next to the bed. He shook his head again; the sun was shining through a window from behind her.

"Are you an angel?" He asked.

She got up and sat down on the bed beside him. "That is the sweetest thing you have ever told me." He felt her fingers gripped around his, and the mellow aroma of honeysuckle. "Yakira." He said. She looked down at him; there was something different about her, she looked beautiful. He reached up and touched her hair.

"You like my hair?" She asked, running her fingers through it. The red at the ends was cut away; it was now solid brown; it had more body, more bounce, with slight curls at the ends. "Andrea gave me a new style." He reached out and she let her hair go. It fell into his fingers, it was soft and fine and he could just pick up the hint of honeysuckle. "I had to have something to do while I was waiting for you to wake up."

He looked around the room at the bright pink painted walls at a neon clock.

"What time is it?"

"Eleven thirty."

Ryder looked out the window past the light pink curtain and could see it was daylight. They had gotten out of the ER around four am. His stomach growled and he placed his hand over it, to quiet it. He lifted up the blanket and saw that he was wearing light blue pajama bottoms. "Dad will bring you another pair when he comes home from the store."

"I thought your family didn't do any business on the Sabbath?"

She looked at him and knitted her brows in bewilderment. "Sweetie, it is Tuesday morning. You have been asleep off and on almost four days. We would try to give you something to eat. Help you to the bathroom, and you would fall back asleep." No wonder he was hungry, he inhaled as he caught a smell of something wonderful, and it was getting stronger, a smell that gave him comfort but made his stomach growl even louder. Yakira's mother-Rebekah-entered the room wearing a bright smile and carrying a tray with a steaming bowl of soup on it.

"Good to have you back. " She said cheerfully as she placed the tray down in front of him. It was the best medicine there was, the fundamental Jewish comfort food- Matzo Ball soup. Rebekah sat down on the edge of the bed beside him; she took the napkin and tucked it under his chin. She took the spoon and cut a chunk of one of the soft floating balls in the bowl, along with a spoonful of soup. She gently blew on it to cool it down. "Eat up." She said, holding her other hand under the spoon.

He glanced over by rolling his gaze over to her, as he opened his mouth, and she fed him. It was a wonderful comforting taste, like a dumpling, with a finer texture, the fattiness and salty flavor of the chicken stock, the richness of the matzo meal that melted in his mouth, with just a hint of fresh chives, and carrot shreds in the soup.

"Eat up!" She said, bringing up another spoonful of the tasty soup. Ryder loved Bubbie's matzo ball soup; it had seemed to comfort him in all his times of trouble, from crashing his bicycle, to losing his mother. Maybe that was what was missing, for he was starting to feel better. She scooped up another spoonful of the soup, "Eat it all up and be *yeladim tovim*." She said, meaning a good boy.

Rebekah suddenly looked up at the clock on the wall. Oh, my kergel! Here, Yakira." She said, handing her the bowl of soup. "You feed him. While I go get it." She got up and quickly left, dashing back down the stairs.

192

"All right, what is going on here?"

"You meant because she is so nice?" Yakira said, scooping up a spoonful of soup and feeding it to him. "That is the strangest thing. Uncle Tony told me what happened and that L.J. confessed; I began giving thanks and praise to Yahweh."

"Wait a minute!" Ryder said pushing himself up in bed. "What does this have to do with the way your mother is acting?"

"They were at the jail getting ready to take me home when we heard about you. Bubbie, as Bubbie does, was talking about all the things she was going to make for you when we got you home."

"What does that have to do with your mother?"

"I was getting to that. Don't be such a *nudnik*. It was just before we getting ready to leave and Sheriff Hart came out and announced that L.J. confessed to killing Annalisa. That is when mom acted real strange. She seemed—I hate to say it but she seemed relieved. Saying 'it was now all over" and you wouldn't have to look into it anymore. Then yesterday Maureen showed up and told her the news; she became a *meshuggeneh*"

"What news?"

"L.J. escaped."

"What! How?"

She hesitated to tell him the rest. "They determined that from your interrogation that he suffered from child abuse and that…" Again she hesitated. "…instead of sending him to prison they are going to send him to a mental hospital in Springfield. They were transporting him, when they stopped at a convenience store. He went to the bathroom and he escaped. She watched for his reaction.

"Guess it doesn't matter." He said as he took the bowl from her hands and placed it over on the nightstand next to the bed. He leaned forward and placed his hand on the side of her face. "You are free, and that is all that matters. *"At chamuda."* He said one of the few phrases in Hebrew that he knew.

"You think I am cute?" She cupped his hand into her hand and kissed it. "But there is still more to the story." He let his hand slip from hers and leaned back in bed and waited for her to explain. "After Maureen visit's mom went to Annalisa's old room, she started getting rid of everything in there; she packed it up and took it out to the storage building at the old farm. "

"The one that Annalisa used as a bedroom?"

"Yes, and every photo of Annalisa is gone. It is like all of a sudden she wants to pretend she never existed. All of sudden I became the good daughter; she is praising everything I do." She paused once again and her face drew up in a frown before continuing. "Then she heard the news this morning. They found L.J. dead; at the Monett South Park. They think the guys from Little Rock did it."

"You sound as if you don't believe that."

"I don't. I think someone else murdered him." She got up from the bed and walked over to the door, opened it and looked down the hall, to make sure no one was coming. She closed the door and returned and sat down on the bed beside, him, crossing one leg under her she lowered her voice and said. "I think my mother did it."

Chapter 28

Rebekah had brought the *kergel* up, a piece for him and another for Yakira, then went back to the kitchen to finish up a cake, a carrot cake with walnuts and cream cheese frosting- Ryder's favorite dessert of all time, plus Bubbie was making *surganiot*, deep fried jelly doughnuts that usually were made at Chanukah; the whole house smelled like an explosion of holidays.

He pushed himself to his feet, and could feet the rush of cold air from the vent on the floor of the central air unit on his bare feet. Having been in bed most of the past four days, he was like a toddler taking his first step. His legs shook under his weight.

"Let me help." Yakira said as he felt her arm wrap around his waist. He reached out, placed his arm around her shoulders, and his fingers stroked her upper arm. Her skin was as soft as the petals of a lily, why had he not noticed this before?

"What makes you think that your mother would have murdered a low-life like L.J.?"

"Maureen came back later that day, they both left in that yellow land yacht of Maureen's. She didn't get back till around one this morning."

"How do you know the time?"

"I had been by your side all day; I was getting hungry so I went down to get a sandwich. I was coming back upstairs when I heard the clock in the living room strike one, and saw her come in; she went to the back bathroom and took a shower."

With his weak legs, they wobbled like a pair of drunks, only to tumble down on a pink cushion on the window seat. She slid down out of his arms onto the hardwood floor. With her legs spread out in front of her, he couldn't help himself. He laughed. He helped her to her feet and pulled her up on the seat next to him and she laughed too, burying her face in his shoulder. He looked out the multi-paned window and down into the back yard, at the red brick patio and the white iron furniture that encircled an oval-shaped fish pond. "I was just thinking of something." He said softly.

"About something that you and Annalisa did?"

"No, that we did." He turned and looked back down at the patio. "You didn't get to dance the last dance at the prom. So we danced under the light of a full moon on the patio." He paused for a moment as if to let the memory rewind in his mind. "It was to '*Love of my Life.*' By Queen. "

"My favorite song. My favorite band." She said looking out the window also. "You remember that? I thought guys weren't supposed to remember things like that."

"We do when it is someone special." He said and she turned her head and faced him. They were nose to nose. He raised his hand to her cheek and lowered his lips to hers, they were almost touching. The phone that was lying on the bed rang, they did not move for just a moment, and then the phone rang again. "Guess I better get that. It might be important." He got up and answered the phone.

"Ryder here." He said into the phone. "Yeah, I understand. We will be there in a little bit." He ended the call. He looked over at Yakira. "That was Thom. He said 'he found something strange' about L.J.'s death."

Chapter 29

Ryder's clothes had torn and spoiled by his blood so Pascal had brought one of his custom-made suits, dark navy blue, with matching pants, and Yakira picked out the shirt; of course it was ice pink. Ryder got dressed and stood at the front door. "I just remembered something." He said as Yakira stood beside him. "I wrecked the Jaguar. I am out of cars."

"Close your eyes." She said.

"Why?"

"Just do it. It is a *haftaa*, a surprise.." She took his hand and led him out the door, across the front yard, and then they came to a stop. "Open your eyes." He opened his eyes; there in front of him was the completed Dodge Charger. The sunlight bounced off the deep dark metallic red paint, and the gray stripes that ran up the center of the hood, and down the back edge of the front fenders, across the air vents where the Super Bee name plate was placed, over the doors and rear quarters, ending with a large circle decal with the words 'Killer Bee.' The center of the circle was a colorful bumble bee with the letter 'S' on its thorax, its back legs spinning wide tires, as flames shot out from under the tires.

Ryder slipped his hand over the front of the hood, the twin hold down pins, and a larger version of the decal that was on the rear quarters was on the hood, at the front edge. Gene was standing there beside the car.

"I thought the best color for you was blood-red. I even matched it to my own blood. Ryder ran his hand over the stripe. "The stripes are for Yakira. Metallic Gunmetal Gray."

"How did you get this done so quickly?" Ryder asked as he looked into the inside of the car, with its black and gray striped interior and the Killer Bee nameplate on the instrument panel, and in the middle of the rear seat back and the door panels.

"By letting all other repairs go, working day and night." Gene said. Ryder rose up and looked over the roof at him. "Your little pal there can be very tough when she wants something done."

Blood Necklace

"I told him we needed a car. This car!" She said as he glanced back at her. "He found the slotted mag wheels, but Gene didn't have any 1971 taillights, so I had him get the ones from your wrecked 1972 down at the lake house." He went around to the back of the car and looked at the thin taillights. It was the final touch that just set this car apart from all the others.

Gene walked around to the front of the car. "Time to see her heart." He pulled the hold down pins and opened the hood. "She may not go quite as fast as your Ferrari, but with 550 horses she is going to come close. She also has a modern suspension under it, so she is going to handle unlike any other Charger out there." Ryder looked at the massive 440 ci power plant, its chrome valve covers, heavy-duty radiator. "And something that no other Charger has- a one of kind handmade Shaker hood scoop. There is only one other thing to do." Gene said.

"What is that?"

"Drive it." He said, holding up the keys. Ryder reached up took the keys. He walked over and held open the door for Yakira. "My lady in pink, your ride awaits." The door shut with a solid metallic clang. He slid down into the driver's seat, and he could smell the freshness of vinyl and hear it squeak as he bent forward and turned the key. The starter whirled and the engine came to life. The Jag had its style, the Ferrari its air of mystique, but there was nothing more pleasing to his ears than this sound.   Ryder's fingers curled around the soft leather rim steering wheel. His other hand slid down onto the floor shifter, he pressed down on the brake and slipped it down into drive. His foot slammed to the floor and the smoke boiled out from the rear tires as the wild ponies roared out of the dual exhaust, and the Charger shot forward. Ryder swung the steering wheel around, and the car executed a 180 degree turn in the street. "You're going to get your crown in heaven for this one, Gene." Ryder said before driving off.

He pulled into the back parking lot of the funeral home, the sound of the exhaust made Thom open the back door; he gazed at the gleaming Charger. "Only you would be driving a car that makes a Ferrari look normal." He walked up to the car as Ryder got out and held the door open for Yakira. "Well come on you two, let's see a different show."

198

"Back to the basement?" Yakira asked, disheartened, that again she would be feeling that cold icy breath breathing down on her.

"Actually, no." Thom said, walking past the elevator door and on through the hall as they followed him. "The feds took his body." He stopped and turned back to them, "My guess is they are going to sweep this all under the rug." He turned and went into his office where he would meet with customers as they planned out the funeral for their loved ones. He sat down in the chair behind the desk. "Who is going to listen to me? After all, I am just some silly county coroner." Even though he had a medical degree, and was one of the top M.E.'s in St. Louis County for five years.

"We will believe you, Double T." Ryder said as he sat down in the chair in front of the desk.

"It was murder, wasn't it?" Yakira said, sitting down in the chair next to Ryder.

"Indeed it was murder." He pulled out a file with photos in it. He placed it on top of the desk, and opened it, revealing photos of L.J. He picked one up and handed it over to Yakira "But unlike any mob hit I have seen. He died of cardiac arrest."

"I thought you said he was murdered."

"Believe it not, a heart attack can be murder. Depends on the weapon used, a triple decker deep fried wrapped in bacon cheeseburger is not murder. But this…" Thom opened the center drawer of his desk and pulled out a Cardio-hypo with a six inch long large gauge needle and placed it on the desk. "This is."

"What is this?" Ryder asked as he picked up the hypo.

"I have seen these on TV; they jam them into the heart of people that are having heart attacks." Yakira said taking the hypo from Ryder.

"Ding-Ding! Give this young lady the prize."

"How do you know this happened?" Ryder asked as Yakira placed the hypo back on the desk.

199

" A few years back in St. Louis. We had a death angel."

"A what?" Yakira asked.

"It is a killer who believes that they are doing God's will, usually by killing those who are terminally ill." Ryder explained.

"Anyway I was the one who spotted it. All the victims had a single red spot on their chest just over the heart." Thom picked up another photo and laid it down on the desk in front of them. "Just like this one!" Ryder picked up the photo of a close up of L.J.'s chest, showing a small red dot.

"Couldn't this have been done by the paramedics?" Ryder asked as he laid the photo back down on the desk.

"Could have, but did not. He was dead when they found him and they did not use this. "

"Could anybody do that?" Yakira asked.

"Yes, it doesn't take any special skill, but to hit the heart you would have to know some basic anatomy. Such as a paramedic, doctor, a nurse."

Yakira turned to Ryder and together they said. "Maureen."

Maureen's house was on top of a hill at the end the street, in a neighbor of working middle class families. The house was the typical city house, a two-story white cape cod with black shutters and a red brick chimney on one end. Slim evergreen trees placed strategically at intervals for interest to the eye, the so-called 'eye-candy' that would most likely please any prospective buyer of the place. At the side and leading to the rear of the house was a white arbor entwined with his stepmother's prized red "Dublin Bay" climbing roses and a "Duchess of Edinburgh" double white clematis, another pleasing sight, and another reason for Ryder to swear he would never have these plants on any place he owned.

Ryder turned the Killer Bee around at the cul-de-sac, and parked in front of the house, behind a white Dodge sedan. The driver of the sedan looked up in the rearview mirror, seeing them; he got out of the sedan. It was Father Anthony. He walked over to Ryder but didn't say a word. Ryder held the door open for Yakira. Again not a word was said as they followed Ryder up to the front door. He started to ring the bell but noticed that door was ajar, Ryder pushed and it opened with a moan and a squeak.

The living room furnished in a formal style with tapestry covered wing chairs flanking the fireplace and an antique sofa covered with silk damask, also more of Maureen's Ozark high society style. He continued through the long hallway with pictures of dead and living family members lining the walls, there was hardly an inch of space between them, all because Maureen said "there should be nothing in the formal rooms belonging to the family." They continued through the all-white coldly antiseptic kitchen out the back door.

Both Yakira and Father Anthony followed Ryder as he stepped out into a flower garden, complete with all the normal flowers of late summer. Everything that could be crammed into hanging baskets and placed in pots was here, from wax begonias to marigolds. Anything that could be bought at the local discount store or any local greenhouses could be found here, showing again that Ryder's stepmother had never had an original thought of her own; she just went along with the "crowd". At the far end of the back yard was a large black jack oak tree, with a redwood bench sitting under its massive shade.

Maureen was dressed in a beige pantsuit with high-heeled sandals, and was sitting at a glass table under a bright yellow umbrella that was directly in the center of the flower garden. In the middle of the table was a large clear pitcher of iced tea with several slices of lemon floating in it, and four glasses. "Richard!" She said, seeing him. "And Father Anthony. Isn't this a nice surprise?"

She looked at Yakira; she had known her since the day she was born. She smiled at her, then turned back to Ryder and asked. "Well Richard, who is this wonderful young girl with you?"

"I am Yakira."

"That is a beautiful name. What does it mean?"

Yakira looked at Ryder, confused, then over to Father Anthony, who was also confused. "Just go along with whatever she says." Ryder whispered.

"It means precious one."

"Well, your name certainly fits you."

Lying on the brick patio near Maureen's feet were a pair of red patent leather high-heeled shoes, and a bottle of bleach, she had used a rag and she was trying to clean something off one of the shoes. He stood there for what seemed hours, but in reality was only a few seconds. "Everyone please have a seat, Father." She said, pouring him a glass of tea, as he sat down in the chair next to Ryder, and Yakira to the right of Ryder who sat directly across from Maureen. "I was so hoping that I would get guests today. So many days go by and I don't see anyone."

She poured another glass and handed it to Yakira and said "for the precious one in my boy's life." She poured another glass and set it down in front of Ryder. "And my son, the greatest detective in the state of Missouri. I have been seeing you on the news, how you caught that nasty killer. And when you were on with Megyn Kelly I had all my friends come." She turned to Father Anthony and continued. "You remember?"

Ryder wasn't sure how to react, what she was talking about happened almost three years ago. Luckily father Anthony knew exactly how to answer. "Yes that was some event, and that pot roast was so good that you cooked." He patted at his stomach. "Really stuck to your ribs."

"Well, I know how you like your roast, father." Maureen looked over at Yakira who had lifted the glass of tea to her lips. "So! How many children do you want?" Yakira choked, spitting out the tea. Ryder wasn't sure if it what Maureen said or the fact that her tea had way too much lemon and way too little artificial sweetener.

"What!" Yakira said gasping for a breath. "But we're not even…" Before she could get the explanation out Maureen continued.

"Just wondering if I was going to be a grandmother."

"I told you that we are not….." Ryder began to explain.

Father Delany reached over and grabbed Ryder's arm and whispered "Remember, love over hate."

"We haven't got that far, we are just planning our wedding."

Again Yakira choked on the tea. "We are?" She looked over at Ryder, puzzled, the corners of his lips turned up. "Oh! I mean yes we are."

Maureen reached over and patted Yakira's hand. "What are you colors going to be?"

"Red and pink?" A confused Yakira answered.

"Oh that would be great! Oh shoot! And I had the perfect pair of shoes to wear." She reached down and picked up the high heels. "But they are stained now."

Ryder looked down at the shoes and the toes were covered with several dark colored spots. He looked back up at her and asked. "With what?"

Without blinking she looked over at him and said "Blood."

"Whose blood is it?"

"I didn't get the name. Just some pig." She said coldly, as she reached down and picked up the rag and went back to cleaning the shoes. "You are a detective." She said stopping and looking up at him again. "You must have gotten blood on your shoes. How do you get it off?"

"You don't." He replied cautiously. "It soaks into the leather; you never get it out."

"Oh shucky darn!" She said, tossing the rag down on the table and holding the shoe up. "I loved these shoes and they were so perfect for the wedding." She set the shoe down on the table. "Hope Pascal can get me another pair. She took a sip of tea. "Mmmm. That is some good tea." She looked over at Father Anthony, grinning insanely. "Don't you agree, Father Anthony?"

"Oh yes, some of the best."

Ryder removed his sunglasses and laid them down on the table. He crossed his arms as he leaned down on the table. "Don't worry, mother dear." He said with compassion. I will buy you some more."

"Don't I have a wonderful son?" She grinned again as she looked over at Father Anthony.

"Mother." Ryder said as he reached over and took a hold of her hand. She turned back to him, she was still smiling. "Can you tell me how the blood got on your shoes?"

"From a filthy pig." She said cheerfully.

"What pig was that, mother?" He said, sounding concerned about what her answer might be.

"That stupid butcher. I told him I wanted liver. He knew I needed beef liver. "He gives me pork liver." She said, looking over at Father Anthony. "As I have told you before father my daughter and my son, they are Jewish." She turned back to Ryder and continued. "I tried to get rid of it, but it fell on my shoes. I have been trying to get it cleaned up before they got here. You know the no pork thing." She turned back to the father. "It says so in the bible. Somewhere. I think Leviticus?"

"Leviticus 11 verse 7. I don't know if I have met your children, Maureen."

"Oh, of course you have, Father. I have a picture of them. Oh, it is inside." She got up from the table and went into the house.

"What is wrong with her, Ricky?" Yakira lowered her voice, leaning over to him. "She acts like she doesn't know who I am."

"I don't know, but just play along." Ryder said, quickly hushing up as she reappeared carrying a photo in a frame.

"Here they are, Father." Maureen said as she sat back down. Father Anthony's eyes opened wide as he leaned forward in the chair, looking at the photo in a silver frame.

"Nice looking kids, Maureen." Father Anthony said, letting his words slowly fall from his mouth before handing the photo to Ryder. Ryder took the photo and saw the photo that was taken on prom night. It was of him and Annalisa and an eight year old Yakira. Ryder handed the photo to Yakira, her mouth dropped open as she saw it. She handed it back to Maureen. Father Anthony added. "So Maureen, where is your daughter now?"

"Annalisa….My dear little daughter." She said softly, again the grin left her face and tears began to puddle up in her eyes.

Ryder leaned over to uncle and whispered. "Get her some help." Father Anthony got up and walked over to stand under the shade tree and made a call. "Mother, when was the last time you saw Annalisa?"

"She came by and told me that blasted L.J. knew our secret, and he was blackmailing my baby girl." She stood up and Ryder stood up also, watching every move she made. Her face twisted with rage. "I had to stop him! I told Becky we had to do it!" She stopped next to a large hanging flower basket. "She didn't want to do it. She said maybe it was time everyone knew and that she had to let Annalisa go. I had to be the one. I had to stop him." Maureen hands clasped together and she looked up at the sky. "God told me it was okay."

She slipped her hand down inside the hanging basket. "I had to stop him." She pulled out a large syringe with a long needle. "I plunge it right into his chest. He gasped and rolled around then he was still. After what he did to my baby I thought it was…" A smile beamed across her face as she calmly added. "God told me it was okay… it wasn't murder…" She turned to Ryder as he stood beside her, and carefully took the syringe from her as she said very harshly. "…it was justice!"

Chapter 30

Three cruisers arrived, parking behind the Killer Bee. Just as Father Anthony requested, they arrived at normal speed, no lights and no siren. Even the ambulance arrived the same way. The paramedics pushed open the side gate and wheeled in a gurney with a straight jacket lying on it. "You don't need to use that." Father Anthony said, holding his hand up.

"Father, you said she has lost her mind." The paramedic said.

"She has." He said, looking over at his shoulder at Maureen sitting at the table, still sipping on the glass of tea, talking about how good it was. He turned back to the paramedic. "But you don't have to destroy someone's dignity. She will walk out. "

"Why do you care?"

"Is she not a child of God?"

"But she murdered somebody. She should be going to jail."

"That is up to the courts of law and God Himself to judge, not you." The father walked over to the table, kneeled down beside Maureen and cupped his hands over hers.

"I am so tired, Father Anthony." She said, turning to him. Her words were low and drug out as if she were very sleepy. "I just want a place where I can rest."

"He who is heavily laden and burdened with a heavy load, put your yoke on me and I will give you rest.' Go with these people Maureen, they will give you a place of rest."

She looked up at Ryder, who had given the officer the syringe that he had placed in a plastic bag. "Will you come to visit, son?"

"I—of course I will."

"And you will bring your sister?" She asked as Father Anthony and Ryder stood on each side of her and helped her walk to the ambulance.

"Sure." He replied as they helped her step up into the back of the ambulance. "Just as soon as they tell us we can. Goodbye, mother." He shut the door and walked back. He sat down on the bench that was under the tree.

One by one the squad cars and the ambulance left, leaving only stillness once again, the pleasant songs of a sparrow resting on a branch, looking down on the neatly manicured back yard surrounded with a wooden privacy fence. A red breasted robin hopped along, turning its head, watching, listening carefully, waiting for just the right moment to go in for the kill, it didn't matter that the worm was nearly as long as the bird itself, it would seem that the bird should just give up, and let the worm go, it would be easier. It was not the bird's nature, so the robin just fought back; never letting up till it gobbled the worm down.

"It is in that house, isn't it. The answer I am looking for?" Ryder stared down at the ground. "I remember what L.J. warned me about, opening a gate to my own personal hell." Ryder turned his head and looked at his uncle. "I know what I am going to find in there. Why I am drawn to find it, when I know it is going to destroy my life?"

"I can't answer that."

"Why?"

"Because of regardless of what you have heard from preachers on TV. God doesn't give the answers to all things. Some we have to find on our own."

"I have to know." Ryder said standing up and walking back to the house and inside the kitchen, passing by Yakira who was cleaning up the dishes. He continued on into the hall of family photos. He looked at the photos, photos of him as a child, in his football uniform, to his policeman uniform the in the row just below photos of Annalisa from a baby to a teenager in her cheerleader outfit, to her wedding photos. "Photos just like any other mother." He said in a whisper.

"What?" Yakira asked as she walked into the hall.

"Blonde hair and blue eyes." He said as he carefully examined the photos hanging on the wall. He came to one, a picture of newborn taken in the hospital nursery. He showed it to Yakira. "Do you know this photo?"

"Yes, it was when Annalisa was born."

"Now I know."

Chapter 31

How many times he had parked here, oddly enough in a Dodge Charger, waiting, watching for the door to open and see Annalisa bound out and race for the car, her arms full of books, making it just in time for the first period at school; walking to the door, waiting for her for a date. Those days would never happen again, for she died and just like her those memories were about also to die.

Ryder got out and walked straight towards the door, just leaving Yakira sitting there, she got out of the car and quickly ran after him. He didn't knock, he just opened the door. Yakira kissed her fingers and reached up and touched the *mitzvah* , he stood there gazing up at the staircase as Bubbie stood on the third step from the bottom.

"Where is she?" Ryder asked with a tone that was more like a detective, than a friend." Bubbie's gaze slipped down onto the photo frame that Ryder was holding.

"You know, don't you?" Bubbie stepped down from the stairs. "I think it is time you know the truth", she said as she glanced over at her granddaughter. "The both of you."

Bubbie turned and led them back past the stairs into the family room that was to the right behind the living room. They followed her into room, decorated with well-worn over stuffed furniture that was covered in faded blue upholstery, and over to a love seat, one that he knew well, having spent many a night sitting here next to Annalisa doing homework. He shook that memory from his mind, as it had to die and die right now, as he sat down next to Yakira. Bubbie turned and walked out of the room as she passed by her daughter-in-law Rebekah in the hall she said. "It is time all the lies stop."

Rebekah nodded and walked into the room and sat down in the chair that was facing the loveseat. "Annalisa was adopted." She said. "And Maureen was her mother."

"I know that." Ryder said as he turned the frame over and removed the backing cardboard. There written on the back of the photo was the date: Annalisa's birthday. "I don't know how I could have been so stupid not to not see it. The blonde hair, the blue eyes, pale skin."Ryder removed the photograph from the frame, and continued. "In biology class when we were studying about genes. Brown eyes are dominate genes and how we get our height, hair color, skin coloring from our parents or other relatives. She reasoned because her great-great grandmother was tall and had blonde hair and blue eyes that was where she got them." Ryder got up and moved over in front of Rebekah and squatted down, he looked up at her. "But then we started studying blood types and how the parent's blood type passes on to the child. Strange thing, both she and I had the same blood type, and a very rare type. AB Negative. We just thought that it made us have even more in common. But we have more in common than just that, don't we Rebekah?" Ryder turned his head sideways and said as calmly as he could. "The same father." He stood up. "She was my sister, wasn't she?"

Rebekah swallowed hard and nodded as she looked up at him, her eyes began to fill with tears. Ryder walked over to the window and glanced out at the back yard looked out. "All the time growing up, when we played together, when my mom died…" He turned back to her; his forehead wrinkled, his eyes narrowed, shielded by the sunglasses. "….our first kiss. " Ryder's raised his voice. "*And you didn't say a damn thing!*"

He marched over in front of her and sat back down on the loveseat next to Yakira again. He sat there staring at Rebekah, waiting for her to say something, anything. Ryder got and walked towards the entry way and she spoke. "I never wanted to hurt you, Ricky, nor did I want to hurt Annalisa." He stopped, but didn't turn around. I don't care what blood says." Rebekah stood up and walked over to him. "She was my baby girl. I was the one who took care of her." He hand shook as she began to reach for him, but she pulled her hand back.

"When did you know?"

Rebekah turned and looked at Yakira who sat there on the love seat facing the wall, her arms fold over her chest. She turned back to Ryder. Annalisa turned five. We got this message saying she was Annalisa's real mother, and if we didn't give her five thousand she was going to let it be known that the adoption was illegal and they would take her away from us. Each year she would call us and demand the payment."

210

"You knew it was Maureen, why didn't you go to the cops?" He said turning around and facing her.

"We were afraid. We saw the news reports where children were taken away and given back to the natural mother and that was with a legal adoption. We couldn't lose her." She buried her face in her hands and sobbed. Rebekah looked over at her daughter still seated on the loveseat. "I am sorry."

Yakira stood up and asked "Mom, when did Annalisa know it?"

"That night?"

"What night?" Ryder asked.

"The night of graduation. " Rebekah lifted her head. "The night you proposed.

Ryder, hearing her, walked out of the room and down to the end of the hall and rested his head on one of the multiple panes of the window. He could feel the warmth from the sun outside. He struggle with holding in his emotions as he continued to listen. "She loved you. There was nothing that was going to stop her. She was going to leave her faith, her family, and her whole life behind. She didn't care; all she wanted was you."

Rebekah drew in a shivering breath then said. "I can still see the look on her face when I told her." Ryder lifted his head and swallowed hard. He looked back at her, then without saying a word he walked back past her, he turned and looked at Yakira standing in the family room; again he didn't say a word. He just walked towards the front door. Rebekah buried her face in her hands again and began to sob even more. "All we wanted was a child. " The front closed with a slam.

"The night she was killed." Yakira asked, fearing to speak of what came next. "Did you see Annalisa?"

"Yes." Rebekah said her words mumbled in her hands. "She was here. She went upstairs and came back down; I told her I loved her. She didn't say a thing; she walked out, slamming the door." She raised her head. "My daughter, my baby died hating me. It is all my fault. "

"Did you kill her?"

"Are you *meshuga!*." She shot back before her tone calmed and she added. "No I did not! L.J. killed her."

"I had to ask, mom." Yakira placed her arm around her mother. She leaned her head over next to her mother's and added in a calm tone. "Annalisa loved you mom. And so do I."

Outside the rumble of dual exhaust could be heard, followed by the howl of tires spinning on the pavement. "You know where he is going." Rebekah said, "Go to him. He needs you."

Chapter 32

Just as he always did when Ryder was confused, he ran. He did it when his mother died, he did when Annalisa turned him down, he did it when she died, and now when he had to let the memories go, he ran to the highest thing he could find in town-Water Tower hill. Yakira knew exactly where to find him, sitting there on the hood of the Charger, the towering silver colored Goliaths glaring down at him as he stared at a approaching thunderhead, rising up into the heavens, looking like a distant mountain, the flashes of lightning from the snow capped tops. How he wished he could be that high, that far away from everything.

"An iced tea for your thoughts." Yakira said as she walked up beside him and handed him a white foam cup. "Sweet. Half twist of lemon."

"You make it?" He asked with a half smile.

"No, but I did *schlep* it all the up here from the drug store." He looked over at her and she tried to grin.

"You don't expect me to get over this quick, do you?" He asked, removing the plastic lid from the cup and taking a drink of the tea.

"She was my sister too, you know." She said, sucking the tea up through the straw of her own cup.

"That is just the thing. Before, you knew she was your sister. Nothing has changed for you. But everything I thought about her, every memory I have of her." The low rumble of thunder made him look at the approaching storm. "That has to change now. I can have no memories." As lightning flashed across the sky he turned back to her. "Where do I go from here?"

"What do you mean, where do *you* go from here?" Yakira said before sucking on the straw again. "Is that all you are here for? Annalisa? "

"Who else would I be here for?"

"*What about me!*" She demanded. "Do I matter in all of this?" She pushed herself up on the hood of the car and sat down next to him. He didn't look at her; he just kept looking at the storm that was quickly approaching. "Can't you see that I love you?" I have since I was eight years old." Dropping her gaze down she watched her feet dangle over the tire. "And nothing has changed."

Thunder rumbled again and a sudden gust of wind blew over them, making her hair blow into her face. He turned to her. "One thing has changed." She turned to him. "You are no longer that little girl." He carefully brushed the hair back out of her face. "You are one beautiful woman. And any man that gets to love you should count himself lucky." He placed his hand under her chin, lifting her head up, letting his fingers stroke the side of her cheek. He kissed her gently as she placed her hand behind his head, letting her fingers curl into his hair. Thunder boomed over them, rattling the windows of the car.

"What to get lucky?" She asked, flashing a broad smile. She tossed the tea she was holding away. She wrapped her arms around his neck. Letting her lips part, she captured his mouth. The kiss was hard and passionate, as she twisted her head around. Her insides were churning, her toes tingled, her stomach twirled as she let her fingers tangle in his hair. Her heart was beating so fast and so loud, she couldn't hear the thunder or anything else but her breath as she pulled away for just long enough to take a deep breath before pushing him backwards onto the hood, his head resting on the hood scoop. She opened her mouth and pushed her tongue deep into his mouth. Her breath was quivering out of her as she pinned his hands to the hood. With another clap of thunder the rain began pouring down on them. She looked up at the overcast sky, then back down at him. "Just blessings from heaven sweetie, that is all it is." Drenched and soaked, she just smiled and kissed him again.

They returned to Yakira's parent's house. "You two took like a pair of drowned cats. What in the world happened to you two?" Bubbie asked as they walked in through the door. She looked at her granddaughter and notice her lipstick smeared down over her chin. "Or should I not ask."

"Bubbie." Yakira blushed, hiding her face with her hand. "We just got caught in the storm."

"We took a walk and got caught in a downpour." Ryder said.

Bubbie walked over to him and patted his cheek. "You may be the professional interrogator, but I am an old Jewish woman and you can't fool me." She took her thumb and rubbed the lipstick from the corner of his mouth before she held her thumb up to her granddaughter's lips. "Perfect match, wouldn't you say, detective?"

She rubbed her fingers over the lapel of his jacket. "Rain and wool do not mix. But I will see what I can do." She helped him removed his jacket and stood there. "The pants, too."

"Bubbie!" Ryder complained.

"Oh *Motek*, it isn't like I haven't seen it all before. Sweetie, I was there when you were born. Come on, give them up. I also changed your diapers and wipe that little *tukhas* of yours." She held her hands out as Ryder unbuttoned, unzipped and pulled his pants off. He stood there, the pink shirt stuck to his chest and hanging down, barely revealing his red colored briefs, the gun still strapped in his holster.. He handed her the pants. She turned to her granddaughter and asked "Have you?"

"Bubbie!" Yakira said, embarrassed again.

All right you two, upstairs and take a shower. They were half way up the stairs when Bubbie shouted at them. "And not together. Separately."

"It is that, or I join you two."

"Bubbie!" Yakira cried out again.

After her shower Yakira wrapped up in a big fluffy cotton towel, then made her way down the hall to her grandmother's bedroom, and sat down on the edge of the big bed, and its overstuffed feather mattress. She remembered when she was a little girl and it would storm, she would run in here and crawl up on this mattress, she could feel her grandmother hug her and tell her that everything was okay and then they would share a chocolate bar.

"So, what happened out there?" Bubbie asked as she sat down beside her on the bed, unwrapping the chocolate bar. "Am I going to be a great-grandmother?'

"Nothing happened!" Yakira said firmly as her grandmother broke off a piece of candy and handed it to her, then broke off another piece and bit it herself. "Well…" Yakira said with a grin as she bit down on the chocolate. "We did kiss." She turned and looked at her grandmother and smiled. "And not a friendly brother sister type kiss." She popped the rest of the piece of chocolate into her mouth. 'It was full of passion."

Her grandmother broke off another piece of the chocolate bar and handed it to Yakira. "Is he going to stay, or are you going with him?" She said as she broke off a piece of chocolate and ate it.

"I don't know, Bubbie. I just know that…" Yakira stood and ate her chocolate as she walked over to the window and saw the droplets of the rain collecting on the screen, some suspended for a moment before running down, leaving behind a crooked trail, till they disappeared behind the window sill.

"Do you know what drives him?"

"I guess…"

" Murder." Bubbie said as she stood up. Yakira turned back to her grandmother. "He has been that way ever since his Danielle died."

"His mother? Are you saying that….?"

"I don't know. But Ricky always did. There are things that boy doesn't want to remember about his home life, that was why he and Annalisa were so close, he found shelter here with us. Those memories of Annalisa are what protected him from those memories. This whole thing is not over. That urging, that need to know, it is going to drive him right back to find out who killed Annalisa. I am just afraid that either you help him or both of you are going to end up the same way.-dead."

****

Many days passed, and days became weeks as the last golden rays of September sun became the biting winds of October. *Yom Kippur* came and passed, and Ryder found himself entwined into the act of letting grievances become forgiveness, of letting go of memories that could never be, and holding on to hope for things that could be.

The leaves began to change color, bright red, yellow and orange, turning the hills of the city of the Seven Valleys into a colorful array, bringing a parade of eyes to gaze upon it, before they packed up their campers, finding their way back to the place that they came from, leaving the campsites naked, waiting to be clothed with the excitement again next year.

Once again Roaring River belonged to the local people; they could be selfish and enjoy the scenes that no others could as the leaves would fall from the trees. Each one seemingly following its own path as they rode the nipping autumn wind to the ground, only to be picked up once again by the wind, to find its final resting place along the banks of the river.

Yakira sat on the rocks of the remains of what is known as Devil's Kitchen. Once a cave that was used during the civil war by rebel troops, and moonshiners, it had collapsed, and now was just a disorganized pile of dark-colored rocks. Wrapped up in a bright pink quilted jacket, she zipped it up around her and shoved her hands down into the pockets, as the wind gusted out of the north, showering her with colored leaves that landed in her hair.

She heard the crunch of leaves under foot as someone approached. It was Father Anthony. She had called him to meet her here. "How are you, my dear?" He said sitting down on the stone next to her. "And how is my nephew? I haven't seen him for awhile."

"Doing great! He went for a walk by himself. This thing with Annalisa; he just hasn't got over it." She said, pulling the leaves from her hair. "But we are both working at the gun shop, thinking of even building a new building. We have every meal together; it is like we are married, but…"

"Without the good stuff?" Father Anthony laughed.

"No—well yes—well huh…." She hesitated; even making her own cheeks flush. "All this time. I have told him I love him, but…"

"He hasn't told you?"

"Yes." She sighed, looking down at the leaves on the ground as they were caught up in a small whirlwind and drifted across the well made trail.

"He is afraid too."

"What is he afraid of?"

"You." He reached over and took a hold of her hand. "More precisely, afraid of losing you." He stood up, letting go of her hand, and stared out into the woods. "Before his mother died Ricky was one of the most loving kids you ever knew, always wanting a hug and telling you he loved you." He turned back to her. "After she died he just shut off."

"So, am I just wasting my time, Uncle Tony? That he is never going to…" She dropped her head down, not being able to finish. His placed his hands on the sides of her cheeks and lifted her head up.

"My dear only you can answer that. But I think someday he will say it and it will knock you right off your feet." He let go of her and began to walk back down the trail, just as Ryder rounded the trail back towards the rock. Father Anthony stopped and turned back to them. "The principal called me and wanted to know if you could come and pick up Annalisa's stuff at school. They want to reopen her room."

Chapter 33

It seemed strange pulling into the parking lot of the of Cassville R-4 school district, almost as if he were a foreigner walking into a land that he never knew. When he was here this was the high school, now it was part of the elementary school. The trees had grown a little taller and the sidewalks a little longer and the freedom locked away behind electronic doors. It almost brought a grin to his face as he remembered how he had thought of this place as a prison, and now it had become one.

"We have come to pick up Annalisa's things." Yakira said as they walked up to the glassed- in office that housed a gray-haired woman with large round plastic framed glasses seated at a desk.

"Oh, yes." The woman said pursing her lips and pushing the glasses up on her nose. "We will send someone down to box it all up."

"That is not acceptable." Ryder said. "We want to remove it ourselves."

"No, you are not acceptable! This is my school! I will decide who gets inside." She pointed her finger at them and then over to the bench next the wall. "You two have a seat over there. And we will send someone down to collect her belongings. It wasn't like it was a crime."

"She was murdered. And you are interfering with an investigation." Ryder said pulling his sunglasses off.

"Are you a police officer?"

"He is a homicide investigator in the state of Missouri." Yakira said.

"You have a badge? Show it to me." The woman said with a smirk.

"There is no need for that, Maxine. I know exactly who this man is." A man said, dressed in a medium blue suit, and dark blue tie. It reminded Ryder of old Mr. Frost, the high school principal. He approached the glass window; he looked about the same age as Ryder, and was nearly a half-foot shorter than Ryder. "Buzz him and Yakira in."

"I do not have them on my list." Maxine snapped back.

"Maxine, either buzz them in now, or buzz yourself right out to the unemployment line."

She did as she was instructed, and as they entered into the main part of school, a door opened and the man stepped out into the hall. Ryder looked at him again; he looked familiar but he just couldn't search his mind for the name. "Don't remember me, do you, Pale Ryder. Maybe I should run down field fifty yards and you throw me a bomb."

"Brad?" Ryder said; take a closer look at him. "Brad ''the Gazelle' Jackson." He turned to Yakira;" this guy was the best wide receiver the Wildcats ever had." He turned back to him. "What are you doing here?"

"I am the principal here."

"Well you did you did spend a lot of time in that office, so it makes sense you would move into it." Ryder laughed.

"Well at least I didn't have to walk down the hall telling every classroom I was sorry for disrupting finals because I rocketed a fire extinguisher down the hall."

"Yeah, I kind of only remember the fun it that, not the punishment. But you did help in carrying in Frost's bug."

"Those were the good old days. Thank God they are gone." Brad looked over at Yakira. "I am sorry about Annalisa. She was a good friend and a good teacher."

"You think we could get a look at her room?" Ryder asked.

"Sure, it is down in the old high school part." He said, leading the way down the hall. The colors had changed, the desks were smaller, and the halls were not decorated with Wildcat spirit, but with artwork that only a parent could love and posters for lunch room rules, how to properly sneeze or cough, classroom rules, eat right, sleep right.

Brad stopped in front of what Ryder remembered was room number 11; unlike all the other rooms, this one was dark. He unlocked the door and turned on the lights. The desks spread out into two rows in a semi-circle pattern.

"Her students loved her." He said. "After she was…"He paused, as if not wanting to say the word-murdered, "...after she died we shut the room up."

Brad continued to talk as Yakira went over to the closet and retrieved her sister's raincoat and umbrella. Ryder sat down at Annalisa's desk, and stared out at the student's desks. He began pulling the drawers open and pulled out her record book. "She liked doing it the old-fashioned way." Ryder flipped through the pages of the grade book, looking at the students names.

"Did she have any problems with any of her students?" Ryder asked.

"They all loved her! Voted favorite teacher five years in a row." Brad walked over to the windows, grabbed the cord and pulled the blinds, allowing sunlight to stream back into the room. 'This is worst thing we have ever had happen in this school. Kids have been asking a lot of questions. Been really tough on some." He glanced out across the yard to another brick building. He turned back to the classroom. . Especially one little lad, Timmy Regan."

"Regan?" Ryder asked, looking up at him. "Why does that name sound familiar?"

"His dad is Bobby Regan, who was the team manager in our senior year."

"Oh, yeah." Ryder moved so that Yakira could clean out the desk drawers and she placed the contents in a box. A box of gold stars, other stickers, and a small wooden box with a heart carved on it.

"Timmy lost his mother about a year ago. He looked at Annalisa as a replacement for her. His grades tumbled, but when he got into her class his grades went back up. Now they are going back down. He says it is because he is afraid."

"What is he afraid of?"

"He tells me that the one that killed that killed Mrs. Warner is going to get him."

Ryder looked over the student's desks. "Do you know which desk was his?"

"Over next to the window." Brad said. Ryder sat down at the student's desk, his legs cramped as he reached down under the seat. "All the children's stuff was collected and given back to them. What are you looking for?"

"Don't you remember being a kid?" Ryder said as he reached further back, feeling along the bottom of the seat. "Where you would hide things that you didn't..." Ryder felt a piece of paper, he pulled it free. It was notebook paper. He unfolded it and saw a child's writing. He grinned as he looked up. "Or maybe... do you remember your first crush?" Hand printed in bright purple crayon was:

"Mrs. Warner

I think you are the prettiest girl in school. You smell so good like flowers. I love you. Timmy.'

"He was in love with her." Ryder said as he stood up and handed the note to Brad.

"Miss Jenkins. He said as he handed the note back to Ryder. Every boy had a crush on her, including me. You know, I would stay after school and come back into the classroom just to see her."

"Brad, you might be on to something there. What if the kid did just what you did, he came back into the room and saw something he shouldn't have? Is there any way I can talk to Timmy?"

"In fact, I think there is. You two share more than just one love." Brad handed the note back to Ryder. "It is football."

The janitor let him into the Wildcat stadium and Ryder stood, right on the twenty yard line, this was where many drives down field began. There was a football lying on the ground and he picked it up, he could hear the cheers in his mind, as they stomped their feet and shouted: "Let's Go Cats! Let's Go!"

"Timmy, I want you to meet someone." Brad's voice brought Ryder back to an empty stadium. Brad walked up with an 8-year-old boy, with light sandy hair, wearing a striped t-shirt. In a way he reminded him of himself when he was that age. "Timmy, this is a good friend of mine. Rick Ryder. Together with your daddy we took the Cassville Wildcats to the state championship.

"Wow! Timmy said, wide-eyed as he shook Ryder's hand. "My daddy said 'they called you Pale Ryder because, when you took the air it put the fear of death into the other team.'"

"Something like that. Heard that you want to fill my shoes and take the Cats back to St. Louis?" Ryder toss the ball to leaned down acting as center as Timmy called out plays. Ryder hiked the kid the ball, then ran about ten yards and turned and caught the ball.

"How was that?" Timmy said after he quit dancing around in celebration.

Pretty good but you have to get a little more spin on. Want me to show you?"

"Yeah." Timmy said wide eyed.

Ryder looked over at Brad. "What about you? Up for Red 21 Kit-Cat."

"Been a long time. Okay." He stood up. Ryder called out some plays, grabbed the ball and drew back as Brad took off running as hard and fast as he could till he got to the 50 yard line, right on the Wildcat logo. Ryder drew back and let go with a perfect spiral that landed right into Brads hands.

"The secret, Timmy, is gripping it by the laces."

"Here—"you two go talk—"some more—"football while I go get a drink. "Brad said, trying to catch his breath as he handed the ball back to Ryder.

Let's go over and sit in the bleachers." Ryder and Timmy climbed till they were at the very top of the bleachers on the side line. You know, my mom watched me play my first game when I was about your age.

"My mom died."

"So did mine.. When I was 12 years old." Ryder handed the ball to the lad. "You know who helped me through it? "Your teacher, Ms. Warner." He glanced over at the boy who was looking down at the football he was twirling in his lap. "She was my best friend back then. Did she do that for you?" He nodded his head. "She was very special, wasn't she?" Again he nodded his head.

223

"Yes, she was real nice." He looked up at Ryder. "And pretty too."

"You know, we grew up together just right down the road. Then we moved away from each other, I couldn't wait to get to school to see her. Were you that way?" Timmy nodded his head. "And when she was in the school play I would stay after school just so I could see her practice." Ryder leaned on the backrest and continued. "You did that too, and when you peered in the room you saw someone trying to hurt her, didn't you?"

Timmy nodded.. Do you know who it was, Timmy? Again he nodded ferociously. "Can you tell me who it is?" He shook his head. "Why not? Because you're scared?"

Timmy nodded his head, and then looked up at Ryder. "He saw me! He grabbed me and told me if I said anything he would kill me."

"I won't let that happen, Timmy. But if you don't tell me who he is I can't stop him.

"His name is Mr. Watterson."

Chapter 34

Annalisa had been dead for more than a month, and it had been weeks since there had been any leads in her death, besides a veiled threat that this man named Watterson had made to her at school. He had no other connection to her. The threat, according to Timmy, was because of her faith, could it be that this was the motive for her murder, pure hatred? When Deputy Brian Thompson ran his name through the computer, it came up.

'Watterson, Steven, age 38, six foot 190 pounds hair dark brown, eyes black, Swastika tattoo on right upper arm, word HATE tattoo on left hand knuckles. Pervious know locations New York, Los Angeles, San Diego. Last known location San Francisco. Last known employment, Dock Worker, US Customs.

Ryder quickly made a phone call . 'Top of Deer Leap, Roaring River State Park. In thirty minutes."

He parked in front of the old CCC Lodge, built in the 1930's, during the depression. Three stories high, with a gray stone foundation that made up the first floor and the ends, the upper portions were wooden planks painted to appear weathered and worn. A second story supported the third floor with six pairs of heavy wooden beams that separated the multiple pane glass French doors that led out onto the balcony; curled wooden beams supported the bottom of the balcony. The third floor featured normal size multiple pane glass windows. The wood shingles, the stone fireplaces at each end, and the wooden hitching railing in front, made it look as it were right out of the Civil War.

Yakira looked up at the third floor, saw the back of a wood rocking chair; she could swear she saw it rocking back and forth. "Ever get the feeling that someone is watching you here?" She asked as she dropped her gaze back down to him.

He twisted his head around, over to the river, up the hills on both sides, over towards the hatchery and to the steps that led up to the second story of the lodge. "I don't see any one here." He took her hand and led her along a sidewalk that was laid along the stone walls that led toward the hatchery and the roaring falls that became just a flash of white water, speeding past underneath them as they walked by and the roar faded.

The fog floated as if it were a disembodied spirit above the lake. Ryder stopped just long enough to look for the solid back sedan, with its government plates.

"She is here. He said. He still continued to guide her along the pool and the up the trail marked Deer Leap. It began if a set of creepy looking stairs leading up the hill to a trail along the side of Spring Pool, as it twisted back to the right, the sound of rushing water could again be heard. As the trees and brushed cleared, it revealed wooden planks, built over the stone pillar that was known as Deer Leap. Special Agent Alexander was dressed in a gray plaid skirt and matching jacket, and a bright red blouse, her hair hanging loosely on her shoulders. She was leaning back against a large boulder, staring up at the bright blue sky.

"Okay, Alex!" Ryder said forcefully as he removed his sunglasses. "I want all of it." He walked over next to her. "And no more holding back! You owe it to me, and to her."

Alex walked over to the guard rail and looked over it into the spring pool below. "I just find it so peaceful here. Watching the eagles fly. Hearing the water the …."

"Enough, Isabelle." Ryder said as he walked over to her. "Watterson. I want him."

"How do you know about him?"

"He threatened Annalisa. When I saw his name I remembered it from the Kansas City Butcher case. He was a suspect. Until after you questioned him and then he was cleared. What did he tell you?"

"I can't tell you."

"Why not!" He demanded as she turned and walked back toward the rock. "And don't you dare tell me it is because it is classified. I want him for murder."

"What about the murder of thousands of people?" Her words made him turn and face her. "Maybe millions of people?"

"What do you mean?"

226

"It is a classified case, I can't tell you."

No more!" He pointed his finger and stormed over to her. "No more lies. No more trying to be cute. Or question me. I want the truth. All the truth! Or I swear to God I will throw you off here!"

"I am trying to prevent the start of the battle of Armageddon."

"What!" Ryder drew back in amazement, lowering his sunglasses and gazing at her over the top of the frames. "That is the dumbest…"

"It is about Black Midnight."

"Never heard of them."

I have." Yakira said as she walked over to them. Ryder turned and looked over his shoulder at her as she continued. "They are the ones that are painting all the stuff on our buildings. They are a hate group."

"They are full blown terrorists." Alex said. "Watterson is my key to them. I am making a deal with him. He finds the ship that a shipment of guns is going out on and I protect him."

"What?" Ryder asked in disbelief. "This isn't New York or D.C. this is Cassville, MO."

"They are everywhere Ryder, and congress won't do a damn thing about it." Alex stood up again and walked over to the rail and looked down at the crystal collective pool below. "They are too concerned with getting reelected next year." She turned back around and leaned back against the rail. "Including the late wonderful *Speaker of the House Scott Warner*." She added with a tone of disgust.

"Are you telling me he was a terrorist?"

"No, he did it for the money, two and half billion dollars; the money is coming out of Iran. Their hope is to make it look as if America has turned against Israel, leaving Israel all alone, bringing on the battle of Armageddon." Alex looked over at Yakira and pleaded with her. "Don't you agree saving Israel is more important than finding your sister's murderer?"

Ryder felt his phone vibrate in his pocket. Someone had sent him a text message. He read it. "Stopped Watterson with a busted taillight. He is in custody. Want to question him?"

****

There was a surprise waiting for Ryder and Yakira when they arrived back at county jail. Deputy Thompson met them outside wearing a broad smile, just as they got out of the car. Ryder held the door open for Yakira as the deputy walked around the car.

"You won't believe it!" He said with delight, proud of his achievement. "I just got him to confess to murdering Annalisa."

"What?" Ryder said, confused how this happened so quickly. He removed his sunglasses and shut the door.

"I went in and within a few questions he admitted it! "You both want to come over for supper? I think Lee Ann is making meatloaf." He turned to Yakira and asked "You can eat that, can't you?"

Something did not seem right to him, Ryder knew what kind of guy this man was. He had questioned him before, he was offensive and aloof, not wanting to answer his questions, why would he suddenly admit to one the most evil crimes known to the sins of mankind?

"He even knew it was yellow colored cable. That is one bit of information that we never released to the public. So he must have done it. So you want to come over for meatloaf?"

"Huh?"

"Meatloaf?"

"No, I suddenly lost my appetite. Ryder said, staring back towards the holding cells. "Did he say why?"

"That is the strange thing about it." Deputy Thompson said as he rubbed his hand over his chin. "He said he 'would tell you.' "

He mentioned me by name?"

228

"Well…" He dragged his words out as if he didn't want to repeat the words of hate. "…his exact words. His words, not mine. His words! 'That big freaking Jew loving cop and his stinking kike girlfriend'." He turned to Yakira. "I am sorry to say that."

"I have heard it more than once in my life, Brian."

Ryder sat in the interrogation room at the table once again, with Yakira right next to him. He didn't like this set up. It was fundamental that during questioning he always have the upper hand, that he would be the one directing the interview; the prisoner could never do it. Now, though, that was exactly what was happening.

The door opened and Deputy Thompson escorted the prisoner inside, dressed in prison issue black and white jumpsuit. His head was clean-shaven and an over growth of whiskers was on his face. His dark eyes were like a diamond tipped drill bit boring right through Ryder as Deputy Thompson helped him sit down in the chair across from them. There were more tattoos on his arms, including a flaming skull tattoo, according to Alex a sign of the group Black Midnight. He looked over at Ryder and snarled a grin. He looked at Deputy Thompson who was standing nearby, next to the door. "I don't say a thing till he gets out of here."

Ryder turned to Deputy Thompson. "It is okay, Brian. If he gets out of hand; I will break his bloody neck."

"Still the freaking tough guy, huh?"Watterson said, leaning over the table toward him. He glared back at Brian. "Get him out of here. Or I don't talk."

"Ryder, I think I should …"

"Go on! Get out of here!"

"Okay, but I will be right outside if you need me." Brian walked out of the room and shut the door behind him.

Ryder sat there, staring across the table at the man, not saying anything. "So big man, I see you still have the kosher taste in women. Watterson grinned maliciously as he looked over at Yakira. "Although when I saw this one getting undressed I didn't see anything that appetizing."

229

"So it was you at the lake house?" Yakira said. "If I knew that I would have took a shot at the back of your head."

"You not gonna ask me?" Watterson said looking over at Yakira.

"Ask you what, you *mamzer:.*"

"What does that mean, big man?"

"Let's just say she insulted your momma by calling you that."

"Oh! This one talks back, unlike it her big sister, who kept calling out for God to help her when I was squeezing the life out of her."

Ryder reached over and grabbed her hands, before she exploded with anger. "Before I lose any more brain cells from listening to you, tell me why you murdered her?"

"I warned her not to be teaching the lies about what happen in World War II. I followed her home and beat the crap out of her. Then she begged me for her life. I squeezed tighter and tighter and she became still. You believe that?' He paused for a moment but not giving them a chance to answer. "You better not 'because it was a lie. No, that is only what I told the other jerk." He leaned forward towards Ryder. "You want to know how I did it. Huh? You really want to know?" Ryder didn't respond and the man continued. "How she looked when I pushed the Amytal into her. How she gasped for air choking on her own tongue."

"Where did you get it?"

"I stole it from the hospital. You want to know where the bottle is? I tossed it in the trash pile behind the house."

Chapter 35

Excited, Yakira didn't even wait for Ryder to open the car door or for the car to come to a stop when they pulled into the driveway of Annalisa's house. She leaped out, leaving the door open as she raced around the house. Ryder quickly shoved the car into the park, and raced after her. By the time he was around the house into the backyard, she was already using her feet to kick the wet musty ashes out of the way. She bent down. "No, don't…" He tried to warn her not to touch it, but it was too late.

"I got it!" She shouted out in exhilaration as she held it up over her head. He came up to her pulling a plastic bag out of his pocket that he always kept for things like this.

"What have I told you about touching evidence?"

"Not to do it." She looked at the small vial, the bright silver top scuffed, the label torn and weathered, still inside a majority of the clear deadly liquid. "Oh." She said apologetically as she dropped the vial into the bag. He rolled it up and put it in his pocket. "This means it is over! This is the guy that murdered my sister."

"Looks like it." He said insipidly.

"And this is going to put him away?" She asked, wrapping her arms around his neck and tilting her head back. Her eyes just seemed to sparkle, maybe it was sun sinking further in the sky; and then again maybe it was something else. She pushed up on her tippy-toes so she could see him face to face. "And this means that we can get on with our life…."She kissed him and added. "…our life together?" He didn't answer her. She lowered back to the ground and released him from her embrace. "It does, doesn't it, Ricky?" He didn't answer her; he just turned and walked back over to the back step and sat down on the edge of it. "Ryder!" She demanded. "Answer me."

"Alex wants that information." He said, looking down and dropping his gaze to the brown colored grass. She walked over to him. He looked up at her. "She is going to get it no matter what." She sat down beside him. "That is why he confessed; he knew she wouldn't let him stay there."

"You mean he is going to get away with this?" She said sorrowfully, letting her head rest on his shoulder.

"That is the way the system works sometimes."

"Well, that stinks." She stood up and the breeze caught her hair, making it flap as it were a flag of surrender.   She pushed her hair back out of her face with her hand as she turned back to face him. "There is one thing we can do. If we find that flash drive Alex wouldn't need him anymore." Ryder shook his head. "And she would turn him over to be charged with murder?"

"Alex? In a New York second."

"Then come on!" She insisted as she grabbed his hand, pulling him up on his feet. "We have to find it."

After a stop at the Sheriff's Department to drop off the vial to be fingerprinted they went back to her parent's house and began to examine the note again, going over it word by word. "Find the heart that is on the chest. There you shall find it hidden in the heart." She read the coded note out loud as she paced back and forth in the dining room.

The dining room was furnished with Bubbie's furniture that she had in storage when she lived in the trailer in the country, when she and her husband moved her from New York. Consisting of a large cherry wood table with matching chairs that with extra leaves in place could seat up to 12 persons. A cherry china cabinet that contained antique Noritake china in the pretty Mimi pattern that belonged to Yakira's great-grandmother and on the opposite wall a large buffet with built in outlets to accommodate hot plates or slow cookers for serving food. One other piece of furniture in the room was a cabinet for storing wine, glasses and other things needed for the weekly *Sader* meal to celebrate the Sabbath in the household. There were pleasing pictures on the walls in gold-leaf frames of flowers and antique English cottage scenes.

It was easy to see that Bubbie and Rebekah were nervous as they did what they always did when they were that way- they cooked. The table was covered with a magnificent sampling of Jewish cuisine, from Smoked Salmon rolls filled with cream cheese and dill to desserts that were too numerous to mention. Rebekah came into the room carrying a small tray of Beet Falafel's and set them down on table. Ryder picked up one of the deep fried beet pastries and walked over to the window, pulling back the heavy antique draperies of crewel embroidery. It was dark outside,

"Ricky, I thought you didn't like beets?" Rebekah said, looking over at him.

"Huh? What?" He looked down at what was in his hand. He hadn't even noticed. "Oh, yeah." He wrapped it up in paper napkin and set it down on the table. "I wasn't looking. Any more Salmon Rolls?"

"I can make some more."

"No bother."

"It would be my pleasure." She said with a small grin.

"I give up!" Yakira who was seated at the table said as she leaned back in the chair. "You want to try, mom?"

Rebekah shook her head. "I never knew what your sis…" She paused knowing what the word sister know mean for both of them.

"Rebekah, you know all is forgiven, don't you?" Ryder asked and she nodded. "Then don't worry, you can say it, she was my sister." The doorbell rang.

"Who could that be?" Yakira asked standing up.

"It is Alex. I invited her over." Ryder turned and looked at the puzzlement on Yakira's face. "She is a code expert; maybe she can break it." Ryder walked out of the dining room and over to the front door. He let Alex in and she walked over to the table.

"Yakira, Mrs. Rosen." She greeted them as she looked at each one of them. "I am only here to help. Is that okay? That is all I want to do."

"Have a seat." Yakira offered with a wave of her hand for the chair across from her. Alex removed her dark colored jacket and placed it on the chair back as she sat down. Yakira slid the note over to her.

"I will get you a plate, dear." Rebekah said, whirling around and heading back to the kitchen.

"I am not really hungry, I…" Alex tried to explain but Yakira interrupted her.

"One thing you need to know about a Jewish home if they offer you food. Oh! And sweetie, they *always offer* you food. You have to accept it, otherwise it is an insult to the cook."

"Maybe something a little bit light?" Alex said, then turned back to Ryder. "You looked everywhere?"

"Everywhere we could think of" Ryder said as he sat down at the head of the table with Alex to his left and Yakira to his right. Even a small box we found with a heart on it, there was nothing in it. The house was trashed, so it wasn't there."

"That is because it is not code." Alex said as she held the note in her hand. "A code has a method to it, numbers that mean letters, letters that changes places, words that meant other words. This is a message, plain and simple, it means what it means. A message that she thought you could understand." She tossed the note down on the table. "Think! This has something to do with both of you. Something only you two would know." About your childhood."

"We are out of smoked salmon." Rebekah said as she walked into the room. I will have to go get some more."

"I will go, mom." Yakira said standing up she turned to Ryder and grinned and blinked her eyes at him "Can I take the Killer Bee?" Ryder reached into the pocket of his pants and held the keys up and asked.

"You do realize that car is a one a kind?"

"So am I." Yakira said with a large smiling, grabbing the keys. She leaned down, gave him a kiss, and said. "Love you."

"Same here." He said as she dashed for the door. Ryder could hear the Charger fire up and then drive away.

"You know, that just drives a woman up the wall."

"What?"

"That you can't say those words"

"What words?"

Alex leaned forward. "I love you." She said just as Bubbie walked into the room.

"I thought you two might like to have some Apple pie." Bubbie said as she walked over to the table carrying a tray with two plates with a slice of apple pie on each and two mugs. She set the tray down and placed one of the plates with the pie down in front of Alex, and then the other where Ryder had sat. She handed a mug of coffee, with cream and two sugars, to Ryder, for she knew exactly how he liked it. "I brought you some tea." She handed Alex the other mug. "Ricky said you don't like coffee."

"Thank you, Mrs. Rosen." Alex said. "What you heard me say I—I didn't mean it like that, I…"

"You don't need to explain." She placed her hand down on Alex's shoulder and said. "And I am Bubbie to everybody." She said as she sat down in the chair next to Alex. "You both are losing hope, aren't you?" She reached across the table and took a hold of Ryder's hand before grabbling Alex's hand and continued. "Never give up hope."

"If we could ever figure this thing out." Alex said, pointing to the note lying on the table. Bubbie picked up the note and looked at it. She reached into her apron and produced a pair of glasses and slipped them on as she read the note, then she looked over at Ryder and asked.

"Is this what you are trying to figure out?"

"Why would she use Hebrew except word that one word?"

"Because it is a name, *Motek*".

"Heart? Is a name?"

"You don't remember your little girl?" Ryder's eyes opened wide as he shook his head. Alex, finding it interesting, rested her elbows on the table and her chin in her cupped hands. "You are only about six years old. Annalisa had been in the neighbors wedding. She was in this little white dress, like a mini wedding dress. She wanted to get married. So we had a little wedding ceremony."

"What does this have to do with Heart?"

"You two went on a pretend honeymoon. I gave you grape juice and strawberry jelly on crackers for wine and caviar."

"Oh, that is adorable." Alex said as she turned to Bubbie, but still resting her chin in her hands. "Please tell me you have pictures of that? I would pay to see those."

"I am sure I do. They are probably upstairs, I can go and get them. I even have one of them in bed together." As Bubbie spoke Alex turned and looked at Ryder and grinned at him.

"We were six years old." He said. "Bubbie ! Heart?"

"I am getting to it. Well she had heard if you sleep with someone you get a baby that way." Bubbie said as Alex took a sip of her tea resting both elbows on the table, her head swiveling back and forth from Bubbie to Ryder. "So the next morning she comes in with a towel stuffed under her shirt, saying she is with child, complaining that her feet were swelling and that Ricky never pays attention to her anymore." Again Alex looked over at Ryder, who was beginning to feel self-conscious and was looking down at the table Alex broke out with a guffaw leaning back in the chair as she laughed. "Well, next time she comes through carrying her doll, telling everyone this is her baby.

Heart!" Ryder said with glee." How stupid can I be? That thing set on her bed for as long as I can remember. The drive is in that blasted doll, Alex! It is upstairs!" Ryder rose up.

"*Motek*, Becky took everything to the farm. It is out there."

****

It could have been the thing of a long forgotten memory, and the doll would have ended its life as most other toys do, neglected and abandoned, tossed away, or the love forgotten and just passed down. Heart was not that kind of toy, she was given to Annalisa by Bubbie for being a good girl and not misbehaving at the wedding. There was hardly a day that went by that

236

Annalisa didn't cradle that doll in her arms. Even that night that Annalisa found out who she really was, it was that doll that she held as she cried, wondering what life would hold for her now.

Bubbie had given Ryder the key to the storage building. He unlocked the door and pushed it open. It was as if he had stepped back twenty years ago, it was Annalisa's room. Her bed, her chest of drawers, her dresser, even the posters that were up on her wall were hung here. Rebekah didn't get rid of Annalisa's memory, she just moved it.

"Where's the doll?" Alex asked as she walked in, shining a flashlight over the bed. "You said it always set on her bed. It isn't here."

"You are forgetting the first part of the note." Ryder said grabbing the flashlight from her. The heart that is on the chest." He shone it around all the corners of the room. "This ring here. He explained, holding up his hand. "Annalisa gave it to me. It has a heart stamped on it." Ryder continued to shine the light around the room. "Yakira reminded me that she put a heart on everything she called hers. Bubbie telling me about the wedding reminded me…" He walked over to the side of the bed and shined the light down on a quilt that draped over something. "Pascal told how he would make her a chest to store her dreams in when she got married. " Ryder kneeled down and grabbed the quilt. "She told him it had to have a heart on the lid." He pulled the quilt off, revealing a handmade cedar chest with a heart carved into the lid.

He lifted the lid, inside was her old prom dress, and a baby blanket that she once hoped would hold a child, and wrapped in the blanket was a haggard doll.. Blonde hair, and fair skin, just likes her beloved owner. Dark colored stains ran down from the dolls eyes, and on its cheeks, as if she had been crying. The eyes frozen open, staring at him blankly, just as if it was done in death. He picked up the doll and shook it: something was inside.

"What deadly secrets do you hold, Heart." Ryder said as he grabbed the head of the doll and pulled it off; turning the body upside down, a USB drive fell out into in his palm. "It would be purple." Annalisa's favorite color.

"I'll take that." He heard Alex say as he turned and saw that she had her service weapon drawn on him. He stood up slowly.

"You are going have to shoot me, Alex." He said, holding up the flash drive. "I am not going to give it to you. Tumanova has to go to jail for what he…" Ryder stopped speaking and looked down at the weapon in Alex's hand. "The gun! You took it away from Annalisa, right?"

"I told you I did." Alex said lowering her weapon to her side.

"It is the one thing he didn't mention." He walked past her and out the door. "Come on! If what I think happened did actually happen, Watterson didn't murder Annalisa. But I know who did."

Chapter 36

Alex wheeled the black sedan into a parking space in front of the Sheriff's department. Ryder dashed inside. "Ryder!" Deputy Thompson said, surprised, but walked over to the door that leads to the cells.

"Where is Watterson! Open this damn door!"

"I don't know if I can."

He buzzed Ryder in and Ryder stormed back, he stood in front of the cell. "Open it!" Ryder demanded again, turning his glance at the Deputy.

"You have your service weapon on you?"

"Anyone who tries to take it will take their last breath. OPEN IT!"

Deputy Thompson opened the cell door and Ryder walked in. He reached down and grabbed Watterson by the collar and slammed him up against the bars. "If you killed Annalisa what did you do with the gun?"

"What gun?"

"The 45 automatic she had on her. If you killed her you had to take it. What did you do with it?"

"Oh that! I threw it in the lake."

Ryder flashed a small grin. "Just what I thought." He patted the man on the side of the face then released him." Ryder walked out of the cell and the deputy closed the door and followed him back out into the main office.

"What is all that about?" Deputy Thompson asked.

"Yakira gave her sister a revolver, not an automatic. It means he didn't murder Annalisa." Ryder said, continuing to walk to the front door and the deputy followed him.

"We got his fingerprints on the bottle."

"Let me guess: his were the only ones, right?" Ryder said, stopping and turning to the man.

239

"Of course."

"That is impossible! When we found it Yakira picked up the bottle. Her prints would have been on it. Since you arrested her, her prints would have had a hit. It means that someone wiped the bottle clean, then put his prints on it."

"But that bottle was here, that means…"

"Exactly." Ryder said as a sedan drove by in front of the department.

"Ryder!" He heard Gene Weston yell. "I just saw your Charger sitting on the road."

"Where?"

"Out on highway 248. It is just sitting there, the door wide open."

Alex was already gone, taking the flash drive with her. Ryder found himself in the passenger seat of Deputy Thompson's squad car, racing through town, the siren screaming, the lights flashing; there was always something about this moment that made the blood just pump through his veins and the adrenalin flow through him like a raging river. It was like it was becoming slow motion, with each breath he took the strobe of the emergency light spanning out on the black ribbon of pavement, bouncing off the trees, and painting across the open fields. As the strobes caught sight of a pair of long slender tail lights he inhaled in a quiver of a breath, letting it out as the siren slow to silence. The Charger was pulled off the side of the road, there was no shoulder, just a small grassy strip and the left rear tire was still on the pavement. Ryder grabbed the Glock and slipped it from the holster with one hand and opened the door with the other.

He held the weapon out in front of him in a nightmarish scene as flashing lights bounced off the car, giving it a gray ghostly appearance. He slid up the side of the car. The driver's door was wide open. He took a deep breath and stepped forward. As he pointed the gun into the interior of the car, he let out his breath in a deep sigh.

"Clear!" He shouted as Deputy Thompson also raced to the car. Ryder slipped the Glock back into the holster. One of the pillows was still in the seat; the other was lying on the ground beside the car. Ryder grabbed the pillow and tossed it in the back seat and sat down in driver's seat. On the console was Yakira's wallet, opened. He checked; $7.38 was still there; her driver's license was removed from the holder and lying on the passenger's seat. As he picked it up he saw a note taped to the flat black dash. He pulled it from the dash and it read.

> *Get me the flash drive or I put Yakira to sleep just the way I did* *Annalisa.* *You have till 7:30 tomorrow night. One minute later, she* *sleeps forever."*

Ryder reached down and pulled the seat adjustment rail and pushed the seat back. He slammed the door shut. He stared out through the windshield into the darkness that was broken by the headlights as he flipped them on. His hands gripped the steering wheel and twisted the key and the hungry ponies under the hood came to life, ripping and snorting as he revved the motor.

"What is going on?" Deputy Thompson demanded.

"If I don't give them the flash drive they are going to kill her."

He started to reach for the microphone on his shoulder. "I will alert the sheriff, we will get everyone…"

"NO!" Ryder said loudly as he grabbed the Deputy's hand and pulled it back down. "You can't do that. I want you to get a hold of Alex and have her meet me at Warner Ranch."" Ryder pressed down on the brake and pulled the gearshift back. "You just have to trust me on this one."" Ryder raised his hand up in a mock paw." Once a Wildcat."

"Always a Wildcat." Deputy Thompson replied, doing the same mocking motion with a growl. Ryder lifted his foot off the brake and slammed it down on the gas. The tires spun wildly in the grass as it sped forward a hundred feet. Then he slammed down on the parking brake as he twisted the wheel around. The Charger spun around in the road and was heading back toward town. Ryder let up on the parking brake and slammed down on the gas again. The tires spun and howled, leaving behind a smoky trail as it sped away.

He pulled into the driveway of the Warner Ranch and slid to a stop behind a black sedan. He got out, his eyes fastening on the blaze that was devouring the barn. He had thought maybe this was where they were keeping her. Fearing she might still be in there, he raced towards it.

"She is not here." He heard Alex say and saw her sitting on the ground, leaning back against the front fender of her car. She hung her head down, trying to draw in a breath. She raised her head and coughed more. "The place is empty and they are burning all the evidence." She dropped her head down again and coughed violently, trying to push the smoke from her lungs. She looked up at him."I don't know what ship the weapons are on."

"I do." He said offering her his hand. "Give me the drive and I will tell you."

"It won't do you any good." She said as she grabbed his hand and he helped her to her feet. "The drive is corrupted; there is nothing on it."

"But they don't know that." He said, putting his arm around her. "If we do this right we can get her back and stop that shipment. Then again, we may just get killed. You up to it?" In the distance he could hear the roar of Butterfield's rural fire truck coming towards them.

"Sure. Who wants to live forever."

He walked her back to her car. "Meet me at the gun shop at seven p.m. tomorrow."

Chapter 37

A sudden gust of autumn wind swept across the yard of the parking lot in front of the high school football stadium, swirling around, picking up bits of trash and leaves. It was strange, it was closer to Halloween than it was Easter, but by the temperature it seemed that bunnies should be hopping down the trail instead of brightly colored leaves falling from the trees. It was eighty-seven degrees and if it weren't for the strong southerly winds blowing, it would have been downright hot again; it just seemed summer had one last stand. There was even the possibility of server thunderstorms and isolated tornados later. In fact there was a line of storms building in Oklahoma right now and heading this way.

Ryder glanced across the parking lot towards the large red brick building that was the gymnasium. A man was there leaning back on the wall, the butt of a cigarette nervously being rolled around in his fingers. It was Sheriff Hart as Ryder approached him the man took one last drag of the cigarette, before crushing it out under his foot on the sidewalk marked with the names of graduates who were listed alphabetically. Ryder glance down it was right on the spot between his name and Annalisa's. Sheriff Hart blew out the smoke, making Ryder's face crunch up.

"You said you wanted to help if I ever need you." Ryder said, cocking his head over to the side as he stared at the man.

"You said these are real—bad guys." The sheriff said drawing out his words. "Gun runners, right?" He kicked the crushed cigarette with the toe of his boot, pushing it over into the grassy area. "Just can't believe we have those types in Barry County. What is the world coming to?" He looked back up at Ryder."

"A man can only run so far before he runs right into himself, sheriff."

"Words of wisdom? Where did you hear that?"

"My captain told me that when we found that the murderer was a dirty cop. I despise a dirty cop, don't you sheriff?"

"Oh ,yes." The sheriff said reaching into his shirt breast pocket for another cigarette. "About the worst thing there is." He placed the cigarette in his lips and Ryder reached up and took it from him and said.

"About as bad as these things? Wouldn't you agree?" Ryder tossed it down on the ground and crushed it under his boots that he was wearing. He looked back at the sheriff who rubbed his hand over his face. Scared?" Ryder asked as slipped his sunglasses down on his nose.

"Aren't you?"

"To die?" Ryder said as he pushed his glasses back up on his face. "Never. To live, that is a different story." Ryder turned took a couple of steps away from him. Then he stopped and said. "Meet me at the gun shop in thirty minutes."

Chapter 38

Ryder stood outside of the gun shop. The Killer Bee was backed up next to the front door, the trunk lid open. He bent down and shoved Yakira's Bulldog revolver down inside of his boot. He stood up just as Sheriff Hart drove up. Ryder carefully shut the trunk lid, not allowing it to bang. In the distant sky lightning flashes were lighting up the entire sky, yet not a rumble of thunder was heard.

"Looks like we are going to get a bad one." The sheriff said as he walked up to the car.

"Yeah, it does." Ryder said without emotion said he reached under his jacket and slipped the Glock from it holster. He pulled the slide hammer back on the Glock and handed it to the sheriff. "Here, loaded and ready to go."

"I have a weapon." The sheriff said lifting up a pistol.

"9 mm?' Ryder questioned as he took the weapon from him. "No stopping power. "That is a forty five; it will bring them down." Ryder walked back over to the Sheriff's car and tossed the 9 mm inside and shut the door.

"What about you?"

Ryder lifted his jacket revealing the Smith and Wesson 500. "Deadly Debra here is all I need." He lowered his jacket. This thing will stop a bull elephant.

"Isn't your F.B.I. friend going to help us?"

"She was, but she had something more important to do. So we are on our own." Ryder walked over, grabbed the driver's door of the Charger and pulled it open. "You ready?"

"Where are we going?" The sheriff asked, grabbing the passenger's door.

"Where it all began." Ryder said, sliding down into the driver's seat and firing up the car. "Roaring River."

The Charger's head lights guided the way down the hill into the canyon below. He guided the car to the right and then on to F-highway. He had just crossed the bridge when Ryder stopped the car.

"What are we stopping for?" the sheriff asked.

"I want you to get out. You can sneak up behind and give us an edge. It is at the old Camp Smokey Camp grounds just down the road; if you hurry you can be ready for my signal." The sheriff opened the door and noticed that the dome light didn't come on. "Imagine that. Gene put everything new in this and the freaking light goes out." The sheriff stepped out and closed the door behind him. He leaned into the window and asked.

"What is the signal?"

"I will say this is some weather we are having, isn't it? Then you come in guns blazing."

Ryder let off the brake and drove forward past the park museum to a point where the road was no more. He did just as he was told to do, 'drive out into the grass and stop, then get out.' He stopped the car and looked up at the rearview mirror at the rear seat back that was loosely in place; he brought his hands up over his mouth and said. "Pray this works." He opened the door and stepped out, shutting but not latching the door, he walked forward as a white Ram van drove up. The back door opened and the interior light spilled out revealing there were five occupants inside: the driver Watterson, a passenger Shawn O'Malley, Yakira, and two gunmen in the back, who escorted Yakira out in between them.

Ryder was within fifteen feet of the back of the van when a voice shouted out. "That is far enough, Ryder!" He quickly recognized Agent Chris who yelled out. "Toss the cannon." Ryder reached under his jacket and slipped the SW500 from the holster and tossed it on the ground. "Let's have the drive."

"Don't think so."

"Ryder! I will waste her." Agent Chris and the other man took a step closer, and Ryder saw it was Agent Simms. "

"Wow! Two idiots. Did Alex know you were morons, or is she involved in this too?"

"She is supposed to be such a hot shot agent. She didn't even know what was happening under her own command." Agent Chris pointed a 10 mm automatic pistol at Ryder. "Now give me the drive or your girlfriend gets it."

"Only when Yakira and I get into my car and drive away."

"That ain't gonna happen. The drive first!"

"No, I get Yakira. And I have the upper hand here."

"I don't see how that can be Ryder, we have your little girlfriend here. And if you don't give it to me." Agent Chris raised his semi-automatic to her temple. "I am going to kill her."

"Because I know what is on that drive." As Ryder spoke Agent Chris lowered his weapon." There is shipment of stolen weapons leavening Pier 11A aboard a ship named the *Virgin Princess*. In fact that is where Special Agent Alexander is right now, boarding that ship with a team of agents, at the same time another team is raiding your house, and yours too, Agent Simms."

"You are lying."

Lighting flashed across the sky and thunder rumbled. "Some weather we are having, huh?" Ryder turned around and saw Sheriff Hart pointing Ryder's own weapon right at Ryder's chest. "Right, sheriff?"

"Think you have it all figured out, don't you Ryder?"At that moment Yakira struggled against the man that was holding on to her arm and broke free; she dashed over to Ryder and he placed his arm around her.

"Yeah sheriff, you killed Annalisa, because she saw you and these bimbos over here loading the weapons that is why she left her ring there. Because as Yakira said, 'she never took it off.'"

"That witch! She was going to ruin everything. The only reason she didn't tell Alex was she didn't know to trust her."

"That is why she only gave her information that if Alex were dirty she would have already known. Smart girl, wouldn't you say sheriff? Don't you want to know where you messed up?"

"The gun that I took."

"That was only part of it. But it was something you said. When they were arresting Yakira you said 'Any more than she could have given her sister that

247

fatal dose.' Alex didn't want anybody to suspect that she drugged Annalisa. So she made the official report read 'death by strangulation'. It didn't come out that she was drugged till Watterson; a confession, and I am guessing you helped him with that. That was another thing messed up on. Yakira found the vial and picked it up, yet the only prints on it were Watterson's."

"He made me do it!" Watterson shouted out. " He told me I would never see a day in jail if I sent the F.B.I. on a wild goose chase. There would be a million dollars in for me."

"Just like he told L.J.

Thunder rumbled in the air. "It isn't going to matter now, Ryder." Sheriff Hart said. "Because you and your little girlfriend are going to die right here, and we are going to hop a plane and get out of here. Because you see, Black Midnight already paid for the weapons."

Thunder rumbled louder. Ryder looked over towards the road and saw a small red light; he began to laugh. "What the hell are you laughing at?" Sheriff said as he pulled the hammer back on the Glock and pointed it at Ryder.

"Not with that gun you are not. It is empty." Ryder said as he kept his eyes fixed forward.

"You are lying?" The sheriff pulled the trigger. *Click.* Ryder grabbed Yakira's arm and pulled her over to the other side of him, leaving his right side free. "It doesn't matter Ryder…" The sheriff said reaching into his pocket and pulling out a yellow Ethernet cable. "…I think it is time for you to have your own blood necklace." He glared at Ryder and lightning streaked across the sky. "Both of you kneel down." Agent Chris pointed his weapon at them. They kneeled down as Sheriff Hart walked up behind him and began to wrap the cable around Ryder's neck.

"I did lie about one thing, sheriff. Alex didn't board that ship; she is coming up behind the van with an automatic rifle right at this moment." Ryder felt the cord tighten around his neck as his Adam's apple was pushed up cutting the air off. He looked over at a red dot beaming on Agent's Chris's chest, right above his heart. He had to give the order. Yakira jumped up and kicked the sheriff in the chin. The cable loosen, just enough that Ryder slipped his fingers in between his neck and the cable, he pulled back and shouted. "RIGHT

NOW!" With those words Ryder fell forward, Sheriff Hart tumbled over Ryder's back to the ground. Ryder drew back his fist down and punched the sheriff in the face. Ryder quickly rolled to his feet. He dashed over to Yakira falling back he pushed her to the ground. Ryder reached his hand down into the boot and pulled the Bulldog free, just as the sheriff grabbed the SW 500 lying on the ground and lifted it up. Ryder pulled the trigger back shooting the sheriff in the shoulder and the man fell to the ground.

Meanwhile Agent Chris looked down. There, right above his heart was a small red dot. He swung his weapon over. "Don't move, agent!" Alex warned then squeezed the trigger of the M4 carbine, a burst of fire rang up and Agent Chris fell to the ground, dead. Agent Simms pulled his weapon up, and another blast of the M4 and the glass in the side of the van shattered as Watterson took off running towards the river. Agent Simms aimed at Alex, she fired the M4 again and he fell back against the van, sliding down the side of it. He too was dead.

Shawn dove for the SW 500 on the ground, he grabbed it up. "Drop it! Deputy Sheriff!" Deputy Thompson yelled as he pulled the slide back on the shotgun. Shawn quickly dropped the revolver to the ground and put his hands up. He quickly moved over to him and pushed him face down on the ground. "I might need a little help now." The deputy said, grinning, holding out his cuffs as he still pointed the hot gun at Shawn.

Ryder got up and snapped the cuffs on Shawn's wrists. "I thought I told you to stay out of this."

"What? And miss all the fun?"

Ryder looked over at Sheriff Hart, moaning and groaning as he held his wounded shoulder, blood pouring down between his fingers. Alex wandered over and looked at Ryder.

"You okay?"

"Yeah?"

Alex glanced over at Yakira, sitting on the ground staring over at Sheriff Hart as the thunder roared overhead. "What about her?"

"She seems okay."

"Well, deputy." Alex said lifting the barrel of the carbine up on her shoulder. "Looks like you are the acting sheriff now."

"Just wish Watterson would have not have gotten away." Ryder said.

"We will get him." Deputy Thompson said.

Ryder looked out over the scene. "There is going to be a hell lot of paperwork to fill out." You two have fun. Ryder caught sight out of the corner of his eye as Yakira stood up, walked over and picked up the SW 500. She walked over to the sheriff. She gripped it in both hands and aimed it right at his right eye.

"No, don't." He said. She pulled the hammer back. "Please don't kill me!"

"Why shouldn't I? You killed my sister."

"Yakira, don't!" Ryder said, dashing over to her. "He isn't worth it."

"He needs to pay. An eye for an eye, a tooth for a tooth." She gripped the gun tighter. "A life for a life." The sheriff held up his hand up over his face.

"He has committed treason." Alex said as she moved closer. "He isn't going to see daylight again."

"Give me the gun, honey." Ryder said, holding out his hand. "I love you."

"You, you love me?" She asked, turning and facing him and smiling as she lowered the gun. "You said it."

"I love you. Now just give me the gun and we will go and have a Texas Burger."

"And date fries?"

"And date fries." He said with a grin.

She handed him the SW 500 and he lowered it to his side as he wrapped his other arm around her and held her close. "It is over. It really is over, honey." He whispered in her ear as lighting streaked across the sky and the minute raindrops began to fall, he could feel them run down his cheeks as if they were tear drops. Meanwhile, Deputy Thompson helped Sheriff Hart to his feet and placed him under arrest, putting the cuffs on his wrists. Suddenly a gun shot rang out and Yakira stood straight up before she fell backwards and slipped out of his arms. Ryder was looking right at Watterson. A rain of gunshots rang out as Ryder quickly raised the huge revolver. He squeezed the trigger, and Alex fired off the carbine. Watterson dropped like a sack of wet cement.

Alex ran over to the man. "He's dead."   Ryder kneeled down and scooped Yakira up in his arms, holding her close as she struggled to take a breath. He could feel her blood soaking through his shirt into his skin.

"You are going to be okay, honey. Just hold on. "Just hold on, baby!" Ryder said as he held Yakira up close to him. She wheezed and gasped for the air.

"Oh dear God, no!" Deputy Thompson said as he dashed over to them. He grabbed his microphone from his shoulder. "I need an evac meccy…!" He said anxiously, trying to get his words out. "I need an air evac and medical team at Roaring River State Park right away!" There was there no reply. "Damn it Lee Ann, answer me!"

"Brian, we are under a tornado warning. All flights are canceled. Lightning has struck a tree, it is blocking highway 112. We will have to reroute through Seligman. But you will have to wait till the storm passes."

"We don't have time! Oh for God's sake Lee Ann, it is Yakira! She has been shot. She is going to die if you don't do something."

"Pray Brian. Pray."

Lighting streak down from the sky, striking a tree in the woods and thunder rumbled. Ryder could feel it vibrate through his chest as a hard rain began to fall, soaking him quickly to the skin, his clothes sticking to him. He looked up at Deputy Thompson. "Help her! Please, Brian!" He shook his head; he didn't know what to do. He turned to Alex: "You are a federal agent, do something!"

"I can't, there is nothing I can do. Except…" She said before dropping her head down, the rain pouring back down the back of her neck. "Pray." She lifted her head. "It is all we can do."

The wind was blowing stronger. Trees were swaying and rocking back and forth; a twister was heading right for the park."Okay God, I get it!" Ryder shouted, the lightning nearly blinding him as it streaked across the sky." Please don't take her, save her. You save her! And I will do something for you." He cried, he could feel the tears running the sides of his face even through the rain. He lowered Yakira slightly and watched as she opened her eyes. She reached up and wiped the tears from his eyes and placed them in hers.

"My tears. Are your tears. I don't cry. You don't cry. But if we weep, we weep together." Her words were as shaky as her hand as she reached up and touched his cheek, and then she went limp.

Epilogue

Three weeks later Ryder found himself once again parking the Killer Bee in front of the Antioch Church cemetery. It was time to say goodbye to a big part of life his life. He carried a bouquet of white roses as he walked through the gate and over to a stone marked with the name Rosen.

"Ryder." Alex said as Ryder stood in front of the grave holding a bouquet of white roses. He stooped down and placed them on the grave. "I am so sorry for your loss, but we did stop that shipment of guns."

"And she gave her life so you could do it." Ryder said as he stood up turning his head and staring at her, his gaze hidden behind the dark sunglasses.

"I guess you heard about Sheriff Hart?" Alex asked as she stepped forward and placed another bouquet of flowers on the grave. It seems the Sheriff was found dead in the hospital, his heart punctured by a cardiac needle. She looked up at him. I hope she liked purple flowers."

"Her favorite color." He said as he looked down at the ring on his finger.

." How is it you knew what ship they were on?"

"I didn't. I just remember seeing a brochure for that ship on the sheriff's desk and took a guess."

"Dang good guess." Alex said as Ryder began twisting the ring off his finger. " So what do you do now? Back to K.C. to rejoin the force?"

"First I have to say goodbye to somebody."Ryder reached into his pocket and produced the heart shaped sapphire ring and placed it up on the headstone."This will always be yours." He held up the ring he had taken off his finger. "You wanted me to never forget you. I can never forget you. But I no longer belong to you. Goodbye, Annalisa."

Ryder took a couple of steps away from the headstone and glanced back at the Charger and saw a young woman heading his way, slow and steady. "I am staying around here. I promised somebody something if they gave me a miracle." He said with a grin as he watched Yakira walk towards them. I got that miracle. I am starting my own agency."

"A private detective?"

"But we do it different. Only charge a dollar a day."

"We?"

"Me and my new partner." Ryder said as he Yakira walked up next to him and he put his arm around her and held her close. "Turns out she is a pretty good detective.

"Somehow I think we may run on to each other again."

Ryder laughed. "I am sure of it my friend, I m sure of it."

THE END